Sundown Apocalypse:

Special Ops

Sundown Apocalypse series

Book 5

By Leo Nix

Sundown Apocalypse 5: Special Ops

The story of the Pine Gap Special Forces operatives.

Thus began the Apocalypse of the book of Revelations.

While holidaying at the beautiful Western Australian seaside city of Geraldton, US Ranger, Staff Sergeant Ben 'Obi-Wan' Kennedy, leads his group of special ops and their female friends through a series of dangerous adventures on their return to home base, Pine Gap Secret Intelligence Facility.

The dedicated and self-sacrificing special ops soldiers join a team of Western Australian Police who have arrested two spies, but the terrorists want them back – dead or alive.

Behind the tragedy and sorrow, leaders emerge. They carry their comrades until they are able to lift the burden by themselves.

A story of betrayal, subterfuge, friendship and love, against a background of survival in the harsh Western and Central Australian deserts.

Setting: Geraldton, Meekatharra, Shark Bay, Darwin, Perth, Pine Gap and the harsh Australian deserts.

Book 5 continues the Sundown Apocalypse series.

Other books in this series:

Sundown Apocalypse

Sundown Apocalypse: Urban Guerrilla – book 2

Sundown Apocalypse: Homeland Defense – book 3

Sundown Apocalypse: Desert Strike – book 4

Sundown Apocalypse: Special Ops – book 5

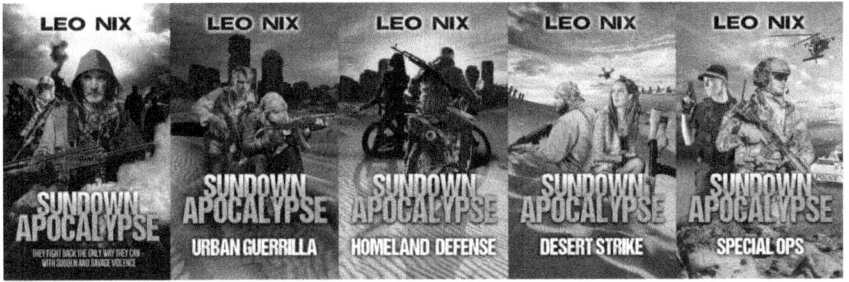

Contact the author, Leo Nix

Email: leo@leo-nix.com

Web: http://www.leo-nix.com/

Cover art: Stephen Kingston

Web: http://www.wingtipdesign.com.au/

A special 'thank you' to Marja for her generous support and the difficult task of proof reading; to my friends Chris and Nicole for answering my many technical questions; to Peter for his ongoing support and technical assistance in all things military. I am especially indebted to Danny for his editing and US military insights without which this book would be far less readable and enjoyable.

I would like to take this opportunity to acknowledge and show respect to the first Australians, our land's traditional custodians, the Australian aboriginal people.

Dedication: To our selfless police and military service men and women who keep us safe in our beds, and to those who support them in their times of need.

Contents

Special Operations soldiers *are a unique breed. Determined, highly intelligent and specially trained problem solvers who train constantly to risk their lives protecting citizens who will never know who they are. These brave men… do not expect parades for their service, in fact, they know that, should the worst happen, not even their loved ones will be given details of their final mission. This selfless sense of duty is only a small part of what makes these operators 'special'.*

http://serioussurvivor.com/wp-content/uploads/2017/01/Special-Operations-Manual.pdf

Chapter 1 - Apocalypse Day

"As George Orwell pointed out, people sleep peacefully in their beds at night, only because rough men stand ready to do violence on their behalf."

Richard Grenier, The Washington Times, 1993.

"How much longer before we move out, Sarg?" asked Lieutenant Norton picking at the scab on his face. His platoon of the Perth Revelationist Church's Hades Battalion, the 'Flaming Damnation', was waiting inside the house and garage for the command to engage their enemy. The platoon had been waiting all afternoon and it was now almost midnight. They were given the honour of taking out the joint US and Australian spy base at Kollarena, which was only a few blocks away.

"Soon, Lieutenant. We've got..." Sergeant Bobbi Francis looked at her wristwatch, it was almost midnight, the time appointed to unleash the Apocalypse of the Book of Revelations.

The spy base was no doubt already under siege by their comrades. These were the 'sleepers', saboteurs planted within the intelligence community by the Revelationist Church years ago. It was now just a matter of walking through the opened doors and exterminating the survivors - if there were any left. Lieutenant Norton's counterpart was waiting in another house a little closer to the base.

Bobbi didn't have time to say more. There was an alarmed shout from their communications specialist monitoring the video display of Australian Federal Police Sergeant Darren McIntosh's house next door. The specialist calmed himself, then called softly to his lieutenant.

"Lieutenant Norton, there's police pulling up outside McIntosh's house. It's their Tactical Response Force... and AFP. We've got big problems!" he said finishing with what sounded like a chicken's 'squawk' as his voice rose in pitch.

Everyone in the garage crammed to stare at the video monitor. They watched as four police vehicles and a Tactical Response Group armoured command vehicle, a Bearcat, discharged eighteen armed Western Australian and Australian Federal Police. They could clearly see their enemy's weapons were drawn.

The terrorists watched open-mouthed as the police Tactical Response team raced to the front and back doors of their informer's home.

"Shit!" grunted the now panicked lieutenant, "Sergeant Francis, get everyone moving, we have to squash this immediately. If we can't rescue our three men we will need to kill them." He paused to squeeze both hands against his greying, sweaty temples, "and that means killing Colonel McIntosh and Captain Landan. They're not to be left for the police to interrogate no matter what."

Turning to his comms specialist, Lieutenant Norton spoke softly, just above the noise of the soldiers preparing their weapons.

"Get on to Captain Lim, tell him what's happening. Tell him that we're going in and that I suggest he go straight to the base without us - immediately. We'll follow when we've dealt with the police."

Corporal Maitland downed the dregs at the bottom of his beer can, gathered his squad and raced to the fence separating the two houses. He kicked down the frail, wooden palings allowing his squad through. Sergeant Francis was already racing towards the front of the house firing at the small crowd of AFP and WAPOL waiting in the driveway and front yard.

"How many times do I have to tell you? I want them back home with me. I can't stand being alone like this," pleaded AFP Sergeant Darren McIntosh. He was the head intelligence analyst at the joint US and Australian spy the base, Australian Defense Satellite Communications Station, Kollarena. It was located twenty kilometres north of the city of Geraldton, on the Western Australian coast.

Thirty-three-year-old Sergeant McIntosh was a spy, conveying top-secret military information to the Revelationist Church. His older brother, Colonel Harry McIntosh, military commander of the Perth Revelationist Hades Battalion, was sitting opposite at the kitchen table. Harry's battalion slogan was 'Flaming Damnation', and tonight, at midnight, they were going to unleash just that, flames and damnation, on all who stood in their way. Apocalypse Day was only minutes away.

"Darren, the girls are safe, so is Debbie. You know our mother wouldn't let any harm come to them?" smiled Colonel McIntosh but it was a little too smooth and this wasn't lost on his younger brother.

"Our mother is fucking crazy, you know that Harry, she's mad. I can't stand the thought of her even being near my kids. Don't you remember what she did to us? A mother is supposed to care for her children, she couldn't even do that. She hired out her own sons for drugs, for her pleasure. How the hell can anyone trust her to look after anyone's children?" Darren was distraught and exhausted after a whole evening of debriefing with his brother and the battalion's intelligence officer, Captain Landan.

Harry's face creased as though in pain. "I know how you feel, Darren. Don't think I can't remember what she did to us. But she's changed, the church changed her. You know that. She's a true believer now, she wouldn't let that sort of thing happen to her own grandchildren, ever."

"The church changed her?" Darren's voice rose in volume to a yell, "that's bullshit! She changed the damn church to suit herself. No-one's game to stand against her, she gets whatever she wants. She's a church Priest, they're Gestapo, and I don't trust her with my family." The fine-boned, dark-haired man sobbed softly as he lowered his face into his hands.

Nearing his fortieth year, Colonel McIntosh looked completely different to his younger half-brother. Where Darren was slim and youthful, Harry was thick-set and ruddy, his face held none of his brother's fine features.

"Darren, after tonight we'll need you," Captain Landan paused and corrected himself, "the church needs you, to continue monitoring Pine Gap communications. We'll still need to monitor the various spy satellites around the world. Do you really think your mother would allow that to be compromised? She loves your girls and she loves the church. With the coming of the blessed Apocalypse you'll have your family back, we promise it." Again both Revelationists glanced across the broken man to stare at each other. Neither smiled. Captain Landan looked at his watch, it was almost time to collect their platoons and initiate the Apocalypse of the Book of Revelations.

The silence was broken by the sound of splintered glass and timber. Into the kitchen crashed five armed and uniformed Tactical Response Group members. Before the terrorists could reach for a weapon they were flexi-cuffed and shoved towards the open door.

"That Sergeant Dyson's a bit of a jerk, isn't he, eh?" muttered Constable Ray Bidder, Australian Federal Police. His voice always went up at the end of a sentence to make it sound like a question. "And that senior constable who drives their command vehicle, that Bearcat, she's a honey isn't she, eh?"

Ray drew deeply on his cigarette as he continued to stare at the Bearcat driver, Senior Constable Nancy Haurenier. She didn't stare back, she was busy on the mic talking to her team inside the house.

The ten AFP, Australian Federal Police, and WAPOL, Western Australian Police, were armed and in body armour, as expected in an arrest of this nature. They stood outside the house waiting for the tactical team to complete the arrest.

"Ray," called the weather-beaten AFP Senior Sergeant, Frenchy, pulling his cigarette packet from his top pocket. In his heavily accented English, Frenchy snapped, "Ray, get your eyes off Nancy's bits and pieces and stay focused. The Revelationists are out in numbers this weekend. Headquarters said there are at least five thousand in Geraldton for their crusader rally. WAPOL have already confiscated weapons from some of the congregation. I've got a bad feeling about this weekend."

Frenchy lit his cigarette and held the packet out to his AFP off-sider, 'Oddie', Sergeant Ogden Danse. The tall, solidly built ex-commando absently took one, leaning forward to light it from Frenchy's now glowing cigarette. He looked around the front yard and down the street suspiciously. All seemed quiet and normal for that time of night.

The Australian Federal Police were deployed at the intelligence base just around the corner. They had been planning this arrest for months. All police and tactical staff knew to keep their mouth's shut if the media turned up. Any news associated with federal intelligence facilities can easily turn into a fireball in moments. All it takes is for one nosy neighbour to call the Perth TV channels and they'd be buzzed by a dozen helicopters before they'd had time to cuff their prisoners.

From inside the house came sounds of a scuffle, yelled orders, then silence. Senior Sergeant WAPOL, Brad Hopkins, nervously fingered the grip of his Glock 18.

"I don't like this," he said to no-one in particular, "it's too easy. Five thousand Revelationists and one undefended spy, all by his lonesome. Nah, somethings not right."

It had been a busy day for the WAPOL team. Earlier that morning Senior Constable Bill Franklin and Constable Danielle Ahmet, attended the violent triple homicide of a mother and her twin, ten-year old daughters, outside Geraldton. The two then had to double up for tonight's warrant and arrest. Brad understood that they were both no doubt exhausted and possibly still distraught from what they had witnessed that morning.

At that moment he caught sight of his favourite tactical police officer, Senior Constable Kerrie Black. She stood in the doorway, waving to him. He walked over, still fingering the grip of his pistol.

"What?" he asked softly, too edgy to say more, something was wrong, he knew it.

"Get your teams to tighten up the perimeter, we've got extras. It looks like we have the heads of the Perth Hades Battalion here too, Colonel McIntosh and Captain Landan. We've got them – shaft, sack and balls. We've scooped the pool, Brad." Kerrie was relaxed and smiling, her face briefly glowed with a youth she had left behind to focus on her career with the police. She liked Brad, he was a professional, like her and the tactical team she now worked with.

Brad nodded but he shivered inside. That was just bloody perfect, more terrorists to handle - he turned to his team.

"Everyone, on me!" his call was soft but firm. "We've got three suspects, two Revelationist accessories not on our warrant. They're the head of the Hades Battalion, Flaming Damnation. Well, we're flamin' damned if we'll let this opportunity slip out of our hands." He let his breath out slowly. "We'll give tactical a few minutes to complete the arrests while we set up the crime scene tapes and then start collecting evidence. Just be on your toes while you do it, anything could go wrong."

Each member of the AFP and WAPOL quickly set about their usual procedure of preparing a crime scene and securing it.

It was about then that the firing started and the police warrant and arrest went pear-shaped - just as Frenchy and Brad feared.

Senior Sergeant Wayne Dyson was an ex-infantry captain in the regular army. He had left the military to join the WA Tactical Response Group so that he could spend more time with his family. He was thinking of them as bullets cracked and whined through the pine-board cottage.

Everyone dived to the floor as soon as the firing started. A bullet hit the Revelationist captain and blood spurted through a hole in his neck. He gave a series of gurgled, wet coughs as he choked on his own blood.

Constable 'Twitch' Frampton twisted sideways as he was hit by a burst of automatic gunfire. Some of the impact was absorbed by his body protection but several bullets found their way below his armour, cutting the artery in his groin. He spun and fell to the floor screaming. Two more officers went down with serious leg and abdominal wounds.

Dyson knew they were now in big trouble. This wasn't simply 'bad guys' firing handguns this was a full-on military-style assault. Then he heard the incoming fire directed at his AFP and WAPOL team waiting outside, the volume of fire was incredible.

'What the hell did we just walk into?' he thought as he lay on the floor hoping the incoming fuselage of bullets stayed high.

Colonel McIntosh saw his friend drop to the floor with the first bursts of incoming fire. He watched as Captain Landan squirmed trying to reach up to his neck wound,but his hands were flexi-cuffed behind him. The Revelationist intelligence officer was now still, the spurting wound pumped a few more times then stopped.

McIntosh rolled onto his side and watched to see what his captors would do. They were competent men and women, he had probably trained some of them during his time in the military. But men and women break under stress, he just might escape arrest - if he doesn't get killed first.

Colonel McIntosh recognised that he was an eye-witness to a truly devastating assault and he was proud of it. But he wasn't pleased to be on the receiving end.

Harry's younger brother, Sergeant Darren McIntosh, was his pride and joy. His personal covert operative had kept the battalion and his Australian counterparts informed of valuable top-secret intelligence for the past three years. Darren huddled on the floor beside his brother, afraid and angry. Both Revelationists were just as vulnerable to the incoming fire as their captors beside them.

The Flaming Damnation platoon had split into three squads each doing their best to exterminate the police.

Sergeant Francis led her squad through the side gate and almost to the driveway. She opened fire as soon as she saw the police.

Corporal Maitland and his squad continued to fire through the timber walls of the house while Corporal Zee arrived at the front of the house to attack the police from the street. For the police inside and out, it was hell in a teacup.

The tactical team had already lost Constable 'Twitch' Frampton while Constable Russell Efferent and Sergeant Guy Luvini were wounded and losing blood fast. Senior Sergeant Dyson now had to extract his team and their prisoners under heavy fire.

Of all extractions this was the worst scenario of them all. Not only were they unprepared for the ambush they were being hit by heavy automatic rifle fire; they had wounded and dead; and they had prisoners, one appeared dead already. But not only were they severely compromised inside the house their escape route was exposed and under heavy fire as well.

"Hooky! Grab Sergeant McIntosh. Lana, grab the colonel." Turning to Senior Constable Kerrie Black he called, "Kerrie, grab Constable Efferent and I'll take Sergeant Luvini." He looked at his good friend, Twitch, "Twitch is dead, we'll collect him later… we extract on three… One! Two! Three!" The Tactical Response Group police officers jumped up and began their extraction. Immediately Lana screamed as a bullet slashed the back of her hand.

"Just do it, Lana!" yelled ex-SAS corporal, Paul 'Hooky' Pan. "Just grab him and run! Come on!" Hooky grabbed his cuffed prisoner by the arm. Pushing Lana and her prisoner, Colonel McIntosh, in front of him, they ran for the door.

As the tactical team burst through the front door they were met by an eruption of noise that disoriented them for a few seconds. They heard Senior Constable Nancy Haurenier in their earpiece, "Get into the Bearcat! Now!"

Nancy had manoeuvred the armoured Bearcat up as close to the front door as it would go. Bullets whined and smacked against its armoured sides and windows but none penetrated. She sensibly put the Bearcat between the terrorists and the police standing outside. All-the-same there were four bodies lying in awkward positions on the front lawn. One of them was her lover, Constable Chad Chopah, a giant of a man with a gigantic heart.

Despite the tears that streaked down her cheeks her mind was cold, frozen. No one was prepared for an arrest warrant to go down like it had. She knew this was evidence of a well-established spy ring with military connections.

In their haste to engage the police the terrorists forgot to cover the other side of the house. It was here that the police had gathered, protected behind the Bearcat. The incoming fire was ferocious and counter-fire almost impossible.

Senior Sergeant, WAPOL, Brad Hopkins looked at his team, only three were still standing, two had gone down in the first burst of gunfire.

"Into the Bearcat!" he screamed above the din of rounds smacking against the Bearcat's armoured sides. "Danielle, help me with the wounded." Both Constable Danielle Ahmet and Constable Cindy Briggs bent to help Brad drag their mates into the cramped interior of the armoured Tactical Response Group vehicle.

Inside they negotiated for space with the tactical team and Senior Sergeant Frenchy's federal police. Nancy pushed the revs up and reversed out of the driveway. The Bearcat roared down the road towards their spy base, Australian Defense Satellite Communications Station, Kollarena, only a few blocks away.

As the Bearcat pulled away from the house three grenades exploded beneath it, one after the other. Although designed to protect its occupants from incoming fire and explosives the massive vehicle had taken a terrific beating. Not a dozen metres down the road it began to misfire.

An exasperated Senior Sergeant Wayne Dyson cried out, "I don't fucking believe it!" He was almost in tears at the horrific battering his team had taken. He crawled over sweating and bloodied bodies to sit beside his driver, Nancy, he didn't notice she was crying.

Dyson grabbed at the radio and connected with his superior in the Kollarena base as their brave Bearcat slowly died beneath him. Every few metres it shuddered, misfiring badly. He finally finished speaking and turned to his driver beside him.

"Nan, get us to the wharf, we'll never make it back to base." Dyson looked down and shook his head, coming back to the moment he called loudly to his team behind him, "Kollarena base is under fire, it seems they've been infiltrated from the inside. All communication with the satellites was cut hours ago. They've just been hit by a massed force of terrorists and they're about to be overrun. Super said we need to get to the wharf and try to escape by boat - he has no back-up for us."

He saw a few heads drop with the terrible news. "Super said they're preparing to blow the base up. He's in the process of holding off the invaders long enough to arm the self-destruct charges and try to get a message to Pine Gap. If we can, we've got to get ourselves and these prisoners to Pine Gap, Perth or Darwin. He said the Revelationist Church have done what they've threatened to do for years, they've set the world on fire."

As he spoke the wharf appeared in front of them. He could make out the base motor launch, several civilian fishing boats, and yachts. Hopefully the launch was fuelled up and ready to go.

In the Bearcat's rear monitor he saw they were being pursued by several cars filled with terrorists. The Bearcat moaned as it approached its death rattle. Nancy kept her mind focused so she could bring it as close to the wharf as possible before it died completely.

"Frenchy, can you and Brad set up a defense when we stop? I need to get the wounded and prisoners on the launch - help yourselves to the automatics in the locker here. I'll only need a minute to get the launch manned and started," said Dyson as he crawled back over the bodies and into the interior. He checked the prisoners and his team. As he checked Lana's bloodied hand she told him in a rushed explosion of words that it wasn't serious.

He turned to the team's head medic, Sergeant 'Oddie' Danse, already flat-out tending to the wounded. "Bandage Lana's hand, Oddie, I need her." His mind was now focused like a laser beam as he readied to exit the Bearcat.

In his minds-eye, Dyson stepped out of his body to observe his team and the other survivors. They looked staunch, and despite the horror of the firefight he knew he could depend on them. He came back to the present and spoke one more time.

"People, we've got to set a defensive perimeter against these pricks. I'm counting on Frenchy and Brad's teams to give us time to board the base launch and start the engines. I'll call you in when we're ready. I'll need about sixty seconds."

He called loudly to Nancy, "Nan, set the self-destruction of the Bearcat to three minutes."

Looking once more at his team Dyson said, "When we stop we've got three minutes so make sure you get to the boat before it goes up." He paused, "any questions?" There were none, all knew what was required. "OK. Tactical! We're up first."

The Bearcat gave it's last choking cough and stopped right at the edge of the wharf, it had served them well. The tactical response team leapt from the side door and ran dragging their prisoners and wounded to the motor launch. Neither prisoner tried to hinder them, they were just as afraid of being hit by their own as the police were.

Brad and Frenchy handed out tactical's Heckler and Koch G36 automatics, there were only a couple of grenades. Each able officer had an automatic rifle, Ray armed himself with a Blasser sniper rifle. There were just six active officers left, they had two dead and two seriously wounded. Ray was sectioned-off to have the two wounded ready for extraction while the rest held the terrorists back.

"Fire!" cried Frenchy as the four terrorist cars came within effective range. He felt damn good being able to fight back at last. The automatics stopped the enemy in their tracks and the cars swerved off the road and into the sparse, wind-swept scrub. In the darkness they could see the enemy rifle-flashes - it revealed that there were about twenty terrorists out there in the dark.

Senior Sergeant Brad Hopkins had one of the tactical team earpieces and heard Dyson call them in. Nancy had already tapped his shoulder as she left the safety of the Bearcat.

"We've got two minutes to get to the wharf before the Bearcat explodes," called Brad to the team beside him.

"Brad, I'll stay back while you get everyone to the boat." Frenchy didn't bother to wait for an answer. He was ex-French Foreign Legion and he loved the wild Australian desert sands. It was better than the jungles of central Africa, his deployment before he retired. Right now, as one of the most experienced heads of the AFP team at the joint US and Australian spy base, it was his responsibility to look after everyone.

"Good luck, Frenchy, we'll cover you once we get to the boat." Brad knew his friend wouldn't budge, he never did once he'd made up his mind. They were in a bad situation but blessed with a comrade who stuck by his mates.

Sergeant 'Oddie' Danse and Constable Ray Bidder firmly slapped Frenchy's shoulder and wished him good luck. They then prepared to race towards the motor launch.

"Ray, you and I'll leap-frog back, we provide covering fire for each other, got it?" yelled Oddie. Ray grunted in reply as he made sure his rifle safety was off, now he was ready. The short, barrel-chested AFP officer hadn't noticed the cigarette sticking out of his mouth, let alone that it wasn't lit.

The last of the police officers made a dash to the boat. By now the terrorists had started to encircle the dead Bearcat - there was just one minute before it detonated. The last two policemen now raced back, leap-frogging each other, firing at the muzzle flashes now appearing on both flanks.

Frenchy laughed, he knew he was going to die, he'd been in situations like this a hundred times before. Not once was he worried about his own life, back then he always knew he would survive. But today, right now, he knew this was no longer so. Tonight he sang his death-song and he shared it with the blood of the terrorists trying to kill his team-mates.

"Come on you arse-wipes! I've killed the likes of you swine a million times over," he yelled, his voice slipping into his native French, "viens et rencontrer ta mort!" - "*come and meet your death!*"

A bullet creased his arm burning like a hot iron. He didn't care, it just fired his determination. The ex-Legionnaire felt bullet-proof as he continued to fire his G36. He heard Oddie and Ray firing from behind him. He knew they were steady types, not given to running from a fight themselves.

Two terrorists ran to the side of the Bearcat and crept around to see Frenchy's legs as he was firing to the front of the vehicle.

"Come on you bastards! Is that all you've got for me!"

The terrorists could just make out his yells and laughter above the ferocious firing around them and the noise of bullets striking the armoured sides of the Bearcat. The bravest of the two stepped around to the back of the armoured vehicle and fired into Frenchy's back. He emptied the entire magazine into him. A moment later the other terrorist joined him. They kicked the bloodied Frenchman's limp body - just as the Bearcat's explosives detonated shredding the three of them into blood and gristle.

The sky lit up as a ball of flames and smoke rose into the black heavens. It was dwarfed by the spire of the exploding Kollarena spy base which detonated only seconds later.

The soldiers of both sides stopped firing to watch, mesmerised by both the Bearcat and then the spy base's demise. To the police men and women it was a sadness that hit them like a punch in the guts; to the terrorists it was a moment to be cherished to the day they died.

Oddie yelled at Ray to get to the boat then turned and raced as fast as he could along the timbered wharf to join him. By the light of the twin fires they were silhouetted against the darkness of the bay, the terrorists now resumed their assault.

"Damn! Look!" cried the raven-haired Constable Danielle Ahmet. She pointed to a streak of white coming at speed towards them. "I think we've got terrorists approaching by launch from the south!"

Chapter 2 – Madness in the City

It was after sunset and still hours before midnight - the official time to launch the glorious Apocalypse. The Revelationist Church members in Geraldton, on the Western Australian coast, were busily preparing for their assault on the city.

The senior commander of the Geraldton operation, Colonel Brandon Newport, couldn't wait until midnight to launch the sister battalion to the 'Flaming Damnation' of Perth. His battalion was called the 'Tartarus Battalion', also known as the 'Be Damned' battalion. He wanted to be the first to execute the Apocalypse in Australia, and 'be damned' to his fellow Perth commanders. He now ordered the assault regardless of the consequences.

Colonel Newport stood outside his motel suite with his officers surrounding him. He revelled in the thought of the accolades he would receive for initiating the Glorious Apocalypse of the Book of Revelations here in Australia.

"Weapons ready everyone, orders are to upscale our assault and make this city a blazing beacon to humanity's freedom a little earlier than anticipated." Lieutenant Serri spoke softly to her platoon of crusaders. They were armed with automatic rifles, pistols, grenades and petrol bombs. Their role was to corral the city residents into the football field and detonate the explosives buried there. These new orders from Colonel Newport meant that they would now execute the city residents as they found them, on the spot.

"Let us all pray." The platoon went down on one knee, bowing their heads as their officer led them in prayer.

There were sounds around them in the dark as thousands of Revelationist Crusader terrorists moved out. They all had flashlights in their hands or around their heads, all the better to see their victims. Each was armed and determined to show their fellow churchmen and women the strength of their faith. Many were stoned or drunk, the church encouraged members to indulge in what the establishment deemed illegal or improper.

As the crusaders spread through the suburbs and into the centre of the city fires sprang up everywhere. The city fire services and police were called in to assist. None of these civilian services knew that it was the end of the world. Within a half hour the electricity network was cut and communications ceased.

"Lieutenant Serri!" cried Tahni, she had a screaming teenage girl by the hair, dragging her to the roadside, "can you give me a hand here? This bitch is trying to run."

Rather than walk over to help, Lieutenant Serri simply fired her Beretta 9 mm pistol into the girls back.

"There, see how it's done! Now get back inside that hotel and just kill them, we aren't supposed to take them to the footy field anymore - weren't you listening?" yelled the lieutenant above the sounds of screaming, the blaze of multiple fires and automatic rifle fire. She fired at another teenage reveller trying to escape, he fell, joining his dead friend on the footpath.

One 'Be Damned' platoon was sectioned-off to scour the beaches adjacent the city centre. Most of the buildings they passed were now alight, the drinkers in the hotels and bars either dead, fleeing or in hiding.

One small group had taken up position in the Freemasons Hotel, just around the block from the white sands of Town Beach. This select group of special operatives anticipated that they would soon be in command of their own weapons, courtesy of the terrorists.

"Obi-Wan, it looks like we might have company, buddy," whispered the tall, dark-haired, Soldier of Fortune. The scar above his right eye stood out, it was proof of the stress they were all feeling.

With the explosive start of the apocalypse most of the drinkers had fled either to their cars parked outside or to their hotel rooms. There remained the six special services operatives and their group of female friends. Emily was a bright-eyed and bubbly, petite blond; Julie, a tall, intelligent and lively brunette, she was a partner in her father's law firm; Tish, a blond who loved to party and already a little drunk, she quickly sobered once the shooting started; and dark-haired Gracie, Julie's office administrator, she had only just joined them that day.

The girls had driven up from Perth to celebrate their friend's wedding and enjoy the sunshine and holiday atmosphere of Geraldton. They'd met the special operatives one night and liked what they saw, that helped them decide to hang around for an extra few days.

The six special operatives now waited for orders from their senior NCO: US Ranger, Staff Sergeant Ben 'Obi-Wan' Kennedy. Although he tried to avoid it he was quite popular with the girls with his blond hair and solid surfer body, kept well toned by his regular work-outs. But it was his calm manner in a crisis that made him a favourite with his friends.

They'd heard the gunfire only a few minutes earlier and knew what it was, a full-on, military-style assault. The special operatives, enjoying a well-earned holiday from Joint Defense Intelligence Facility at Pine

Gap in the heart of the Australian continent, had heard those sounds before, many times before. The sound of automatic rifle-fire usually meant death.

Within moments they had rounded up their friends and a few other revellers, moving them deeper into the hotel. Obi-Wan, and his buddy, Corporal Gary Fortune, a member of the U.S. Army's famed Delta Force, remained in contact with the terrorists. They wanted to gain more information and, with luck, weapons. Off-duty servicemen and women do not carry firearms, especially in Australia where the laws prohibit it - they were feeling naked without a weapon to defend themselves and their friends.

Their buddies, Petty Officer Second Class Matt Murphy, with his blond crew-cut hair and solid build; and Petty Officer Third Class Peter Liner, 'Pipeline', whose skin was as black as the oil that flowed through his namesake, took the girls and a few other hotel patrons towards the exit at the back of the building. Both were the U.S. Navy's elite Sea, Air, and Land forces, known as SEALs.

The flaming red-haired and short, thick-bearded Australian, Ollie 'Skip' Stone, looked more like a Viking marauder than a SAS Corporal. Skip and the tall, good-looking Samoan, Corporal Laurence Burger, another U.S. Army Ranger, stayed back to maintain contact and provide support for Obi-Wan and Soldier of Fortune.

The special operatives of both countries knew the drill, they'd done this before and they now performed as they were trained to do. The first thing they needed was intelligence, the second was a weapon. Fortunately for them, five terrorists arrived, smashing their way through chairs and tables to get to the liquor behind the bar.

"Cheer up, Sammy, 'Milk Tits' still loves ya. She'll be as horny as a lioness on heat after this," laughed one of the terrorists as he threw a bottle of Creme De Menthe to his mate. "Give it a few hours and she'll be begging for more of that man-meat between your legs."

"You guys make me sick with your sex talk. That's all you do, talk about sex and tits and cocks. We're Revelationist Church members, we're the pillars of our church, we should set an example. Besides, Lieutenant Serri said she didn't like that name, it embarrasses her," Tiny lectured. She was so petite that even her tailored uniform dwarfed her elfin figure. Her heart-shaped face was framed with a blond pixie cut, adding to the impression she could pass for being a child's doll.

Looking closer, the M1911 pistol she held in each hand destroyed the illusion. She sat in the tall bar-stool and lay the twin pistols on the bar, struggling to raise her elbows high enough to rest them on the bar's top. Eyeing the abandoned bottles left sitting on the bar, she reached over and poured herself a neat whiskey and soda, knocking it back in one gulp.

"Damn it's hot tonight, and my hands are shaking. Look, all that firing, I can hardly hold my pistols anymore. I need another drink," she said.

"Yeah right, as if the lieutenant cares," continued the loudmouth private who was pouring himself another bourbon and coke. He thoroughly enjoyed killing as much as he enjoyed sex. "Milk Tits has already humped everyone in the platoon bar you, Tiny. If you had a dick I'm sure she'd hump you too."

"If I had a dick to match Serri's tits I'd be pretty darn popular with the whole battalion," laughed Tiny. Her face was red from the whiskey, the exertion of throwing firebombs through shop-front windows and firing her pistols. She poured herself another drink, her third.

"If I had a bigger dick I'd fall over too," called a very drunk Corporal Mandy, an older, non-commissioned officer. She tried but with pathetic regularity failed to fit in with the younger members of the platoon.

"Girls don't have dicks, Mandy, but if you want one I've got mine right here." Tall and good-looking with his black hair and tanned skin, Sammy grabbed at his crotch and pretended to open his trousers to release his manhood.

"The corporal said bigger, not smaller, Sammy," joked Ivan. The thin, well-built ex-infantry private was staring through the front door of the hotel. Ivan knew that some of the spy base staff frequented this particular hotel on the beach front. Despite their initial success and zero opposition, he was certain that they'd eventually need to confront armed survivors. He wanted to be ready.

"Hey, Corporal Mandy, did our team finish poisoning the water treatment plant in Perth? And what's happening with the rest of the world? Any news?" Ivan asked as he turned to accept a cold beer from the loudmouth at the bar.

"Yes, they've poisoned the water, it should have hit the city reservoirs by now. When everyone wakes up to make their morning cuppa they'll have to drink it and… bingo! We've had to start the apocalypse early so we won't find out what's happening world-wide until later. Just give it time." Mandy replied as she tossed off a triple bourbon and coke.

While the terrorists drank and laughed, Obi-Wan and Soldier of Fortune had crept from the darkened corners through the maze of bar stools and tables tossed loosely around the room. They emerged, knives in hand, at the back of the bar behind the two terrorists serving up the free liquor. On the other side of the bar Skip and Burger manoeuvred to the kitchen entrance, positioning themselves to take out the guard at the front door. They were also in a position to take out the girls now sitting at a nearby table drinking.

Skip waited for Obi's signal then threw a coffee mug through the broken glass window. It smashed five metres beyond the ex-infantry guard at the entrance. All eyes turned disinterestedly to see what the noise was.

Obi-Wan was now within striking distance to take down the first soldier, the foul-mouth passing out liquor. He stood and put him in a stranglehold cutting off his airway. He snapped the youth's neck as he dropped back down to a crouch easing the body to the floor.

While Obi-Wan took care of victim one, Soldier of Fortune had grabbed Sammy by his long greasy hair as he too looked to see what the noise was. Sammy found himself spinning to the floor paralysed from a crushing karate palm strike to his neck. The terrorist's larynx was crushed, it's delicate cartilage and tendons a pulp of blood and tissue. As he fell, Fortune grabbed and eased him to the floor. Sammy died quietly with Fortune's hand over his gaping mouth.

Within seconds two of the five terrorists were down. Now both Obi-Wan and Fortune were armed with AK47's and pistols. Obi-Wan nodded to Fortune, together they rose from behind the bar to put two bullets into each of the surviving terrorist's foreheads.

No-one spoke as they stripped the enemy bodies of weapons, knives and ammunition. Anything of use was taken, even down to their webbing, backpacks and water bottles. They might not have a chance to gather supplies like this again. Skip and Burger were now armed and they had a spare AK47 for Murphy and a pistol for Pipeline.

From listening to the terrorist's conversation all four knew that something very serious was happening. It wasn't just local it seemed to be world-wide. The four soldiers dragged the bodies into one of the rooms off to the side of the drinker's lounge. It was unlikely they'd be discovered unless someone deliberately went through each room.

"What's this say, Obi? It looks like it's written in Arabic." Skip held up one of the terrorist's bandannas, it was black with white writing on the front.

Obi-Wan snatched it out of the air as Skip tossed it to him. He studied it for a moment then threw it to the floor.

"It's ancient Aramaic, it says *'Apocalypse'*," replied Obi-Wan disgustedly.

Skip handed the spare weapons to Murphy and Pipeline when they got to the back of the building. They were waiting there with the four girls. The other patrons had disappeared.

"Guys, this sounds like the Revelationists have started the apocalypse like they've been praying for these past few years. One of them said that they had poisoned the water in Perth and that the rest of the world is also under attack, probably much like this. Something started the firefight early but I don't know what that was. Maybe their plan was discovered, I don't know." Skip spoke softly, urgently.

"Obi, from what we've seen, this city is dying, there's explosions, fires, smoke… I think we need to contact base and head back to Pine Gap, what do you reckon?" said Murphy scratching at an insect bite on his exposed ankle.

There were the six, off-duty Pine Gap special operatives, and the four girls they were drinking with. The girls were calm but clearly afraid and confused. They didn't want to be separated from their rescuers, they stuck close to Murphy and Pipeline in particular.

"I think we should head to Kollarena, meet up with the AFP at the base there. They'll have weapons and intelligence. We should be able to contact Pine Gap base from there too," suggested Soldier of Fortune.

"Yeah, good idea," agreed Obi-Wan, "but how do we get there? They've got, what did the news say, five thousand Revelationists here in Geraldton? We can't just hijack a car and drive out, they'll have the roads blocked and manned with automatics and heavy weapons by now."

One of the girls, Emily, spoke up quickly, her breath labouring with tension. "My dad's got a boat... it's moored just around the corner... I know where the key is." She took a deep breath then continued. "It's going to be a lot safer if we go to Kollarena by boat."

Murphy, an avid yachtsman in his hometown near San Francisco, replied, "Great idea, I'll take the helm first and get us away from the wharf."

Emily led them through a series of back alleys and then through a park on the beachfront. At one point they saw terrorists firing on a group of civilians hiding on the water's edge. The terrorists walked into the waves and continued to fire, it was a bloody slaughter. Some of the victims dived under the waves in an attempt to swim to safety. The terrorists just waited until they surfaced for air then shot them.

The group held back in horror hidden by a screen of bushes. The sounds of screaming echoing in their ears.

"Obi-Wan, no, we've got to get to the base," said Pipeline softly, putting his hand on Obi-Wan's shoulder. They all knew they could take this group out but the whole city was swarming with laughing, drinking and murdering terrorists. On every corner there were groups of them dressed in black shirts and bandannas covered in white Aramaic writing. "Our priority is survival, we have a duty and right now that is to get back to our base."

Obi-Wan nodded but inside he shuddered. He'd seen wanton murder before but this was different, this was pure evil.

"It's that one, there," the pretty blond pointed out her father's launch. It looked solid enough and should easily hold the group of ten survivors. "I'll get the key and unlock the disabler dad put on."

Murphy was already checking the launch driving compartment. The broad-shouldered SEAL took the keys from Emily's outstretched hand and started the motor.

"Cast off, Pipeline. Skip, get that rope off, yeah, that one," he pointed to a small line holding the bow to the wharf. "OK, hold on and take station everyone." The two sailors were members of the US Navy SEAL Team Six, the team that had killed Osama bin Laden over a decade earlier.

The boat roared into life and shot forward. The group of terrorists on the beach heard them and ran forward, some crouched and opened fire. At that distance it was unlikely they'd take any hits, but Burger escorted the girls below decks anyway.

Once they'd escaped the beach and put some distance between them and the city, Emily slipped behind Murphy and hugged him tightly.

She shivered in the cool breeze. "Murph, you are my hero." Emily kissed his neck then went to check that all was as it should be on her father's boat. She too was an experienced sailor.

Like Murphy, Pipeline had handled boats all his life too, even captaining a racing yacht for his uncle while still in college. He set about securing the launch and checked the fuel and battery. These were essential to their successful escape to the Kollarena spy base roughly twenty kilometres away.

"Don't worry, Pipeline, we'll get to Kollarena without running out of fuel. We've done that trip heaps of times," called Emily as she curled up in one of the wet-weather jackets she'd brought out for the girls to wear.

"Emily, can you please give me your radio unlock code. I'll try to raise the base from here. I might be able to listen in on the chatter from the terrorists too." Emily walked him through the radio setup, it was a standard marine-style CB. Obi-Wan nodded as he keyed in and tried to contact Pine Gap or Kollarena base - without success.

Skip sat down to join his friend, Obi-Wan. Together they listened to the chatter from the terrorists. It appeared they were having a great time. They'd met no opposition from civilians or police. They laughingly described how they had hit the police station earlier, they took no prisoners.

"Idiots, they don't have secure radio protocols," said Skip, "they must think they'll get away with all of this."

"Skip, I'm worried that they just might. If this is worldwide and they've poisoned the drinking water; and if they've exposed whole populations to something deadly like the SARS virus; they just might destroy enough of civilisation to make things impossible to come back from." Obi-Wan was clearly upset at what he'd seen at the beach, it had stuck inside his head.

"Bud, we're in it deep you know. If they planned to take out the police station I bet they've done the same with Kollarena base, maybe even Pine Gap." His head dropped. "If they've hit America too those assholes may have even taken out my hometown…" He didn't finish what was on his mind, it hurt too much.

"I'm sorry, Obi-Wan, I know what you're thinking, mate." Skip stopped for a moment, he recalled an image of his ex-wife and their children in Victoria. "Once we regroup at Kollarena we can then contact Pine Gap. The Commander will want to fly us back as soon as possible. We can think of other things then."

Chapter 3 – Ocean Escape

"Look, that's a firefight. There's a shit-load happening up there too," called Skip straining to make out who was firing on whom around the spy-base wharf.

The lighting from the weapons could be seen reflecting off the ocean surface. Then the noise came to them, light crackling at first, then, as they approached closer they could make out individual cracks of automatic rifle fire. There was also the distinctive 'pop' of a Blaser sniper rifle.

Fortune said softly, "Well, we now know that Kollarena is in the thick of it. I hope they have the terrorists by the throat and not the other way around."

Skip leaned forward and readied his weapon, he paused a moment to wipe the sea-spray from its sights. The rifle fire at the wharf started up again. He yelled to his comrades, "I have a feeling we'll be needed, folks."

"Burger, what can you see through those glasses?" asked Obi-Wan. He needed to know what they were approaching. He already felt the motor launch slow as Murphy backed off the revs, waiting for Obi-Wan to decide what they should do next.

Just then there came the vision, followed by a thunderclap of sound, as the Bearcat exploded in a sheet of flames illuminating the battleground around the wharf. Within seconds a second detonation rent the air as the self-destruct explosives inside the Kollarena base detonated. All firing ceased as everyone stopped to stare in wonder as the twin-spires of flame and smoke lit the night sky.

Burger spoke slowly but clearly. "Obi, we've got a group of police in the boat at the wharf. They're firing at what looks like terrorists approaching from three directions. They're surrounding the wharf and firing on the launch."

"Murph!" called Obi-Wan, "can you get us in close enough to fire on those terrorists on the shore?" He paused, thinking, "we'll need to get in and out, fast."

"Sure can, boss, just keep me posted when to get the hell out of there," replied Murphy pushing the revs up to top speed.

Their launch picked up speed like a thoroughbred racehorse. Burger sent the girls back down for their protection and the five soldiers waited to get within comfortable range then opened fire on the muzzle flashes on the shore.

"They're firing, Sergeant! They're firing at the terrorists!" cried Constable Danielle Ahmet, tears formed at the corners of her eyes, "they're ours."

The joy and surprise in her voice gave the small group of police officers hope as their own motor launch pulled away from the wharf. It skirted the yachts protecting them momentarily from the terrorist's incoming fire.

"Hooky, get us out to sea and meet up with this other boat," called Dyson as he organised Brad and his men to get the prisoners and wounded below. The others were preparing to fire their automatic weapons on the enemy once they cleared the cover of the yachts.

It was a busy few minutes as both motor launches pulled strongly to get beyond the range of enemy fire. They slowed as Hooky set course to take them north to one of their stations in Shark Bay, three hundred kilometres away.

Once well out of range Murphy motored closer to the base launch. They both slowed to a crawl as Obi-Wan and Pipeline leapt across the gap to join Senior Sergeants Dyson and Hopkins. The two newcomers noted the stressed state of the officers and the damage taken by the launch in their escape.

"Hi Brad, hi Wayne," said Obi-Wan, shaking hands with his two friends. "I didn't think to meet you guys under these circumstances."

"Yeah, it's pretty shit-house isn't it," replied Brad. He handed Obi-Wan a hot cup of coffee then went below to make another for Pipeline.

"We've got four civilians with us and six operatives. I can see you've got a bit of a mess here too, how are your wounded? Do you need any help?" offered Obi-Wan, noting the two surviving wounded propped up on the floor of the cabin.

"We're OK for now, Obi. It was perfect timing for you to come and help us out back there. We were up shit-creek with only the one paddle." Dyson paused, his shoulders sagged momentarily. Obi-Wan and Pipeline knew the senior sergeant was exhausted as he struggled to decide what to do next, as they all were.

Dyson lifted his head to continue speaking, "We're heading to a secret training base up the coast, Shark Bay. We'll need to drop into some of the caravan parks for fuel on our way there. We'll decide what to do next once we get to the bay."

"Wayne, we saw Kollarena base go up, was it that bad?" asked Pipeline quietly as one of the wounded men on the cabin floor groaned and began to wreath in pain.

"I spoke to Super before the end, he said they had terrorist infiltration within their staff. It sounded like they didn't stand a chance. I'd say there were no survivors on either side. We lost Frenchy, too, did you know?" asked Dyson.

Pipeline was good friends with Senior Sergeant Frenchy Wahib, they both served together at Pine Gap on his first deployment a few years ago. They were firm friends, often spending time at each other's homes during their holidays.

"I liked Frenchy, he always made me laugh." The tough SEAL closed down after that.

"I'm sorry too, Pipeline, he was a brave man. He held them off us while we got to the boat. Frenchy knew he'd be staying behind." Brad coughed to disguise his own sadness. The shock of the assault, the violence of the terrorist incoming fire, the smell of blood and guts… He wasn't the only one in shock though, no-one was prepared for the apocalypse, except the Revelationists.

"What do we do when we get to this training base?" asked Obi-Wan, he wanted to build a picture in his mind that he could go back and work on later. His capacity to take information and step into it, like he was walking through a garden or a park, was what made him such an exceptional analyst as well as a first-class team leader. His mind-palace was perfectly formed for intelligence analysis. He specialised in solving complex problems in his head, he didn't need computers though he certainly knew how to use them.

Dyson groaned softly, "I'm sorry, Obi, I'm shattered. I've lost nearly half my team to those bastards. I've got two spies in custody that I just want to throw overboard, but I can't. I guess without them we might have been caught up at Kollarena and be dead by now. And no-one knows what's happened to our families back home either."

Brad decided to swing the conversation away from family, it was too dangerous for them all.

"The place in Shark Bay has camping gear and supplies, but that's about it. We're trying to contact Pine Gap for instructions but we've had no luck." Brad paused and thought for a moment, his eyes lit up. "You're the Pine Gap communications expert, you and Skip know more about that than our boys, what say you give it a try?"

Obi-Wan smiled. "I was just about to ask you, Brad. I tried to get our launch's CB onto our frequency but it would take a hell of a lot of modification. Give me a half hour with your radio, I think I'll have those instructions for you."

Within the half hour Staff Sergeant Ben Kennedy, 'Obi-Wan' to his friends, called Senior Sergeants Wayne Dyson and Brad Hopkins to join him.

"I've contacted Commander Cullen at Pine Gap, they know of this secret base in Shark Bay. They're sending in the choppers to pick us up. They'll take my party first then they'll take the rest of you."

He noticed the two visibly relax, Dyson even smiled, a tired, tight smile.

"No matter what happens, we need to get to Pine Gap." Obi-Wan continued, "Commander Cullen also informed me that this event is global, those Revelationist terrorists have initiated their 'Apocalypse'. We're cut off from the rest of the world down here, no one's interested in Australia, it's a backwater. That means we have to look after ourselves."

Brad's face shifted through several emotions before he asked, "What's happened to the US and Europe? Did they get hit too?"

Obi-Wan didn't answer straight away, his face went rigid. "No idea, buddy. We won't know if they've been able to frustrate the terrorists for some time yet I guess. The Revelationists must have friends in high places for it to have gone global - it's probably much like we've experienced here."

"What?" cried Dyson. "No, that can't be right, we've been monitoring these bastards for years. We've had our own network monitoring them and not a word slipped that this was about to happen."

"We knew, Dyson, we knew enough. We knew they were planning it, their weapons stockpiles, their rallies and drives to recruit members. We've known of the billions of dollars in their secret accounts. But they were protected, protected from the very top, everywhere. Who knows what they offered as bribes. Yeah, we knew, but no-one believed they would ever go through with it."

"I guess you're right, Obi-Wan, we did know, at least we knew they were planning this crazy apocalypse, but..." Dyson's voice trailed off, no one spoke about it again.

After a few minutes of silence, Obi-Wan stood and made his way back to his boat. Pipeline was already there, sitting silently with Murphy at the helm. Emily sat with them, chatting brightly to keep them awake. It was almost dawn - the first dawn of the Apocalypse.

They anchored in Shark Bay some days later. Their breaks at various caravan parks along the coast were fruitful. The CB chatter between holiday-makers, grey-nomads with their caravans and four-wheel drives, and other park occupants, made for lively discussion when the police and special operatives arrived with their uniforms and weapons. Everyone wanted news, news of the apocalypse, the terrorists, their hometown, and, most importantly, advice on what they should do next.

"Like we've told everyone else along the coast: we are all under siege, the terrorists have wiped out almost the entire Australian population. You'll have to organise yourselves into military-style camps. Find weapons, set outposts, develop a secret CB radio code to communicate with and prepare for an invasion of terrorists. We can't paint it any nicer than that, I'm sorry." Murphy said it like it was. He was always willing to help but he was also a straight shooter. A lot of people were shattered at hearing the news they may have lost their loved ones.

By his side was Emily, the petite blond with the bubbly personality and good looks. She made it easier for the residents to listen. Most of the time one of the constables went with them, a police uniform helped settle the restless crowds.

"Where is the army? What about the police, aren't they doing anything about this?" asked one holiday-maker. His caravan had everything that opened-and-shut, everyone around appeared to be fed-up with him.

"I'm sorry bud, there aren't any. As far as we know the police are either dead or scattered. The terrorists targeted them first. The military had terrorists planted within their units, you can only imagine what that would have been like. You've got to sort yourself and your community into some sort of defense. If you don't you'll just become fodder for the terrorists," explained Murphy.

"Well, that's not good enough, mate. You lot have weapons and you're all police of some sort. As a citizen of our country I demand that you stay here and protect us. You have no right to come here and take our supplies and then leave. We have rights and I demand you respect those rights." With his chest puffed out the bull-necked man sounded like a lawyer - or a politician. Some of the crowd laughed, some sighed and some just walked away.

Emily tried to find ways to better explain the situation to blow-hards like him. She was certainly more tactful and successful than Murphy.

"Sir, we know you're all worried about your families at home. We are too, we've lost loved ones as well. But we all have to do what we can to help our community." Emily stopped to point to the woman beside the grumpy old man. "Is that your wife, sir?" she asked and waved for the lady to join them. The woman was quiet, like a frightened mouse, she too looked like she was fed up with her husband. "What did you do before you came here on holidays, to Western Australia?" she asked. And so Emily worked the crowd trying to build confidence in their ability to develop a safe community.

By the second day on board the two wounded had died. They each had serious gut wounds and once peritonitis set in there was little anyone could do for them. Their scant supply of antibiotics proved ineffective. The police were down to nearly half their original numbers - plus the two spies.

The team's minor wounds began to heal in the salt air and judicious use of the first aid kit's remaining antibiotic ointment.

The food from the boat's pantry was running low, especially instant coffee and tea bags. The UHT milk went in the first 24 hours. Every evening when they pulled into a deserted beach they would fish, snorkel and gather rock oysters, crabs, lobster and shellfish. They certainly didn't go hungry, and the mud crabs and lobsters were delicious.

When they arrived at Shark Bay the group found themselves living on one of the most beautiful beaches on the west coast and quickly set up camp. It seemed that the word 'idyllic' was invented to describe such a scene. By their third day in Shark Bay everyone was beginning to relax. The trauma they had been through was slowly fading into the mists of the past.

Each morning they would go for a swim to freshen up then they would sit around the campfire to cook the leftovers from the previous night's meal and drink tea and coffee - until it ran out.

The smokers were hardest hit. The first aid and survival kits didn't cater for smokers. Rather than go without they resorted to drying the used tea leaves. The resulting herbage was wrapped in whatever paper they could get their hands on and smoked. It wasn't very nice but it helped satisfy their addiction.

With such a beautiful beach right on their doorstep the group spent a lot of time swimming and collecting food when not standing security with the prisoners or patrolling. Their clothing was beginning to rot in the damp heat. It smelt of mould and stale body odour and was basically unwearable. The group fell into the habit of gathering at the ocean's edge to strip naked and wash themselves and their ragged clothing. By day three no-one was all that bothered about their nakedness. Life in the services gave them plenty of opportunity to see naked bodies, attractive or otherwise. Soon most discarded their clothing altogether when they were lazing around camp.

Julie, Danielle and Kerrie walked to the end of the spit to check for signs of visitors. On their way back they met with Skip and Burger. Some members had begun to tan to a deep, honey-brown, like

Burger and Danielle, but fair-skinned Skip just went straight to beetroot-red no matter how hard he tried to cover up.

The two men were in the water collecting shellfish buried in the sand, the delicious 'pipis'. Sitting on the sand was a bag of the flavoursome shellfish they'd already collected, neither of them noticed the group of naked girls strolling towards them.

"Mind if we join you, that looks like fun," called Kerrie wading into the sea beside the boys. She started the special 'wriggle' that pipi hunters use to dig their feet into the sand locating their prey by feeling for the shells with their feet.

The two other girls joined in. Soon they were wriggling, digging and splashing in the waves together. It was about then that Danielle spied Burger, she liked what she saw and subtly moved to be closer to him. It also meant that Burger saw a little more than he was prepared to see of Danielle. It soon became obvious that Burger liked what he saw too.

Skip looked up when he heard the girls giggling and staring at the naked Burger.

"Hey, Burger, be careful, mate," called Skip, laughing, "we don't want any sharks seeing that bit of flesh between your legs and thinking it's a giant worm."

Burger realised that he had grown a few inches since the girl's arrival. He looked down, saw his engorged manhood and immediately sank beneath the waves. There was an embarrassed silence as the girls tried not to giggle, but as soon as Burger lifted his head from the water they engaged in some friendly banter.

"Hey, Burger, don't worry about it, we've seen it all before," offered Kerrie, the eldest of the group. "Besides, you've got nothing to be embarrassed about, believe me."

That, of course, only made Laurence Burger's tanned face turn almost as red as Skip's beard. He slowly moved away from the group mindful to keep his manhood beneath the waves.

Danielle felt the need to go to Burger's assistance, but she could only think of one suggestion - and there was no way she'd be saying that in public.

At night the campfires burned low as they placed a guard on the sand dunes with the prisoners and another in each boat. The rest slept in their sand beds, exhausted.

It was late spring and on some days the heat was almost unbearable. One morning Skip was sitting with his friend, Burger, trying to light their camp-fire for breakfast. Burger laughed at Skip as the wind kept blowing the matches out.

"Why is it, Burger, that one single match can start a bush fire, but it takes a whole damn box to light this one tiny twig? I'm damned if I can work things out sometimes," he chuckled.

The chatter on the CB radio indicated there was little chance they would meet with a terrorist patrol. They were well fed, healing with the salt water and sea air, and everyone seemed to be getting along well.

The two prisoners were cuffed and placed under guard, away from the group. Dyson interrogated them for information, of which they offered none. All Dyson wanted to do was be rid of them.

Each member of the group carried wounds, not necessarily physical but certainly psychological. No-one was prepared for the end of the world and no-one had time to say goodbye to their loved ones. They had left behind husbands, wives, children, boyfriends and girlfriends, and they knew in their hearts that there was little chance they would ever see them again. The Americans in particular felt the keen loss of never being able to return home to be with their loved ones, it hit them all hard.

Each evening Obi-Wan and Skip sat radio watch listening in on the terrorist's communication while also maintaining contact with the secret intelligence facility at Pine Gap. They often spoke with lone CB enthusiasts around the country. The story was always the same: the terrorists had taken out huge populations in all major cities and towns right around the country, right around the world. Their occasional contacts from overseas were particularly distressing. For Obi-Wan it served to reinforce that he may never see his family again.

Sometimes, when Obi-Wan was off duty, Julie would sit with Skip to keep him company while he was on radio watch.

"Hey, big fella," she called as she approached the launch in the dark, "want some company?"

"Hi, Julie, yeah sure. It's always a pleasure to have someone as good-looking as you drop in." Contrary to his mother's protestations Skip had actually learned some manners while gaining his engineering degree at Oxford.

"You flirt, flattery will get you everything, at least from my experience it does." Julie giggled lightly as she sat beside Skip in the launch. She handed him a hot cup of herbal tea made from fresh picked bush herbs.

"Not bad is it?" she asked as Skip finished his cup.

"Better than nothing, better than I've had in a lot of five-star hotels," he said as he handed the cup back to his companion.

The tall beauty sat close and snuggled into Skip's shoulder to get out of the strong evening breeze. She put her arm around him as she began to talk.

"Skip, how come Obi-Wan is so shy with us girls? He only talks to his soldier friends and the police but hardly ever to me and my friends. Even when we were in Geraldton, he sort of ignored us. Is it because we're female, you know." She petered off into silence leaving the question hanging there.

Skip chuckled softly, "Julie, that's funny. Obi-Wan is as horny as any of us but he is different, that's all. He's married, he's got a dozen kids and doesn't play around. He's just straight, you know, up and down. He doesn't fool about."

Julie listened, "Then he's not that way?" she asked at last.

"No, but autistic, maybe," Skip chuckled, he liked this girl, she was funny. "He definitely likes girls but he's shy around them. Cripes, haven't you watched him around you girls at all?"

"Yes, I did. I was sort of hoping he'd invite me to his bed, but he never did. I dropped quite a few hints too but he didn't pick them up. That's why I wondered, you know, men don't usually say no to a bonk or a rumble in the hay." Julie giggled and snuggled closer.

"Well, now you know. He's a genius too, and you know genius' are one step from crazy. He spends so much time inside his head he hardly comes out to see what's going on around him, especially when he's on holidays."

"So how'd he get that funny name, is he a Jedi too?" Julie laughed, it sounded like music.

"Ben's called 'Obi-Wan' because he loves Star Wars, he's fixated on it. When he's not cracking codes and running tests or developing protocols for counter-espionage, he's collecting Star Wars memorabilia for his kids." Skip cupped his mouth and whispered in Julie's ear like a conspirator, "he even dresses up in Star Wars costumes and goes to those Star Wars conventions. Plus… get this, he's also a serious Trekkie. He has a massive collection of Star Trek original movie posters, figurines and all sorts of obtuse memorabilia. I'd say he'd be worth a fortune if he ever sold it."

Julie stopped rubbing Skip's arm and looked at him. "No way! He's a Star Wars geek, so am I! We should make love and make Jedi babies." She laughed again. It delighted Skip to share his boring shifts with someone as bright and bubbly as Julie.

Julie wasn't finished, she had more things on her mind. Just like all lawyers she had to have answers to her questions. "Skip, I've got a question I've been meaning to ask you but I don't know whether I should."

Skip rubbed gingerly at his face, it was sunburned and peeling in places. "OK, well, if you have to ask then you just have to ask." He leaned across Julie to adjust the radio dial. It sounded like voices and he wanted to get a clean signal but it was just noise.

It had been a quiet shift and seemed like it would remain so - except that Julie's hand on his thigh suggested otherwise.

"OK, I hope I don't upset you, but… what does it mean to kill someone?" Julie didn't know any other way to ask such an emotive question so she just jumped right in.

"Wow. Now that's a deep and meaningful question, Julie," replied Skip, a little shocked.

"I'm sorry, you don't have to answer that. Just... well... I want to know. You're a soldier and you have to kill sometimes. Like those people at the hotel and now we've got those two terrorist prisoners. How, you know... how do you make peace with yourself afterwards?" Julie chewed at one of her fingernails, she was now a little nervous wishing she hadn't asked.

Skip considered the question before answering. "We train to be the best and for me that's radios and computers. I build them and maintain them as best I can. I also studied how to code and write software for all kinds of military communication systems. I was offered a position at Pine Gap because I am considered the best." He started with what was safest.

"I joined the military because they offer positions in what I love doing and I'd heard that signals staff get the best postings, at least I thought so back then. It was suggested that I apply for a signals position with the Special Air Service, the SAS, and I got it. I had to accept that sometimes I would need to fight and sometimes I might have to kill." He paused for a moment trying to think how to say the next part, the awkward part.

What saved him was Julie, she had always been impulsive, a bit like Tish, she spoke before Skip was ready. "So... I've seen you catch a fish and then hand it to the other's to kill, what does that mean?"

Once again Skip carefully considered his answer. "I've seen too many dead people. I've also seen animals killed in warfare. We live on a planet that is hellbent on killing for revenge or as an expression of power. That's not me, I hate killing, anything. Life is way too rare and precious in this universe to want to destroy it."

"That's why you won't even kill to eat?" she was curious and wanted to know, even if it meant pushing her friend like this.

"Julie, if I was starving or had to protect myself or a friend I would kill. I'm human, it's in my DNA to kill to survive. But if I had a choice I wouldn't do it."

"Does that mean you would go vegetarian?" Julie gave a pixie-like smile knowing Skip was doing his best to be polite.

"Ha, ha, that's funny, I didn't fight my way to the top of the food chain just to eat vegetables!" he chuckled. "Seriously though, Julie, it's impossible to be vegetarian in an environment like this. If we tried to stick to vegetables we'd all be dead by now. In the bush, living off the land like we're doing, it's downright impossible."

Julie smiled, "I'd miss all that lobster and fish and the oysters, yum."

"You've got me on your hook, girl, and I can't get off it, just like those fish," he said, smiling back at her.

It wasn't hard to like Julie, he decided. She was almost as tall as he was, she had a beautiful smile and complexion. She was manicured and toned, wore the most expensive clothing and had a nicely sculptured feminine body. Julie had money and she had brains, she also knew what she wanted and when she put her mind to it, she got it.

Skip decided he had to change the subject. "Hey, pretty girl, that's enough about me. I'm the most boring person in the world. You don't want to know anymore, I assure you." He patted her hand which had mysteriously moved higher up his thigh.

"I don't know about that, big boy," she smiled again, knowing how to play the game, "but I'll let you off the hook if you…" she leaned forward and kissed him lightly on the lips.

"Mmmm," moaned Skip, his sunburned back hurt and his loins ached, but his heart leapt for joy. "OK," he moaned softly, "you win, I'll do anything you want. I'm your fish caught on your hook to do with as you please."

Julie laughed, a delightful sound against the soft slap of the waves on the beach. "See, I told you flattery would get you everything." Julie eased herself down into the chair drawing Skip down with her - and then she did exactly as she pleased.

Besides her pleasant body, which he'd enjoyed viewing when they went swimming, it was her dark, smouldering good looks which attracted Corporal Laurence Burger to Constable Danielle Ahmet. He would sit and talk with her whenever he had the chance. There was more to Danielle than her sensational body, he discovered.

"I've got a wife and kids back home in Berkeley, we broke up a year ago," he said as he leaned back into the scooped-out sand-bed readying himself for sleep. "She went and found someone who didn't spend half his life overseas. I've not seen my kids since. I sometimes can't even see them in my head when I want to."

Danielle sat down beside him and peered into his eyes. "I wish this damn apocalypse never happened, Burger, then we could all go back to our miserable lives." She part giggled part choked back a sob. Things were so messed up and each member still had no idea whether they themselves would survive.

The lean, honey-skinned Ranger shifted his body to make room for Danielle in his sand-bed, he put his hand on her arm briefly. "Do you know what, Danielle? We're surrounded by the best beaches and the best seafood on the planet, but it's inside us that's starved."

She placed her own hand on his and left it there. "We've got each other, Laurence. We have to look after each other no matter what. Now we're at Shark Bay waiting for the helicopters to rescue us we can pretend to play 'Survivor' and run around naked for the camera's," she said trying to sound as though life was still fun.

Burger said nothing, he could now hear her softly crying.

"It's all so wrong, Danielle." He pulled her to him and crushed her in his arms. She sobbed into his shoulder as they lay beneath the starlit sky.

"I've got a brother in the army," Danielle admitted, breaking the pulse-throbbing silence, "he's a sergeant in the cavalry in Darwin, I hope he's OK."

"I've got a brother in the army too, in the states. I wonder what's happening over there," mused Burger, staring at the enormous night sky filled with countless stars.

Danielle liked this simple, uncomplicated man. She snuggled deeper into his shoulder and closed her tired eyes.

"I expect anyone in the military will be busy with this apocalypse," she mumbled shifting herself to brush her lips on his bare neck.

"We may never know, Danielle." He pulled her closer burying his face in her hair. Breathing in her scent he sighed in ecstasy. Burger finally realised what it was that he was experiencing. It was something he didn't expect to ever feel again, the desire to be with another woman, this woman.

It was during the early hours of morning that they both woke. The stars of the Milky Way were so bright that it almost hurt to look at them. The lean Ranger groaned softly as he felt Danielle's hand lightly brush his firm stomach as she sought his manhood. Automatically he sought out her lips and they kissed.

Their embrace awakened a powerful longing that surprised them both. Danielle's soft, sensual touch aroused the sexual heat of the handsome Ranger. They clung tightly to each other as they made love beneath the heavens. Not wanting to waken the others, only metres away, the frantic lovers tried to dampen the gasps, groans and sighs of their lovemaking.

It was the most exciting thing Danielle had ever experienced - making love under a canopy of stars and their ancient, mythical constellations. It felt as though their love was imbued with the blessing of the Gods and Goddesses of the ancient Greek and Babylonian pantheon. All too soon it was over, they fell asleep in each other's arms until the chill wind of dawn woke them.

Each evening Obi-Wan and Skip sat together to plan the coming day. They were close friends, complementing each other's personality and skills. Where Skip knew radios, Obi-Wan knew code and how to access the secret frequency bands - he could easily decipher codes in his head. Skip was amazed at what his friend discovered amid the scrambled noises they listened to.

"It's an international code, buddy, the scrambler is one I helped invent." Obi-Wan smiled as Skip shook his head. "Seriously, I've been around longer than you think. I was a little late to the party after the first Gulf War, but everything you hear now has had my input in some way, shape or form."

"You're not that old, mate, you're what, thirty-five? Nah, no one that young knows so much about radios and codes, no way," argued Skip.

"You make me laugh, Skip. It's not my age that counts it's what I've done to learn about cryptoanalysis that counts. I specialise in cracking codes. To do that you need to know how to create codes, and that, my good fellow, is what I've done since I was two years old," added Obi-Wan tuning into Pine Gap at their appointed time.

"Bullshit, Obi, you were still playing with dolls when you were two - just like I was," laughed Skip as he passed the cup of warm tea to his friend.

"Laugh while you can, Skip, but now we have work to do." Obi-Wan smiled to himself at Skip's good-natured teasing. Over the next few minutes the two friends were busy interpreting the code from their CB and replying to their superiors in Pine Gap.

Chapter 4 – Rattlesnake Strike

Senior Sergeant Wayne Dyson continued his investigation with the two prisoners, but all he got were complaints. It bothered him that his prisoners forced him to compromise the safety of his team. Not only did they participate in the destruction of the world, forcing it into something equivalent to the dark ages, but they considered themselves reasonable human beings who did what they believed to be in the best interests of their God and humanity.

"Come on, Wayne," pleaded AFP Sergeant Darren McIntosh, the spy of Kollarena. "We've spent all this time handcuffed and my wrists are bleeding and scabbed like blazes. I'll get an infection any day now and then you'll never get me an interview with Commander Cullen."

Colonel Harry McIntosh, his older brother, agreed. "Wayne, we promise not to try to run away or sabotage anything. We just want our hands free so we can wipe our own butts when we shit. You'll get more from us this way, I promise it."

Dyson was curious about the two brothers. Although they seemed to get along well enough, Darren exhibited a covert enmity and distrust of his older sibling. He decided to talk it over with his fellow senior sergeant, Brad Hopkins. They'd unsuccessfully interrogated their prisoners many times but the two had remained tight lipped.

The senior policemen walked along the beach as they talked.

"What is it between these two, Brad? I don't get it. They're both Revelationists, both up to their necks in terrorist activity yet Darren hates his older brother. I can't see any outward signs that Harry dislikes his younger brother, though," said Dyson stopping to scratch shapes in the sand with a piece of driftwood.

Brad looked at Dyson for a moment then the intensity of his stare intensified as he answered. "Wayne, I think something happened the morning of the raid. I recall some of our team were sent to investigate a homicide… the name McIntosh rings a bell… hang on, I'll get Constable Danielle and Sergeant Oddie."

They met up with Oddie after he returned with an armful of lobsters he and Ray had collected diving off the reef.

"Oddie, do you remember Darren McIntosh's wife, Debra?" asked Brad, watching to see Oddie's reaction.

"Yeah, I do, Debra, she was a sweet little thing, totally dominated by her mother-in-law. They had twin girls I think, Nina and Gina, beautifully behaved kids they were too. Why?" asked Oddie.

Brad then turned to Danielle, "Danielle, do you recall that triple homicide on the day of McIntosh's arrest when the apocalypse started? You were on call-out weren't you?" continued Brad.

"I do, it was a mother and her twin daughters, aged 10 years… holy cow! They were those people you just mentioned, Sergeant. Only the woman's name was Johnston, not McIntosh." Danielle was chewing her top lip as she tried to recall the details of that crazy day.

"Brad, that's Debra's last name, they never married. So, the poor bastard lost his wife and daughters on the morning of the apocalypse. I wonder if Darren knows," said Sergeant 'Oddie' Danse brushing his hair out of his face in the light sea-breeze.

Senior Sergeant Dyson looked at Brad and they both nodded knowingly. He said, "It seems Harry knows and Darren doesn't. Maybe something has been going on behind the scenes with these two. We know the McIntosh mother is one of the top Revelationist Priests, and she is a right nasty bitch from what we have on her. An ex-drug addict and prostitute, rumours have it she prostituted her sons for drugs. I wonder…" his voice trailed off. "OK, thanks, Constable Ahmet. Sergeant Dance, would you and Sergeant Hopkins like to come along with me and see what we can make of this?"

Harry McIntosh's face brightened when he saw the three senior policemen approach and sit down with him and his little brother, Darren.

"I see that you've been thinking about releasing us," he joked, "maybe we could do a deal now?"

"Maybe," said Dyson as he lifted Darren McIntosh to a standing position. "We want to talk to Darren first and see what he can offer us in return." Together the four walked off down the beach leaving Colonel Harry McIntosh seated, tied to his tree.

When the four sat down on the sand overlooking the ocean Dyson began his interrogation.

"Darren, we may have some bad news for you. Before I say anything, is there something you would like to tell us? Like, why you allowed yourself to sink so deep, handing out intelligence to the church?"

Darren looked at the three sergeants, he had worked with all of them during his deployment over the past three years. He could read their every mannerism, he knew something was up.

This was his first formal interview with all three senior police officers, they didn't look happy or comfortable. In fact, they looked like they did have bad news. For him that would mean just one thing, news about his wife and kids.

Darren's face grew pale and he whispered, "What have they done to my wife and daughters?"

He was already sobbing when Sergeant Hopkins spoke, "I'm sorry Darren, and I mean that. We've just put together some information we had from the local police who investigated a triple homicide in Geraldton. The victims were a Debra Johnston and her two daughters, Nina and Gina, aged ten years... I'm sorry to have to give you the bad news." Brad felt terrible, as he always did when he had to deliver the news of someone's death to their family. It was the worst part of his job.

Darren roared in pain. He tried to stand but his hands were tied behind his back, he fell rolling to his side. Bending over he beat his head against the sand and screamed. It was a traumatic sight, one the three policemen had seen countless times before.

"Darren, why? Why did they do that? Why did your mother and your brother allow them to be murdered? You mentioned that your mother was caring for them but why did she allow it? They were her own granddaughters," said Dyson softly.

Darren burst into tears. "My fucking mother is a psycho, she... she... she took my wife and kids hostage so I'd have to keep sending them intelligence. Now you know why I did it! I had no choice! I had to join the church and then I had to hand my family over to them. They said they'd look after them for me... why did they do this? Why did my brother let them kill his beautiful nieces?" He screamed and rolled on the sand once more, he didn't try to rise, he just lay there, paralysed, crying.

Dyson looked at his fellow police sergeants. "Boys, we may have solved the mystery. I don't know about you two but I'm about ready to execute Harry. I've had enough of this shit." For one of the rare times

Senior Sergeant Dyson, Tactical Response Group leader, wanted to take the law into his own hands.

"Sergeant, we won't be doing that. We've got to get them both to Pine Gap for questioning. They know things vital to our own survival as well as the country's," said Brad putting his hand on Dyson's arm. "It's going to be hard enough as it is without the weight of that on your conscience."

Dyson shrugged his friend's hand away. "Give me five seconds with him and it'll be done... Forget it, I'm stepping away from this," decided Senior Sergeant Dyson. His face creased with anger and frustration, and perhaps there were elements of compassion for David McIntosh.

"I think you pair had better take over supervision of the prisoners, I've done my bit." Dyson got up and walked away to be by himself amid the solitude of the sand and the waves.

Pine Gap Intelligence Facility, a joint US and Australian secret spy base right in the middle of Australia, was one of a few such facilities in the world to survive the initial onslaught of the apocalypse. On every continent such spy bases were heavily targeted by the terrorists. Those bases infiltrated by terrorist spies prior to the apocalypse were swiftly sabotaged and the base staff overwhelmed and executed. Despite the penetration of Revelationist spies not one base fell into the terrorist's hands. Each base has a self-destruct device that would detonate when a specific code was entered into its mainframe - or a specific code failed to be entered at set times. The Kollarena base was one that was deliberately detonated by its commander to prevent the terrorists gaining access to their intelligence and thus control of their coveted network of military satellites.

Pine Gap, thus far, had experienced no terrorist attacks, not as such. The exception was a single, or a small group of persons, who had managed to manipulate and control their satellites - and all communications with the outside world. Pine Gap base harboured a spy, or spies, and Obi-Wan was not the only one pissed off - so was his commander, Commander Sue-Ellen Cullen.

In her early forties, the attractive blond, US Navy intelligence officer, relied on her staff to find the traitors. Unfortunately her two key investigators, Staff Sergeant Ben 'Obi-Wan' Kennedy and Corporal Ollie 'Skip' Stone, were just surviving on the Western Australian coast, three thousand kilometres away, and in desperate need of rescue.

Pine Gap had two helicopters. One was a recently acquired stealth MH-X Black Hawk, call-sign 'Maverick', which was kept in an underground warehouse for stealth purposes. Her Black Hawk aircrew were all US Navy, they had been together for several years and were a tight-knit team. She likened them to Siamese quintuplets, they were like family to her and to her husband before her.

The Black Hawk aircrew went by the name of the 'Four Musketeers'. Major Sam Samuels had the same black moustache as the American movie comedian, Groucho Marx, from the Marx Brothers movies of the fifties and sixties.

One other helicopter, a utility MRH-90 Taipan, was the base helicopter. They used it to ferry personnel and stores back-and-forth from Darwin to their base in the middle of the desert. It's call-sign, 'Wagontrain', described it's purpose with a tribute to the wagon-trains of America's yesteryear. Right now Commander Cullen needed them both to bring back her precious special ops team.

The helicopters had a range of about 600 km and could carry up to 11 people each. The Taipan was now employed ferrying fuel, food and water to form a series of caches for their route to Shark Bay and back again. With twenty odd survivors she wanted to ensure they all made it back safely.

Commander Cullen dearly wanted to interview the McIntosh brothers as well. They no doubt had useful information for her and they even knew who her spy was. Her orders were simple: bring the Revelationist prisoners to Pine Gap.

Hades Battalion had other plans for Harry and Darren McIntosh. Priestess Lauren McIntosh, otherwise known as 'The Black Widow' but never to her face, was their dysfunctional, and some would say psychopathic, mother. The Black Widow wanted her sons back with her. As head Priestess of the Western Australian Revelationist Churches she held enormous power and got the things she wanted, no-one had the courage to stand in her way.

It was rumoured that she had executed two of her own teenage staff members for failing to follow her orders. Their bodies were never found. Their families were told that the teenagers had been sent to serve with the church in Istanbul, Turkey. No-one dared cross The Black Widow after that.

Each time Obi-Wan communicated with Pine Gap the spy within their facility passed his communication directly to the Hades Battalion. The first receiver was always Priestess McIntosh. She liked to work closely with the head of the Revelationist Church in Perth, General

Ethan Lawson. It was said that she worked a little too closely with him.

"Lawson, I want the Hades Battalion sent to Shark Bay, now. I want them to take out those helicopters as they come in to pick up the survivors… and bring my sons home." She held his gaze long enough for her young lover to turn his eyes away.

The tall, thin priestess of the Perth churches, had been his choice for Head Priestess. She had mesmerised him with her sparkling eyes, wide smile and perfect teeth the moment she introduced herself to him. He wooed her for months until she finally decided it was time to bed him. From that day she held the Perth Revelationist congregation under siege. By controlling the general she controlled the Western Australian church, and The Black Widow wielded her power with an iron fist.

"Darling, please, why don't you call me 'Ethan' when we're alone like this? It makes me feel, sort of…" he searched for words. "I feel abandoned and naked if I think you don't like me." He lay on the opulent king-size bed in his y-briefs as the 'Freemantle Doctor', Perth's cool, afternoon sea-breeze, blew in through the open window. "I've been very naughty," he teased, "would you like to… you know… punish me, and show how much you love me?"

"Ethan," Lauren said slowly and deliberately. Although she thought he looked ridiculous it was time to reward him for agreeing to her 'suggestion'. She dropped her dressing gown to reveal her toned, wiry nakedness. The youthful-looking grandmother ate healthily, thanks to her personal chef; she went to the gym twice a day for her workout with her personal fitness coach; and she used bottled Perrier Natural Spring Water for her tea and coffee.

With the generous support of the church congregation she also managed to fit in weekly manicures, massages and hair treatment. Her cosmetic surgery was done by the best surgeons in Thailand - her lovers considered her physical augmentations well worth the church's investment.

Ethan reached up to caress her enhanced breasts.

"How would you like it today?" She nudged his organ roughly with her knee as she straddled him. "How about I just sit here... like this..." she was surprisingly agile for her age. The Black Widow smiled inwardly as her lover's face contorted, he groaned loudly. "Or would you prefer if I just... did this?" Ethan's manhood grew larger as she crushed his scrotum. She enjoyed watching her victims suffer.

The Black Widow excelled at gaining revenge on those who tried to oppose her. If there was one thing she excelled at and enjoyed the most it was the manipulation of weak underlings.

She also wanted her son, Darren, to receive his punishment for failing her. How dare he allow himself and his brother to be caught by the police? Besides, it had been too long since he had felt the buckle of her belt.

"Base said they might need a week to place the caches and prepare for the extraction." Obi-Wan informed everyone that evening around the campfire. "They're having all sorts of trouble with their satellite communications. It seems someone is playing games, changing the code and sending it all over the world other than here."

Obi-Wan's blond hair was bleached almost white from the sunshine on the west Australian coast. His week of surfing and diving with his friends at Geraldton had toned his body and he now looked like the

Norse God, Thor. His commander, Sue-Ellen Cullen, said he looked more like Yoda, the wizened Jedi master.

"Obi-Wan," called Nancy, the tactical team's driver and sometimes master chef, "if the spies at Pine Gap can manipulate the big board satellites that means they can manipulate the other satellites. Is that right?"

Obi-Wan liked Nancy, her short brown hair, brown eyes and straight-up-and-down manner reminded him of his first teenage love.

"I've been busy working on that, Nancy. Skip had an idea that we might be able to vaccinate the satellites against the terrorists with our own Trojan or a virus. I haven't been able to crack the code the spies are using though, not with the radio equipment we have here. But I will once we get back to Pine Gap."

Ray was sitting with Cindy, the two had been on and off lovers for the past year and it seemed that his wandering eyes had finally settled on the one girl. That was his problem, his eyes were bigger than his brains and he could never keep his eyes from wandering. Cindy and his other girlfriends simply got fed up with his flirting. He never quite understood why they dumped him.

Since the apocalypse something had happened to Ray, he began to settle down. He and Cindy got back together and soon became inseparable. Ray was powerfully built from his daily work-outs but to his dismay he was an inch shorter than his girlfriend. Never-the-less he was enjoying his time in the sun and the sand. For him the crisis was a holiday – it couldn't get any better.

"Obi-Wan, I think there's a good chance we might be stuck out here for a while. Not that I don't mind and all, I've got good food and a good woman, and I don't have to polish my shoes every day." He squeezed Cindy's hand like they were young lovers.

Danielle, the girl with the brown eyes and attractive, dusty smile, was seated next to Burger, his hand was resting on her leg.

"If base can't see what's happening here or Geraldton then we don't know if we've been betrayed and the terrorists are listening in to us," she said.

Skip pulled a woollen jumper over his broad shoulders as a cool wind blew in from the sea. He had once skippered Sydney's Newington College senior rowing team. When he went to study engineering in the United Kingdom, he soon became skipper of Oxford University's successful men's rowing team as well.

"Danielle," said Skip, "Commander Cullen is using her own ultra-secret channel and protocols. The only way the terrorists would know where we are is if they were told by someone in Pine Gap who had access to her secret channel. It's on the cards the Revelationists are on their way here right now but we have little choice other than to sit tight and wait for orders. Commander Cullen may have other satellites she can use but if they're compromised too then we just have to keep a sharp eye on the horizon for the enemy ourselves."

"So that means we could be tracked here through your conversations with Pine Gap?" asked Ray, he had a ragged home-made cigarette sitting between his lips, it seemed to be part of his anatomy. He and Cindy sat a short distance from the others. The wind had picked up and most of the group moved closer to the warmth of the fire. Ray and Cindy stayed where they were, they just snuggled up closer to stay warm.

"Yes and no, Ray," answered Obi-Wan. "It means our transmissions might be passed on to the terrorists. If the spies are able to scramble our communications with Pine Gap, plus control the military satellites, then they can just as easily get a message to Perth or Geraldton of our whereabouts. It won't be easy to avoid detection if that's the case."

Obi-Wan stood up and stretched. "OK, folks, Sergeant Dyson has the watch roster for tonight. Just to remind you all - if you get caught you will be tortured and killed, there is no doubt of that. We are currently basking in a false paradise. There's a rattlesnake out there waiting to strike - we will only be troubled if we blink first."

It was way past midnight as Commander Sue-Ellen Cullen sat with her second in command, Major Will Binks, in her office. They each had a drink in their hands as they discussed the events of the day, as they did most evenings.

The couch at the back of the commander's office had become Sue-Ellen's bed since the apocalypse. She had barely slept these past few weeks and felt somewhat responsible for the events that had occurred on her watch.

"Will, we've got to get Obi-Wan and Skip back here, we're flying blind. It's like there's a little mouse loose inside our computer and he's chewing through cables and messing up our networks. Communication with our satellites have all gone down and we have no control over them. We need them here to sort it out." Sue-Ellen ran her hand through her short, blond hair and wondered when was the last time she'd washed it. It was as though she never had time for anything these days. There was always just one crisis after another.

"And the big board, Will, what have our comms guys done with it? It works then it stops working. I tell you, I'm losing my patience with everyone." She slurped the last of her dry martini and reached to pour another.

"Sue-Ellen," said Will. "We've got the best IT specialists here with us, they're working flat out, they have since the apocalypse. They know what they're doing but I still think it's coming from an outside network who have taken control of our computers and satellites." Will was tall, over six feet. He was once slim and well muscled, but lately, he'd begun to put on a lot of weight. Tonight, under the artificial lighting in the commander's office, he looked tired, obese and ready to drop where he sat.

"I know I know, they just have to work harder, Will. We've got two helicopters busting their balls right now, working twenty-four-seven to bring our team back to us and we can't even tell the crews if they'll arrive to find our boys alive or dead. We're blind, Will, damn blind to the entire continent."

"I've had our investigators working back to back shifts trying to sort out the problem, Sue-Ellen. They've uncovered nothing. No suspects, no evidence, just more errors. Now we have what appears to be a damn Trojan, or virus of some type, controlling some of our satellites." Will pulled a handful of pages out of his case and held them out for Sue-Ellen to read.

"What are these?" she asked as she leafed through them. "So you've definitely found a virus in our network? Is that responsible for our computer blackouts and communications problems with the satellites? What about the International Space Station, can we still talk with Dr Tantoni?"

"Sue-Ellen, the IT guys think this is caused by the virus that attacked our system yesterday. We can't communicate with some of the satellites. We can't get Dr Tantoni and his team in the ISS up either." Will leaned back in his chair and tossed back the last of his bourbon. "I've got to get back to the big board, Sue-Ellen. I'll wake you if anything comes up. Get some sleep." He stood and leaned across to kiss his commander on the cheek. "I've got it tonight, you can take over at dawn. I'll be needing a break by then." He strode to the door and closed it quietly behind him.

Once he was out of the room Sue-Ellen clicked her computer awake and checked the base security protocols. She then tried to establish contact with the big board and satellites using her personal, ultra-secret code, but nothing worked. She slammed her fist on the desktop in frustration. Suddenly she noticed that there was something wrong with her computer screen background image. Sue-Ellen always used a picture of herself and Reece, her deceased husband.

'*So… what is this*?' she asked herself. She studied the picture carefully. All looked fine except a small smudge in Reece's left eye, it wasn't like that before, someone had changed it.

She sat for a few seconds then had an idea, converting the image to raw code she saw her message. It was from one of her and her deceased husband Reece's most trusted spooks - an enigmatic ghost who went by the call-sign, 'Goldmine'.

"Sue-Ellen, your man's left a thumbprint - goes by the call sign 'beeprep'. I found a message today to your man in Adelaide Alpha Army, Major Daniels. Your base spy has asked for an upload of special porn. He has top secret possibly ultra security clearance. Be

careful, I can only guess that he is a 'He' from the message. Watch your back, he's very close to you. Your best clue is his call sign, work that out and you've got him, 'Goldmine'."

Sue-Ellen sat back in her chair and closed her eyes. 'My God I'm tired,' she thought as she instinctively rubbed at her face and straightened her mess of hair. 'So Goldmine has a lead, but there's only me, Will, Obi-Wan, Skip and a half-dozen staffers at top and ultra-secret level.'

The call sign, 'beeprep', made no sense to her. She left her mind there as she put a call through to the Black Hawk. Captain 'Curly' Moe confirmed they would be ready before midday tomorrow.

'Reece, where are you? I need you now my love, I miss you so much.' She felt tears forming behind her eyes and let them flow down her cheeks. It helped, it usually did.

It was late and she really needed some sleep if she was to be of any use tomorrow. She felt the weight of responsibility for her staff and that of their families now living under her roof since the apocalypse. Sue-Ellen crawled into the messy couch she used as a bed, pulled the blanket over her shoulder and fell asleep.

As she drifted off she had a thought to check the personnel files of all top and ultra-secret staff - perhaps that is where she would find a match to Goldmine's clue.

Revelationist Captain Lim took control of the four-wheel drive patrol vehicle for the last hundred kilometres into Shark Bay. His battalion signals operators were wise to the skills of the Pine Gap experts, Obi-Wan and Skip, and kept their communications systems turned off.

The terrorists were going to stage a two-pronged assault right at the moment the Black Hawk and MRH-90 Taipan helicopters arrived to pick up the Pine Gap group. They moved into the Shark Bay caravan park to meet up with several of their covert operatives and began their preparations.

Chapter 5 – Chopper Down

Sergeant Darren McIntosh staggered across the sandy beach back to his brother. He looked like a dead man.

"What the hell's wrong with him?" ejected Colonel Harry McIntosh. Harry's beard had grown long and bushy but it was quite clear to the police officers that he knew his secret was out. His face went from red to white as he looked into his brother's eyes.

"What bullshit did they tell you, Darren? Did they say something to turn you against the church?"

Darren didn't respond he just stared at his brother, an unnerving, dangerous stare. Sergeant Brad Hopkins tied him to a tree trunk away from his brother.

"What?!" Harry yelled, his voice becoming hysterical, guilt written all over his face. "What! They told you bullshit about me didn't they!"

"You lying, deceitful, blood-sucking scum bastard! You knew, didn't you! You knew our mother would execute them the day of the apocalypse, that's why you visited, wasn't it! I thought it was strange, not once in twelve months have you been to Kollarena to see me yet it all happens exactly the day of my family's execution. You knew and you let her do it!" The venom in his voice was worse than a blow to the face. Harry sagged against his tree trunk and mouthed soundless words.

Brad looked at Oddie and the two walked away to leave them to argue it out. They'd be back in a few hours to pump Darren for information. He'd then willingly testify against his church, of that they were certain.

The sandy beach was idyllic. White sands, fresh fish and other seafood delicacies, that, plus mild sea-breezes by day and pleasant tropical nights. The team of special ops and police felt more refreshed each day. The sun was high in the sky when Brad and Oddie made their way back to where they had placed their captives, but the space in the shade beneath the trees was empty.

"What the hell?!" exploded Oddie, "where have they gone?"

"Shit!" Brad exclaimed, then he saw the knife a short distance away, towards the water. There were traces of blood and it looked as though the knife had been deliberately thrown there. There were scuffle marks showing there had been a fight. But there was no body or bodies, no trail of blood.

Brad and Oddie raced to gather the team together. They left four to guard the boats and the rest separated into pairs to search the beach and the bushes behind their camp. They found nothing.

"Damn it, Brad, what else do they have if they could get a knife off us without anyone knowing?" said Dyson looking closely at the site where the two prisoners had been.

"Sergeant, Burger and I'll head inland," offered Skip, he had his AK47 as did Burger. The two got along well, both were experienced in the bush. "We'll track them if we can and fire three shots if we find something."

The two loped off into the bush where they soon came across tracks and scuff marks of a fight. They followed for twenty metres when they found Darren's body. It looked like he'd been strangled. Skip fired three rounds and they waited for their comrades to gather.

"It's possible Harry was the one who had the knife. He must have cut himself free, forced his brother here to strangle him after he'd lost his knife," said Skip, examining the ground. He began walking in ever-growing circles to try to cut Harry's tracks.

"Harry's our man then, if we find him we'll string him up. We're the law now and I don't give a donkeys-arse if Commander Cullen wants him for an interview and cup of tea." Ogden 'Oddie' Danse, ex Australian commando and now AFP sergeant, had known Darren McIntosh well. He'd worked beside him in several investigations for the AFP. He liked the guy and had met his family at several social outings. They were such a nice, gentle family. Like Dyson he was shattered by the events that had unfolded. The horror and the evil that had visited their land had finally broken him too. He now knew what his colleague, Senior Sergeant Wayne Dyson felt: a loathing fanned by a savage, primal lust for revenge for all the innocents executed by the Revelationist Church.

Skip and Burger failed to locate Colonel Harry McIntosh, he'd obviously escaped them in the dense undergrowth. Night was falling and it would soon be too dark to see.

Realising that there was a good chance that Colonel McIntosh would survive to contact his battalion, Staff Sergeant Ben 'Obi-Wan' Kennedy suggested that the group should move to the mainland side of Shark Bay straight away. It was easier for the helicopters to pick them up as well as a strategic move if they needed to escape by vehicle. If the terrorists came now they would be trapped on the peninsula with their only escape being the water.

Oddie called their new campsite 'Bush Bay', it looked much like anywhere else on the Western Australian coast. Over the next few nights they went by launch to collect fuel and brought back four, off-road vehicles to transport them to Pine Gap across the desert if the choppers didn't make it. By their fourth night they had a collection of fuel, fresh water, packaged food from abandoned caravans plus dried and salted seafood - they felt prepared for any emergency.

Captain Lim was now ready to set and initiate his ambush with the help of their operatives from Carnarvon and Geraldton. A half-dozen nights after the group had relocated, Lim's company silently made their preparations to assault the camp at Bush Bay. They now settled in to wait for the signal from their spy in Pine Gap to launch their assault.

Obi-Wan's group had made good their time while waiting for their evacuation as well. They'd set their defensive perimeter and were confident they could get back to Pine Gap regardless of what was thrown at them.

'*Just hurry with those choppers,*' thought Obi-Wan.

"We have a scrambler on our system, some bastard's screwing up our radar and radio," said Major Samuels in his lazy, southern drawl. "Can you isolate that signal and clear it?" he asked Captain 'Curly' Moe, who was in the co-pilot seat of their MH-X Stealth Black Hawk helicopter.

Samuels then called up the MRH-90 Taipan, their companion in the rescue mission and slightly ahead of them, approaching their destination at Bush Bay.

"Wagontrain, this is Maverick, do you have a fix on that signal trying to scramble us? Over." Before Wagontrain could answer he received a call from Pine Gap.

"Maverick, this is Downtown, we've got the scrambler and we're working on it. I suggest you stay at altitude until we get some clarity on the situation, out." The call from Pine Gap made its way through some horribly scratchy noise that set the crew's nerves on edge.

"Damn, this is just shit," said Captain Moe, "Wagontrain's due to touch down in one minute. Where's Obi-Wan's call? This is just another damned screwed up mission!"

"We could put Wagontrain upstairs on watch while we load, then swap." Samuels growled in frustration, "damn, what's wrong with this blasted radar? We've had nothing but problems since we left the Gap."

Although Captain Lim's soldiers were highly trained and outgunned and outnumbered their opponents, they were also naive and reckless. The three crews manning the shoulder-fired, Surface-to-Air-Missiles, simply couldn't wait for the order to fire.

"Sir, there's something down there, at 9 o'clock, two dots. Looks like SAM's. They're coming in fast," called Crew Chief Lance Trudeau, his voice strained but calm. He was stationed at the port door with his M240 machine-gun at the ready.

Captain Moe looked to his left and saw them, two Surface-to-Air Missiles. "We've got missiles at 9 o'clock heading for Wagontrain." He was already switching to their sister helicopter to inform them. "Wagontrain, this is Maverick, you've got SAMs at 9 o'clock. We're going upstairs suggest you do likewise."

"Roger, Maverick," came Lieutenant Panela, "engaging counter-measures…" he paused, as the two missiles exploded harmlessly, their counter-measures worked faultlessly.

"Maverick, we have eyes on dust and vehicles heading towards ground zero. I believe them to be terrorists..." there was static as his signal went off the air. A missile from a third position, hidden along the rocky shoreline, exploded just inside the exhaust of the Taipan.

The Stealth Black Hawk pulled up sharply as another set of missiles veered off and exploded close to their own counter-measures. They quickly moved out of range and eventually were out of sight, leaving the group below alone, stranded. It was as they moved out of range that the 'Four Musketeers', as they were affectionately known, noticed that something just didn't seem right with the computer systems running their Black Hawk.

Staff Sergeant Obi-Wan had been listening in to the conversation but the scrambler used by the terrorists now prevented all communication between himself and the choppers. However he did note the missiles and comments about dust clouds, he knew that they really were in the shit now.

Murphy cried out, "They've taken out the Taipan! It's coming down." He put his hands over his face and remembered. It was in Afghanistan, two years ago, a skirmish with the local Taliban - over nothing, a barren valley and a lazy, winding creek. Murphy had been waiting his turn to be evacuated, providing covering fire as his squad leap-frogged backwards to their rescue helicopter.

For some reason the chopper lifted and left him there, alone, stranded. Within seconds he was witness to it bursting into a ball of flame, falling back to earth in a blaze of smoke, fire and pieces of metal and bodies. Over the following twenty-four hours he lived in terror, fearfully evading Taliban terrorists by stealth and his silent knife.

Emily was watching the helicopters with excitement, relief and anticipation, but now she felt horror as the huge machine fell from the sky. She suddenly felt alone and betrayed, leaning forward she screamed, clenching her hands in shock.

Glancing up she saw Petty Officer Second Class Matt Murphy, the SEAL who had so bravely helped save their lives only a few weeks ago. He was standing still, his face a mask of shock and horror. Reacting instinctively the petite Emily stepped over and drew him to her.

"Hey, big fella, it's OK, I've got you." Then the sobs started deep inside her too, they just spilt over and possessed her. So much had happened, so much had been lost.

At thirty-one she was still single, a series of failed relationships, domestic violence, several miscarriages - then one day she just gave up. No one wanted her, all she had to show for her life was a career in business administration, depression and post-traumatic stress. She would look in the mirror and cry, "why?" Why was she the one left standing beside the bride at every wedding she attended?

Murphy held on to her tightly as his body shook with the emotions he'd kept locked away for the past two years. He finally forced the tears to stop but his body held the memory and he couldn't stop shaking. Twenty-four hours he waited for rescue, pissing in his pants as the Taliban stalked the valley looking for him. He cried then too. Murphy couldn't tell his own friends and family back home of how he cried in fear, of how his urine soaked into his trousers. The only reason the terrorists didn't smell him was because they smelled twice as bad.

At his debrief he tried to explain what it felt like to kill someone, up close, forcing a knife through their ribs. The powerfully built, crew-cut SEAL was surprised at how lean the Taliban youth was. The boy was strong too, much stronger than he expected. As Murphy grabbed at his throat the boy twisted ferociously trying to escape. He stabbed, over and over he stabbed at that poor kid. He'd made sure to cut the boys airway with his left arm locked around his throat but it wasn't enough. The boy was so wiry and skinny that he had trouble keeping his grip. Murphy recalled how scared he was that the boy would slip free, just slip right out of his arms.

He'd stabbed over and over, feeling the boy squirm in terror. Murphy could taste the boy with his face tight against the youth's scalp. He could still smell that stale, acrid sweat - the smell of fear. Then the memory of when his knife finally found the gap between the boy's ribs to slip smoothly into the boy's body. It was almost sensual, like entering a woman's sacred place - but it gave no pleasure, just death, and he immediately felt an enormous shame. He was ashamed that he'd killed that kid. So many times since that nightmare twenty-four hours he had wondered how old the boy was: thirteen, maybe fifteen at the most?

Watching the MRH-90 Taipan helicopter burning its way to the ground was like he was watching his buddies falling to their death leaving him alone in that valley of evil. It was a mixture of guilt, terror and horror. He felt himself collapse to his knees, lifeless with shame and guilt - '*I killed that boy, he was just a kid.*' That thought triggered his other shameful nightmare, '*why did I survive when I should have died with my buddies?*'

Emily didn't let go. She could feel him trembling, slipping, hearing his mumbled cries. As she eased them both to the ground she pulled him into her breast like a mother does her injured child.

"I'm not going to let you go, Murph, I won't let you go," she sobbed into his shoulder. It seemed as though they stood like that for ages. They didn't notice the movements around them or the yells as their team prepared for battle. They were locked into a parallel world, clutched in an embrace so tight, afraid that this sacred moment of connectedness would slip away.

"Sweet Judas! Get yourselves back under bloody cover! Murphy, what the hell do you think you're doing out there!" cried Sergeant Dyson. He was in a panic fumbling with his G36 assault rifle to swing it towards the incoming terrorists.

In spite of their best efforts, they were soon overwhelmed and separated into small groups by the terrorist numbers and fire-power. Fortunately, over the past two nights they had hidden their vehicles and gear in a dry creek bed nearby.

Captain Lim was kept informed of the incoming helicopters by his superiors in Perth via their Pine Gap spy. What they didn't appreciate was that the group they were fighting was made up of determined, highly trained, service men and women. They were like hornets defending their territory and would rather die than give up.

The Perth Revelationist company from the Hades 'Flaming Damnation' Battalion now skirmished forward through the low, bushy scrub.

Staff Sergeant Obi-Wan had taken command of the perimeter defense for the chopper extraction. But now he led his team of special ops in a determined effort to halt the enemy pushing forward and overwhelming their position. He was grateful that his team knew exactly what to do in situations like this. They kept up a continuous automatic rifle fire as the rest tried to extract to the vehicles.

Senior Sergeant Dyson, the tall, sun-tanned ex-infantry captain, led the survivors of his anti-terrorist team to block a squad of enemy forcing their way behind a screen of thick, coastal scrub. The sand dunes were low but provided sufficient cover for him to quickly place his team.

"Hooky, take Lana and Kerrie to that position!" he tried not to yell. Next, turning to his remaining team member, Nancy, he said, "Nan, we stay here and hold it. No matter what, we don't move until we know the others are safe." Dyson pulled out one of the grenades he had salvaged from the Bearcat and placed it beside him.

He nodded to Nancy as she kept a close watch on the surrounding bushes. She knew what he wanted from her, she also knew quite well that she was capable of delivering it too.

Nancy, the Bearcat driver with the short hair and brown eyes, had found courage in the midst of her grief since losing her lover, Constable Chopah. She found comfort, to her surprise, with Senior Sergeant Brad Hopkins. Brad was an old hand and had been in the Western Australian Police force most of his adult life. He was quiet, kindly and competent, she had always got along well with him during their shared time in Geraldton. But right now he was the furthest thing from her mind as heads popped up in front of her.

"Firing!" she called as she raked the bushes only ten metres away. Her Heckler & Koch G36 cut through several of the terrorists. She heard screams and grunts as her bullets found their target. Nancy saw three more terrorists stand up and fire back at her, two were already in her sights and they fell to her fire. But the third had time to put a burst of 7.62 mm bullets into her chest.

Dyson heard the bullets slamming into his colleague beside him as he too rose to return fire. He felt a chill run up his spine as he saw Nancy drop and slowly slid down the face of the sand dune. He cut his grief short as he leapt to another defensive position and fired at the enemy that rose to peer above the dense bushes.

Now he wished he had kept another member of his team with him. To his left he heard them firing and screams as they too hit their targets. There was movement to his front and then to his right. He reached to pull the pin from his grenade but never completed the action. Senior Sergeant Dyson's body twisted as bullets hit his side, he mouthed a cry as more bullets hit his trunk and head.

Ex SAS corporal, Hooky, and his two companions, Senior Constable Kerrie Black and Constable Lana Wosniac, were trying to prevent a rush of terrorists to their front and right flank. Their automatics sounded loud in the mid-morning air as they fired short bursts to drop several of their targets.

"Come on, follow me," he called softly leading them to assault the right flank of the approaching terrorists. Hidden behind a low sand dune they rose and Lady Fortune smiled upon them. There were four terrorists crouched in enfilade position not more than five metres away. They cut them down in seconds.

"OK, on me, this way." Again Hooky led them to get behind the terrorist platoon but they slammed into a group of terrorists who had the same idea. A vicious hand-to-hand fight ensued.

Lana's wounded hand was now inflamed and swollen from the effort of running and fighting. It gave way as one of the terrorists, a tall woman in her forties, knocked her sideways with a blow from her AK47.

Dropping her rifle Lana reached for her Glock 21 pistol but the woman was fast and strong, she smashed her rifle butt into Lana's face. Lana's nose broke with an audible crack and her lips split like jelly from the force of the blow.

The small, dark-haired policewoman fell backwards as the taller woman followed through, plunging the blade of her bayonet into Lana's stomach.

It was five against two now as Kerrie threw her empty rifle at one of the terrorists. It gave her enough time to draw her Glock 21, she fired as fast and as furiously as she could.

As a senior member of the state's anti-terrorist team, Kerrie spent more time than most on the range and at the gym. Each time she was betrayed by another loser lover she would burn out her anger and grief in heavy physical training. Today that training paid off in spadefuls but not before a bullet tore a chunk of flesh from her arm.

Hooky took a savage blow to his shoulder which knocked him to the ground. He instinctively rolled to one side, as he did he let go of his empty rifle and drew his pistol, a Beretta 92, an old favourite from his army days. He fired as he rolled and took out the last of the enemy, a big woman lining up to bayonet Lana a second time.

Senior Constable Kerrie Black stood panting, her pistol by her side and blood streaming down her left arm. Hooky moved to stand beside her. They looked at each other, then at Lana, squirming on the sand at their feet. Lana was already dead but the nerves in her system hadn't quite registered it yet.

"Bastards!" cried Kerrie. She choked back a sob as she gently closed Lana's eyes with her fingertips. "Lana was my friend."

"Yeah, she was a good one, I liked her a lot." Hooky spoke softly but then sagged and grunted as a shooting pain lanced through his left shoulder. "Kerrie, we're ineffective here. I think I've broken my shoulder and you've got a bad wound." He gingerly eased his arm into his shirt and tried to immobilise it with his webbing.

"Here, let me help," said Kerri as she tried to ease his arm into the make-shift sling with her uninjured arm. She noticed her hand was shaking. "I think we need to pull back to the vehicles, we're damn useless. We'll be of more use holding a fall-back position there." Kerrie bent down and picked up her rifle and slid in another magazine, awkwardly. Hooky did the same but had to hand his rifle for Kerrie to reload for him.

The AFP and WAPOL position was also under heavy, continuous fire. Already ex-commando Sergeant Oddie Danse was down and his team pinned behind a low sand dune.

Sergeant Brad Hopkins took command. "We're fucked if we stay here," he panted, slamming another magazine into his G36. "Ray, take Danielle and Cindy, get to the vehicles. I'll provide cover as best I can." He too had a single hand grenade now held in his right hand ready to throw. The three police constables knew they had few choices, they nodded to their senior and said their goodbyes.

"OK, when this explodes, you lot run. Good luck, give my love to Nancy if you see her." Brad knew that she might not survive this massacre either.

He looked at each in turn, to imprint his staunch friends into his memory. Like his good friend Frenchy, he knew he wouldn't be joining them on the road to Pine Gap.

"OK, ready?" he said, not really expecting a response. The three had fresh magazines and were crouched, ready to run. Brad pulled the pin, counted then threw the grenade into the scrub where most of the firing was coming from. They heard the thud and crack of an explosion followed by screams. Brad then stood up and opened fire as the three raced towards the creek bed where the vehicles were hidden.

The three ran across open ground as they sought to gain the cover of another sand dune. Only two made it. Ray, the smart-mouthed life of the party screamed as bullets smashed into his leg and he crashed to the ground. He was only halfway to the safety of the sand dune. A burst of automatic fire stopped his screaming.

"Fuck!" cried Constable Danielle Ahmet gulping air deeply into her burning lungs. "Where's Ray?" she asked as she turned to her friend, Cindy Briggs. Danielle choked back a scream. Cindy had collapsed beside her, her back against the sand dune. Blood seeped from her uniform top. She tried to speak but bubbles foamed from between her lips. It was ghastly and it was wrong. Danielle leaned across to her friend, tears streaming down her cheeks. Just then Cindy shuddered and stopped breathing, Danielle had just lost another good friend.

"You bastards!" she moaned as she peeped above the dune. She could see three terrorists running towards her, she raised her rifle and fired. Two fell and the other skidded to a halt and raced back to their cover. "You pricks! You stinking bastards!"

She now saw Ray lying on the sand in a pool of blood.

'There's no-one left,' she thought as she turned towards the vehicles in the dry creek-bed, then she ran for her life.

Obi-Wan's team of special operatives had the added task of protecting the four civilian girls who had stayed with them from the hotel in Geraldton. His team were the only ones who had any success in forcing the terrorists back.

Pipeline and Murphy were assigned to protect the girls, which they did while also firing on the flank of the enemy. The girls did their best to remain calm, but it was in vain as one by one they forced their screams into their hands or stuffed their shirts into their mouths.

Obi-Wan led Skip, Soldier of Fortune and Burger forwards and split the enemy into two groups. One group fled towards the road and their transports while the other moved across only to be met by the incoming fire of Murphy and Pipeline.

"We've got them on the run, Obi. We'd better retire to the vehicles and get shifted. That's only one squad we've pushed back, there's more out there," called Burger. Obi-Wan and Fortune listened to the firing all around them as their police colleagues fought just as viciously as they did. The firing stopped for a moment as an explosion indicated someone had thrown a grenade off to their flank. Then the firing started up again.

"Yep, we've got to keep moving. Come on, let's get back to the girls and shift ass to the vehicles." Obi-Wan pulled his team back to the cover of their initial position and together they all ran to the vehicles. They stopped briefly beside Brad's limp body on the sand.

"Looks like Brad's team have pushed off too," said Burger. He turned when he heard a burst of gunfire and one of the girls screamed, a bullet had knocked Gracie to the ground. It had gone in one ear and out the other. She was dead and her friends were clearly in a state of hysterics.

"Shit," Burger said under his breath as he turned back to gather the girls to force them to run with him.

Obi-Wan spun on his heel and fired as he saw movement out of the corner of his eye. He instinctively waved his hand to send his team off once more while he and Fortune laid down covering fire at the movements behind them.

"Loading," he said softly, slipping one of the few remaining magazines into his AK47. Fortune nodded and did the same as soon as Obi-Wan was ready. Together they fired and ran to join the others, leap-frogging each other towards the vehicles. Bullets followed them as the terrorists realised they were escaping.

When they arrived at the four-wheel drives, ready packed for just such a situation as this, they noticed there was only eleven of their group left: Burger, Fortune, Skip, Pipeline, Murphy, Kerrie, Danielle, Emily, Julie, Tish and Hooky.

"Where is everyone?" asked Obi-Wan, he looked around and unconsciously noted how well the team had positioned themselves to defend the vehicles.

"We passed the police team, they were all dead," replied Pipeline his head hung down as he gasped for breath.

"Damn it. And we saw Brad, he was dead too," offered Gary Fortune.

Danielle announced softly, "I saw Ray and Cindy, they're dead." She was clearly exhausted clinging tightly to Burger's arm for support.

Hooky shook his head and said, "We lost Dyson and Lana, and both Kerrie and I are ineffective."

Obi-Wan nodded. "So it's just us then. OK, into these three vehicles - stick with me." In moments the vehicles roared into life skidding up the dry creek-bed towards the desert.

They left the terrorists confused, wondering where their enemy had disappeared to. The vehicles were below eye level and all the terrorists could hear was the sound of revving motors disappearing into the desert.

Captain Lim sat in the air-conditioned cabin of his luxury Range Rover. It was the very model and colour he had always lusted after but would never own on his bank-clerk salary. He listened silently to the reports from his staff through the window and considered his next course of action.

The captain had done extremely well. He had knocked out both helicopters, killed most of the police and scattered the remaining few into the desert. He needed to freshen up at the hotel in Shark Bay and consider his next move.

There was no need to contact his superiors until later that afternoon. So he decided upon a swim in the pool, a few drinks with his friends and then he would report in. Lim felt expansive enough to invite his NCO's to join him for a drink when they arrived at the hotel.

"Well done everyone. Sergeant Francis, take Corporals Santos and Hawker and bring in anything the police left behind. Send a squad to determine the direction they've headed and post them to block the main road. Set up for an overnight stay and we'll relieve them in the morning. The rest of you will be heading back to our base at the hotel for drinks and dinner.

"We'll convene at 2000 hours tonight after I speak to headquarters. I'm not sure if they'll send us after them but just in case have your troops prepared. OK, driver, let's head off to the hotel." Captain Lim pressed the button of his window to close out the world. It slid smoothly upwards to keep the cool, air-conditioned air in and the desert heat out.

On his arrival at the hotel he was disappointed to find his colonel waiting for him. Colonel Harry McIntosh had indeed escaped. He'd commandeered a car at the caravan park and beaten Captain Lim to the hotel. He now took command of Captain Lim's men and sent them to form a wide umbrella to capture or kill the police and special operatives. Meekatharra was one township he considered worth sending a squad to investigate.

"Captain, get me some prisoners. I want to see them bleed and hear them scream."

Chapter 6 – The Four Musketeers

They saw the incoming surface-to-air missiles and fired off their counter-measures. Major Samuels pulled the chopper lift and stick sending them higher. No sooner had they started the climb when a second set of missiles came at them. The warning blast signalled the missiles were locked-in so Samuels manually hit their second set of counter-measures. Again the missiles exploded harmlessly but no one noticed several pieces of shrapnel hit the Stealth Black Hawk deep in its under-belly.

Once they had settled their bird and prepared to return to assess how best to attack their enemy, Captain 'Curly' Moe did a double take at the dials on the dash.

"Hey, Major, something's going on here, it looks like we've been hit." Quickly flicking a series of switches to diagnose the problem the major looked carefully at the diagnostics.

"What the hell?" Samuels frowned and checked again, this time running specific diagnostics manually. "We've got a problem here. Curly, take the stick, I'm going to get BB to have a look around inside."

"Hey BB, what's up with the electrical system? It looks like the hydraulics are working, the pedals and flaps are fine but the engine indicators are all over the place," he called to Crew Chief Brian 'BB' Bingley.

BB unclipped his headgear at the side door where he manned his M240 machine gun, then clipped back in at his own computer to run his checks. Next he pulled up the access floor panel and climbed down into the space where various electrical systems were housed and began running through his systems checklist. This was something they'd diligently trained for many times but it was never much fun in a moving aircraft.

"Major, I can see it," he called into his mic. "We've got several pieces of shrapnel and they've taken out one of our computer servers. It's still working but there's damage and I'd say we'd better get her down where we can do repairs. I doubt this baby can get us home, nor will it carry a load."

"BB, is it that serious?" asked Samuels, his brow was creased but his demeanour calm, professional.

"Sir, it's serious enough that I crapped my trousers as soon as I saw the damage."

"Right you are, BB." As Major Sam Samuels settled back into his pilot seat he had his copilot plot a course to the nearest airfield. "Curly, I don't care where it is as long as it's close. I can smell BB from here - so it must be serious."

"Sir, we've got one airfield just south of Exmouth on the coast up north, it's not fully manned and I doubt they'll have the electrical parts we need, but it should do us fine," said Curly.

"Chief, how long do you think we have? I need two hours to put down at... RAAF Base, Learmonth," called Samuels into his mic.

"Sir, I think we've got two hours. I'll keep working on it, but no longer than two is my guess... shit!" he said dropping his screwdriver, it fell between the panels. Fortunately it was attached by a hand-strap. Slowly, carefully, he drew the lanyard up - but it caught on a piece of broken panel right where the shrapnel had entered. He cursed and tried again.

'*This is going to be a fun trip,*' Crew Chief 'BB' Bingley thought to himself.

They didn't make it to Learmonth, things began to fall appart near the West Lyons River quite a distance from their destination.

"Moe, check the controls again will you. I've got the helm but she's sloppy as all-shit." Samuels spoke calmly into his mic, "BB, we've got slack here in the controls, what can you see in there?"

"As I said earlier, sir, we're just about done. Hang on, there's smoke coming up through the panels - I'd say right now is a good time to put…" there was the noise of a fire extinguisher. "Sir, we've got flames here. Let's do it now before fate decides for us." Before he had finished speaking BB could feel the rapid acceleration towards the ground and knew he had better get his ass up into the body of the Black Hawk and belt-up.

"Crew, we are in a controlled dive… at this stage. It looks like we'll make a soft touchdown but prepare for a crash landing." Samuels had performed many systems-fail simulations over the years but this was his first real crash-landing in his beloved stealth Black Hawk. As they side-slipped he searched for a place to land his craft. It had to be flat and large enough for the giant helicopter - then he saw it, at the bottom of a canyon, alongside a flat, narrow dry riverbed.

"Moe, what's this place called?" he asked his copilot.

"Sir, by my calculations it's a region called the Pilbara, that must be the West Lyons River… not much of a river is it?" he replied. "We're quite a ways from Learmonth and even further from the Exmouth township."

As the Black Hawk settled to the ground both BB and his crew-mate, Lance, jumped out and hosed down the underside of the aircraft with their fire-suppression equipment. They took their time knowing full well that if they lost their helicopter now they may-as-well kiss their lives goodbye.

Lance came back from his reconnaissance towards dusk. He was tired, depressed and he collapsed beside the campfire without speaking.

"Thanks," he croaked accepting the cup of coffee from Samuels' hands. "It's a maze of buttes, canyons and dry creeks, this place is a labyrinth. But I saw water, the creek has some shallow pools with some scummy water in it. If we boil it we should be able to drink it."

"Did you see any sign of habitation? People? Smoke? Anything?" asked Curly. Lance shook his head as he downed the rest of his coffee. Putting his mug out for BB to fill again he continued. "Nothing, Captain. It looks like this desert maze we're in goes on forever." He lay back in his camp chair and poured a little precious water onto his shemagh scarf and gently rubbed at his face and neck.

"Buddy, you'd better drink some more water after walking about in this heat." BB brought a water bottle over and placed it next to his friend. "I've got some food, chicken and spiced vegetables, it's nice too." He left the plate on a small table beside his friend.

"We're now locked-out from all communication with Pine Gap and Obi-Wan's crew. We've got no other form of communication, even if we try the alternative satellites we get kicked. Radio communications has been well and truly jammed," BB said to his friend. "But the good news is there's plenty of food and there should be more water here, somewhere. In fact this is probably a favourite holiday destination of the rich and famous. Unfortunately they're not here to rescue us."

Major Samuels looked side-ways at his crew chief. "We keep getting this radio interference, BB, it may be a local signal, someone who can hear us... we'll keep calling Pine Gap regardless. We never know, the jamming may stop and some local might receive us and come to our rescue. That's about all we've got to hope for right now."

Lance finally sat up, he'd only now realised how hungry he felt and began eating his stew. "So what's the damage bill, BB?"

"We've got a stuffed computer server, a simple remove and replace job but we've not got the parts. We have the tools, the access to the computer and we've got fuel and caches all the way back to Pine Gap, but we're stuck out here in the desert holding our dicks in our hands." The solid, blond-haired mechanic stood up, took a second serving of stew and sat back down. His mind becoming fixated on his machine, he felt responsible for its repairs and his crew's safety.

"Sam," offered Curly, "is it worth one of us heading through the bush and trying to contact Learmonth or Exmouth? I'm sure there'll be someone there who can help us?"

The tall, thin major put his cup of coffee on the sand at his feet. Looking in the direction of the setting sun he considered the idea.

"I'll send you and Lance out in the morning, together. Head out at dawn and get as high as you can. Take the maps and create a search grid. If we're going to be here for very long then we need to know every square inch of this place. Our bird is possibly the only stealth aircraft left. If we compromise it then we might as well be dead because Sue-Ellen will surely want our heads on a platter if we don't bring it safely home to her."

After three days of doing everything they could to fix the electricals and what minor damage was done to their aircraft, the crew of MH-X Stealth Black Hawk, call-sign 'Maverick', settled in for their long wait. On the third night they were surprised when they received a clear channel on their radio console. A previously empty slot was now working. It had zero jamming and no noise. It was as clear as though they had been standing next to the stranger on the other end.

"Maverick, this is Goldmine, do you copy?" was their first communication with the outside world since their aborted rescue attempt at Shark Bay. Captain Moe was on radio watch, he spilt his coffee over his shirt front when he heard the voice.

"Holy shit! Major! We have a contact!" he called. Quickly wiping the coffee from his shirt he acknowledged. "Goldmine, this is Maverick, I copy you, over."

"Maverick, welcome to Goldmine's channel, over."

"Goldmine, please identify yourself, and how the hell did you make this connection, over."

"Maverick, I've been listening to your sorry story for the past week. I know things and I can help you, but first, you have to pass the test. Please put Major Samuels on, over," continued the strange voice with the strong Australian accent.

"Goldmine, I think you need to identify yourself first. Who are you and how did you contact us? Over."

"No deal Maverick, get Samuels first, then we'll parley. Over."

By this time Samuels had climbed into the helicopter and was now seated, waiting to take the mic from his 2IC.

"Goldmine, this is Maverick Actual, Major Sam Samuels, and you are?"

"What a pleasure to meet you, virtually, sir. I will give you what you need. But first I want to know that you are who you say you are, over."

"Go ahead, Goldmine, ask away. Over."

"One question Major, name your commanding officer's husband and why he isn't there with you now. Over."

"Goldmine, that's easy, but I have a question for you, if you don't mind humouring me. Who is my commanding officer's child and where may they be based? Over."

"Maverick, good question. OK, I'll go first. Name is 'Tanner', and he's based about six hundred kilometres north of you. Over."

Samuels smiled and looked across at his three crewmen now crowded inside the chopper.

"Thank you, Goldmine, it's now my turn. The name is 'Reece', and his absence is due to an unfortunate accident some years ago. Over."

"Nice work, Maverick, now we can get down to business. I must say that I knew who you were anyway but thirty years as a spook is hard to shake. Before I start, do you have any questions? Over."

Samuels nodded his head thinking of a million questions he'd like to ask, he settled for just two.

"Right, firstly who do you represent and work for? Secondly, how did you make contact with us? Over."

"I'm a retired spook, ASIO and beyond. I'm working covertly with several of your friends whom we shall not name, even though this connection is ultra-secure. I'm on your side, Major." There was silence as they heard the disembodied voice mumbling something.

"OK, I've sent you a detailed data file of your location and I will inform your friend of your position and situation."

"Friend? Over."

"The Star Wars guy, you know him I presume?"

"Roger that, Obi-Wan's one of ours. But you haven't answered my second question, over"

"Maverick, I'm an ex-communications engineer, a bit like a souped-up Obi-Wan. I've created my own code, uploaded it as a Trojan into the bases military satellites, and inoculated them from the spies currently present in Pine Gap. I have a direct connection to the world from here, no one can break my code, it isn't in the books. No-one can access or control the satellites now, no-one but me. I have some friends on the network too, you will be talking with Joey, call-sign 'Tonto' over the next couple of weeks while I organise your rescue."

"Goldmine, that's great, but can you put me through to Commander Cullen? Call-sign QE3? I need to speak with her, it's urgent."

"That's a negative Maverick, that place is crawling with spies - they're all bloody spies for fuck sake! I won't talk to them and neither will you - nor can you, period. I've had to lock-down Pine Gap for security purposes."

"Goldmine, that's an order not a request!" came Major Samuel's terse reprimand.

"Fuck you!" Goldmine closed down the connection.

Chapter 7 – Desert Hell

Staff Sergeant Ben 'Obi-Wan' Kennedy kept his foot on the accelerator pushing the four-wheel drive to its limit. He kept his foot down until he was satisfied they were out of danger. Once they'd left the cover of the dry creek bed and were on higher ground he stopped and pulled out his binoculars.

"Not much out there, mate," said Skip, his face was smeared with blood and sweat – it matched his short, red beard. "We've got the HF CB in the back. I'll try to get Maverick, he must be somewhere... did anyone see him go down?"

It had all happened so fast that no one quite knew which helicopter crashed. Hooky said he saw the Black Hawk fly away but it looked like it dropped suddenly, like it was hit, but he wasn't sure.

Burger was still in his vehicle, Danielle sat beside him, her arm around his shoulder. They'd both lost friends and so they sat comforting each other, as lovers do. The three girls from the bar in Geraldton were with Murphy and Pipeline. They stood outside their vehicle drinking from their water bottles. The girls hugged each other in their grief and shock at losing Gracie.

"Come on girls, we've got to get you to Pine Gap. We'll look after you as best we can but you have to help us," said Pipeline in his deep, southern drawl.

"We can help drive if you need us to, Pipeline, we're not useless," offered Emily. She was standing next to Murphy, claiming him as her own. She felt that she was on some sort of firm ground with him - and she wasn't going to let one of her friends take him, not now, not after what they'd just been through.

Kerrie Black was being tended by Fortune, the Delta medic. She was feeling faint and Fortune knew she was in shock, for many reasons. It was a combination of the heat, the horror of the fight, the loss of her friends and the loss of blood from her wound. She was exhausted and needed rest.

"Burger, help me out here, buddy," he called as Kerrie fainted in his arms. Burger climbed out of his vehicle and jogged over to help Fortune ease Kerrie into the back seat of the Landcruiser. "She'll be out for at least an hour," said Fortune as he injected their last vial of precious antibiotics into her arm, "you'd better keep an eye on her while I see what I can do for Hooky."

Fortune then attended the tactical police officer, ex-SAS corporal, Paul 'Hooky' Pan. His collarbone didn't appear to be broken, it looked like his shoulder had dislocated and then popped back in during the fight.

"How's that feel, Hooky?" asked Fortune as he gently moved Hooky's arm back and forth.

"Yeah, it's a bit better now. I was sure I'd broken my shoulder or something in there," Hooky replied, his eyes scrunched up tight as Fortune moved his arm back and forth again, this time in slightly larger arcs. "I'll be right soon enough. Don't worry about me, mate, just look after Kerrie, she's a gem."

"Kerrie's asleep, Hooky, it's rest she needs more than anything. She's lost too many friends today, we all have," said Fortune fixing a proper sling for Hooky's arm. Fortune's scar stood out bright on his sunburned face. "You just take it easy, buddy, we might need that arm of yours to hold a weapon. We have a lot of desert to cross and no idea what we'll meet on the way."

Obi-Wan took another bite of the salted lobster they had packed for just such an emergency and studied his map.

"This road heads towards the Northern Territory. We'll have to head cross-country to get to this place, Meekatharra. There are a few farms out here too, we'll stop at them for fuel and supplies." Obi-Wan lifted his cap and squinted into the sun as he rubbed his sweaty forehead. "Skip, can you get anything on the radio?"

"Nothing, no satellite, no Maverick, no Pine Gap, nothing." Skip left the radio set and walked over to Obi-Wan. "I wonder what happened to the chopper? It's stealth, has the best counter-measures on the planet. Hooky said he saw it drop downwards like it was hit by one of those SAMs, but we don't know what happened to it. It could have packed up and gone home for all we know."

Burger was in hearing range and walked over to the two. Danielle was now with him still holding on to his arm. Hooky noticed and felt a sense of loss. How he wished he was the one she was holding onto.

"I think they might have gone to the first fuel cache, what do you reckon?" Burger asked.

"Yeah, makes sense..." said Skip, "but this scrambler jamming our signals and those bullshit stoppages we're experiencing from Pine Gap, it pisses me off. We're blind and we've got, what, two, three thousand kilometres of desert to cross? We'll be driving forever. If we don't run out of water we'll run out of fuel and if none of that happens our vehicles will fall apart on us."

"Hey, buddy," said Burger, the good-looking Samoan Ranger, "come on, you're supposed to be our Aussie tour guide here, we'll make it. It might take us a month but we'll get to Pine Gap, just chill out a bit."

Skip smiled, his face was covered in grime and dried blood, the cut to his cheek was starting to scab over and it burned when his salty sweat entered the cracks his smile made.

"Damn, it itches when I smile." Skip ran his fingers gingerly through his short, thick red beard, then wiped at the sweat dripping down his face. "Yeah, you're right, Burger, we'll make it. Not by tomorrow like we planned, but we'll do it." Skip left them to go back to his radio.

The scorching sun beat down on them as Obi-Wan called everyone together.

"Right, we've enough food and water for about three days. We'll eat now then we'll head off. We've had to leave some of our gear behind in the other vehicles but there are some farms on the way into the desert itself that we can visit for supplies." Obi-Wan pulled at his short, unkempt blond beard then drank deeply from the water bottle Murphy handed him. "Thanks, Murph. We've got about three or four hundred k's drive to get to Meekatharra. We'll stop there and stock up on fuel and food, then we'll drive night and day until we get to Pine Gap." He paused to straighten his map. "We'll only stop to swap drivers, no CB chatter unless it's an emergency. Questions?"

Julie, the tall, attractive lawyer, spoke up. "Obi, we're deadbeat, do we have to drive all night? Why not spend a few days at Meekatharra and get some proper sleep. We've got three thousand kilometres of desert driving ahead of us. I think we'll all be needing a few nights of decent sleep before we leave Meekatharra."

Tish looked at Julie and gave a slight nod. "That's a good idea. I'll second that. Even one night in a proper bed won't hurt."

Obi-Wan nodded his head up and down as he processed the many possibilities. "Sorry, girls, we're too close to the enemy. All they need do is send a patrol to Meekatharra or get word that we're in the vicinity and we're history. Don't forget we have wounded and civilians. We're not a fighting patrol we're compromised and retiring to home base."

"It's going to be tough, Julie," said Skip, his beard still a mess of dried blood. "We can sleep in the vehicles while we drive. It's not the best but we have little choice. Maybe once we're in the deep desert we can take a day off but right now, I'd prefer not to."

Julie nodded as she stepped up to Skip to wipe some of the blood off his face. The two had grown closer since the night they made love - they now spent most of their free time together.

The girls looked at Obi-Wan, they saw he wouldn't change his mind. "OK, it was just a suggestion," said Tish, the bubbly party girl. She scuffed her feet in the dry sand, "but at Meekatharra I bags buying the first beer!"

Ranger Corporal Burger struggled with the reality of having a new love in his life, Danielle. He realised that he still grieved the loss of his wife and family. Sitting in the vehicle he had time to reflect. '*This is all too much, too fast. I need to pull back a bit before I get hurt again,*' he thought as he sat in the driver's seat and started the engine.

The three vehicles made a convoy as they drove cross-country to Meekatharra. It took them much longer than they expected. Fortunately they met some healthy kangaroos, wild goats, and even some cattle on their journey, and ate them. The farm stations were few and far between, they decided to only visit when desperate. They had enough food from their rations and what they shot and dried; and enough water from the few dams and water-holes they came across.

But fuel was getting low as they approached the mining township of Meekatharra.

"Shhh," whispered Obi-Wan, "they're probably all sleeping." Murphy, Pipeline and Burger were lined up behind him on the outskirts of Meekatharra. The convoy had arrived late that evening. Immediately Obi-Wan organised a reconnaissance of the town with the intent of filling their fuel tanks. He also considered that a meal and a beer or two at the Royal Mail Hotel would be good for morale. After their gruelling desert crossing the possibility of a cold beer was worth investigating.

"Burger, you and Pipeline check out the petrol station, meet me back here in five." Obi-Wan turned to Murphy. "Murph, I need eyes inside that hotel, you're with me."

The fuel station was close to their entry point and proved to be a winner. Electricity was supplied by solar panels to the entire Meekatharra region. All they needed to do was switch the pumps on from inside the station and they could pump as much diesel as they needed. Pipeline and Burger investigated the station itself, the door was unlocked and by shielded flashlight they checked to make sure they could fill their cans in the dark. Once satisfied the two headed back to their rendezvous point.

While Obi-Wan waited for Murphy he saw a half dozen four-wheel drives parked in the rear car-park. It looked like they belonged to visitors staying at the hotel. Carefully shielding their flashlights they saw, lying on the backseat of one of the vehicles, magazines of AK47 ammunition and what was definitely female underwear.

"If these are our friends from Geraldton then we've got a fight on our hands. They could be dingo or kangaroo shooters but those panties and bra just don't quite fit my image of a rugged, outback kangaroo shooter," whispered Murphy with a grin. He wanted so much for the Perth Revelationists to be sleeping in the hotel, he was spoiling for a fight.

They made their way to the back door of the Royal Mail Hotel. The rear door was unlocked so entry was simple. It was pitch black inside, there wasn't even a night light.

Silently the two began the slow but thorough examination of the downstairs bar, lounge, toilets and kitchen. They found nothing to suggest terrorists were staying there. Obi-Wan motioned for Murphy to follow him up the stairs.

They found a lounge room with a wide-screen TV, the room was large enough for a dozen or more visitors. This was where they found their first confirmation that the enemy were staying at the hotel.

In an ancient armchair slept a large man, beside him leaned an automatic rifle, an AK47, and an empty bottle of Bundaberg rum. Murphy looked at Obi-Wan and opened his eyes wide in anticipation. There was enough light for Obi-Wan to recognise Murphy wanted to put the man into a deeper sleep, one he wouldn't wake up from. Obi-Wan finished searching the room then motioned for Murphy to do the deed.

The SEAL grabbed the man by his greasy hair and slashed his knife across the man's throat. As he sliced deeply through both the terrorist's jugular vein and carotid artery he whispered, "This is for killing my friends, you bastard." He released his grip on the man's hair letting his head drop to his chest, the man was very dead.

Obi-Wan had kept guard, now he inspected the man's weapon and ammunition. He collected what he could including a grenade and a knife. He handed the AK47 and webbing pouch filled with ammunition magazines to Murphy. He then motioned for his buddy to leave the gear in the stairwell while they went from room to room silencing the terrorists - at least that was their intention.

The first room they came to wasn't locked, they slowly opened the door and crept in. The blinds were pulled down and the room was pitch black. Murphy switched his flashlight on and covered it with his hand. The glow was enough to show a man and a woman asleep in the bed, curled into a spoon shape. Obi-Wan had the terrorist's knife in his hand. It had a razor sharp, 8-inch blade, perfect for killing.

'Right now I'd just love to have my old Ruger GP 100. Damn, I'd have some fun,' he thought. The pistol he had in his webbing was an old M1911, one he'd taken from the terrorists in Geraldton. *'There just aren't any decent pistols in this whole darn country.'*

Obi-Wan held his knife in his hand as he deliberately slung his automatic rifle over his back, keeping it well out of the way of his killing arm. With a swift and decisive movement he plunged his new-found knife into the neck of the sleeping male. Immediately he withdrew the blade and plunged it into the back of the female. Their bodies stiffened then relaxed. The solidly built Ranger staff sergeant leaned on the twisting bodies until they'd settled to a deathly stillness. It wasn't pleasant and he didn't enjoy it. It was a task that just had to be done.

Something then fell, crashing beside the bed. The noise was so loud that both special ops froze where they were - listening. Murphy turned off his torch and they waited, pistols drawn.

"Can't you pair stop having sex for five minutes? We've got a big day tomorrow! Arseholes!" cried a male voice from the room next-door. The walls were so thin they could hear him fart as he settled back into his bed.

The two soldiers now checked the room for weapons and gathered what they could carry without compromising their stealth, and executions.

The next room was also unlocked. Inside was a female, sound asleep, snoring softly. With the blinds up there was just enough light to see her lying on her back, naked except for a sheet covering the lower part of her body. Murphy drew his knife and stabbed upwards, up into the woman's chest and into her heart. She stiffened then slumped. There was no noise except her release of breath, it made no more sound than her snoring had.

So far they had been successful in delivering death to four of their enemy, but Obi-Wan was getting nervous, something was wrong, his breathing accelerated.

Murphy noticed and checked the room. He held up a pair of men's trousers for Obi-Wan to see.

'Damn,' thought Obi-Wan, 'she's got a lover and he must have gone out for a smoke or a pee.' He motioned for Murphy to step behind the door while he positioned himself on the other side. Murphy indicated that he would take the man down. Just then the sound of an approaching pair of bare feet came to them through the closed door, the door swung open.

"What the..!" cried the man loudly, just before Murphy's hand found his throat. The man didn't have time to say anything else, his guts spilled onto the floor as Murphy's knife sliced up through his stomach and into his heart.

But that was enough to waken the terrorists. There were sounds of movement, voices calling to each other, a door swung open.

At a nod from Obi-Wan the two raced quietly along the hallway and down the stairs. The Ranger set up position ready to fire into anyone coming down the stairs while Murphy raced for the door to signal to their two buddies.

"What's going on here!" cried the same male voice they'd heard earlier, he stomped loudly along the hallway. "I've fuckin' told you lot to shut-the-hell-up and get some sleep. It's 4 o'clock in the fuckin' morning and we've…" his voice suddenly ceased and Obi-Wan knew the man had found the dead bodies. The light in the hallway came on as the sounds of movement grew into shouts and orders. The hotel now turned into a boiling cauldron of terrorists.

"Perfect," whispered Obi-Wan removing the pin from the terrorist's grenade. He waited for the sounds of movement to approach his position then pulled the pin. He gently lobbed the grenade into the hallway above, then raced for the back door.

There were shouted yells then the sound of an explosion. This was followed by screams, all hell broke loose as Obi-Wan was joined by his recon team.

Smoke billowed out of the windows and doors, flames illuminated the terrorists as they ran to escape.

The special operatives positioned themselves at all exit points and opened fire as the enemy tried to escape the building. 'Fire superiority' in a situation like this is a strategy that not only kills but it also terrifies and forces the victims to make mistakes. The terrorists made the big mistake of trying to get out of the building where they were quickly cut down.

The sounds of gunfire not only woke the township it also alerted the remaining special ops team waiting beside their vehicles parked not far from the hotel itself.

"Fortune, I'm going in to see what's up. Get the girls ready and have the vehicles started. I'll come back with news, give me five minutes," called Skip as he raced towards the sound of firing.

He could now clearly see the action centred on the hotel, as he got closer he saw his team members firing. There appeared to be no return fire. He saw his friend and called out to him. Obi-Wan motioned for him to stay where he was. Skip immediately prepared for any terrorists who may have been billeted in some of the houses in the town.

With the intensity of firing into the hotel no-one noticed Burger hit by gunfire and slump to the ground. The big Samoan Ranger knew that he was hurt bad. His jaw stiffened and his chest wouldn't let any air in. He tried to crawl towards his buddies, tried to call out, but he hurt too much inside. The bullets had gone deep into his chest smashing muscle, bone, organs and punctured his lungs.

Pipeline looked to see where his friend was, it was standard practice to know exactly where friendlies were. Burger wasn't at his station. When he scanned the ground a second time he saw a figure curled-up on the ground.

"Obi!" he called, "Burgers hit, I'm going over to check on him."

There was no longer any movement or noise from inside the hotel, so Obi-Wan motioned for Skip to come to him. Before he could get a word out they heard Pipeline's voice rise then catch in his throat.

"Obi, Burger's dead," he cried with a rush of emotion that choked his voice, it came out more as a sob than a statement. "He's just dead." Pipeline had to say it again. The big man collected what he could of his friend's gear and trotted over to Obi-Wan's position. "He's dead, Obi," he repeated to himself, his head bowed.

The township was now alive with movement but no one had come near the firefight around the hotel. It appeared that the terrorists were either dead or subdued. Obi-Wan made the decision to bring the vehicles in and fill them up, now, before the terrorists re-organised, if there were any left.

Skip left with Burger's gear and ran back to the vehicles, he didn't say anything just tossed the gear into his Toyota and signalled for the girls and Fortune to follow. They silently filled their tanks and jerry-cans at the fuel station.

Obi-Wan took a confused Danielle aside and told her that Burger had been killed. It was an unpleasant task that had to be done. Danielle burst into tears and collapsed to the ground. Julie and Emily saw and raced over to comfort her.

By now the garage owner was there. He was confused and angry, as were some of the townsfolk who came to see their precious hotel going up in flames.

"What the hell is going on here?" asked Joey the mechanic and garage owner. "I go to bed with the missus and wake up at 4 am to gunfire, the hotel's in flames and some bastard's stealing my diesel…"

He moved to stop the boys from helping themselves to load up their vehicles and jerry-cans - with his fuel.

"Now you can't do that, fella's. Come on, I've gotta make a living." He stopped when he saw the look on Skip's face.

"You had terrorists living in that hotel of yours, you lot should be ashamed of yourselves," said Skip, his face reflected his fury and grief at the loss of his good friend, Burger. "I'd suggest you cooperate or you'll be one sorry bastard." His voice was cold and hard.

Obi-Wan came over to ease the tension. "Buddy, when did the Revelationist soldiers turn up here?" he asked, mindful that some of the residents might be Revelationist members too.

Joey was of medium height, thin but solidly built. He scratched his balding head. "Couple-a-days ago, just rolled up and took over the hotel. They've been partying pretty hard, they've not paid a cent for their fuel, their drink or their beds neither, proper bastards they are. Poor Dominic spent a lifetime in the mines to buy this pub too, he's made it the best watering hole we've had. They beat him up you know, hurt him, broke some ribs. They said the worlds ended, something about an apocalypse has hit the world. Maybe you jokers could tell us what's really happening out there." Joey was now on a roll and couldn't stop talking. "We've no TV, no radio, everything is static... we got power because that's from our solar panels, but we've had no news, now the church people have guns and won't let us leave..."

Obi-Wan cut in, he didn't want to spend all morning listening to Joey ramble on. "Bud, the church people are terrorists, they've destroyed the world as we know it. You folks had better arm yourselves and organise a defense of some sort. Stick together, appoint a leader, fight them."

Joey looked at the two special operations soldiers and asked, "Who the hell are you guys anyway?"

Skip looked around at the growing dawn, in another few minutes the sun would rise.

"Mate, we're the good guys, that's why we haven't killed you yet." He smiled to take the edge off his remark. "Do as my friend suggested. Organise a resistance, gather as many people as you can, get them armed and fight to protect your precious community."

Chapter 8 – Meekatharra

It was dawn, smoke from the hotel rose like a funeral pyre in the warm morning air. They stood around Ranger Corporal Laurence Burger's grave, each said a few words, it was a morose affair.

Danielle stood crying on Kerrie's shoulder, the two constables had a lot to cry about. Everyone felt miserable and depressed. Not only were they simply exhausted from their trek through the searing heat of the desert but they had lost too many friends. Obi-Wan noted everyone's mood was low so he called them to 'gather 'round' at his Toyota. It held the long-range HF radio which was like a security blanket for them all.

"This morning we hit the enemy hard. It looks like we took out the local hotel while we were at it, for which I am personally responsible and very very sorry." The sound of Danielle sobbing made everyone uncomfortable and miserable. Obi-Wan pressed on. "I was hoping to take today off and rest up but that's not going to happen - especially now that we know the Revelationists are looking for us, or they will soon enough." He was interrupted by one of the elderly locals wandering over towards them.

"Hey, my name's Walt and my lovely missus asked if you'd like to join us for breakfast? A cup of tea and some toast? We can see that you'll be heading off soon but another ten minutes won't hurt. You can have your meeting at my place." He pointed to his wife standing outside a comfortable looking house on the main road heading east, towards Pine Gap. That made it easier for Obi-Wan to nod in the affirmative.

"Thanks, buddy, we'll take you up on that." He turned to his friend, Corporal Gary Fortune. "Gary, can you get on top of that building over there and have a look around. We'll send some breakfast up to you."

The tall, dark-haired Delta, silently nodded then trotted over to the tallest building in the town. Climbing onto the empty rain-water tank and from there to the flat roof he settled down for a stint of guard duty.

The group were already walking towards the house. Obi-Wan followed his head down thinking of all the things that could go wrong - and those that could go right.

Inside they gathered in the large lounge and dining room where the lady of the house had already placed toast, jars of marmalade, vegemite, jam, and even a jar of fish paste. For the desert trekkers, it was a veritable feast.

"Welcome, everyone," said Walt's missus, Maisie. Her wrinkled face was all smiles. She looked the sort of country woman who could generously feed a host of thousands with her last loaf of bread and a fillet of fish in the fridge.

"We're grateful to you for kicking those terrorist vermin out of our town and we're sorry that your friend died. We want you to know that we will honour and tend Mr Burger's grave when you're gone. He came from far away to shed his blood here, at Meekatharra, for us. He'll never be alone, he's now one of us, he's now our son." Maisie paused when she saw Danielle drop her head into her hands. She knew how the poor girl felt having lost her own husband in a mining accident some years ago.

"I'm Maisie, by the way," she introduced herself. "We know you've had a hard time of it, from what Joey said, he's my son." She then pointed to the weathered old man handing out toast to their visitors, "and you've already met Walt. We work at the hotel you just shot to pieces. But we've survived worse." Putting on a bright smile she lifted the pot of tea and started pouring into the mugs lined up on the table. "Help yourselves, if you're too slow you'll miss out."

The coffee was instant but it was hot and tasted just awful enough for the hungry, tired group to enjoy. The tea was mostly black, Maisie ran out of milk after the second serving. She apologised that she didn't have any cake to give them. No one complained they were just so grateful to this lovely couple for their generosity.

The girls sat with Danielle and comforted her. She didn't eat anything so Emily took her for a walk outside under the rosy dawn sky. Emily knew that walking sometimes helps.

Walt had invited Joey and his wife, Gina, to join them. They asked a lot of questions as they too sipped their tea and ate their breakfast with the visitors. Obi-Wan left the talking to Skip and the others, he was too busy planning their next move. Through the noise of the many diverse conversations, Obi-Wan's ears pricked up when he heard Joey mention a friend who lived on a remote property – this fellow had a radio that was linked to the satellites.

While Obi-Wan digested this new and important information, Maisie and Gina hovered over the two wounded police officers like mother hens. They fussed over the strength of their tea… "*or did you want coffee?*" They buttered their toast for them, "*is this the right amount of vegemite? Or did you want marmalade and jam?*"

Gina was especially attentive to the handsome Hooky, his smile was a winner and it appeared that Gina couldn't do enough for him.

Kerrie appeared to be recovering. She was able to move her wounded arm a little but it was still inflamed and swollen. Fortune, the team medic, looked at it regularly. His greatest concern was sepsis, if that set in she had little chance of surviving their trip to Pine Gap.

Obi-Wan was feeling the loss of his friend Burger, too. He took his cup and plate of toast to sit outside. Walt noticed and sat beside him.

"I guess it's been a hell of a journey for you and your friends?" he asked lightly, trying to make conversation. The old man pulled his tobacco pouch out of his top pocket and offered it to Obi-Wan. Obi-Wan put his hand up, no. He'd not smoked since he was a kid, it had triggered the worst asthma attack he'd ever had. He was never tempted to smoke again.

"I'm fine, Walt, but you go ahead," he said politely. Walt made his cigarette and leaned back in the timber-framed chair and lit up.

"This terrorist thing, is it going to end?" he asked.

"In a word, no," replied Obi-Wan. "The world as we knew it has ended. There'll be no more TV or beauty pageants or surfing contests or new cars to buy, nothing. It's finished. All we can hope to do is survive in this new world."

Walt nodded, drew on his rollie and politely blew smoke up into the air away from Obi-Wan. "That means we have to pull our community together and do the best we can..." he was clearly thinking of how to go about life in this 'new world'.

Obi-Wan sat back in his chair as well, he closed his eyes and put his hands behind his head. "You know, Walt? I've got family in the states and I'm a long way from home, I doubt I'll ever see them again... but I have my duty to my 'family' here, those people inside, they're now my family. If I keep that in mind I'm not going to go crazy. If I think of anything else, then, well, I just might have to put a gun to my head and leave this God-forsaken world."

Walt turned to look at his companion. He saw a thirty-something year old, good-looking man. He noted that Obi-Wan looked confident, a professional, there was nothing to suggest someone who would let go of life and give up that easily.

"Yeah, I guess that's the best way to manage it. We often lose in life, most of the time the promises we hear end up in disappointment. At eighteen I thought I was going to turn into a man, I didn't. Then at twenty-one I thought I was going to be mature and successful. I was married, had a little boy and had just started a business, that didn't work out either. My wife left me when the business went belly-up and I was left to care for my son."

Walt paused to lift his cigarette to his lips and drew back slowly, luxuriously, then continued. "I expected life to be a piece-of-cake, instead I ended up with a shit-sandwich."

Obi-Wan smiled, that was a description he had to remember. His friends, and not-so friends, always reminded him that he never got their jokes nor did he have a sense of humour - maybe this was what they meant.

"I've had to live by the seat-of-my-pants, raising a child and working three jobs. I ran from dawn to midnight for years trying to make ends meet. Now those terrorists have taken the meaning of life away. Does that mean all those years where I sacrificed my needs for those of my son, and then for Maisie and Joey, were wasted?" He drew back again on his cigarette then dropped it into the tin sitting beside his chair. "Maybe this will be better, no more taxes, no more bosses, no more government..." he laughed as he began rolling another cigarette.

"Walt, I know what you're thinking, maybe the shit-sandwich that life handed you has made you better, better prepared for Part Two. And this is now Part Two of life," said Obi-Wan. His eyes were closed and his mind was back in its 'palace', he was already thinking of their drive to Pine Gap.

"Obi-Wan, do you know what? Maybe this Part Two thing is the piece-of-cake I've been waiting for." Walt laughed out loud as he leaned back in his chair smoking, just as quiet but perhaps a tad more contented than his friend beside him.

Tish managed to juggle two cups of black coffee in one hand and a plate of toast covered thickly with a mixture of apricot jam and vegemite, in the other. When she arrived at the base of Fortune's building she called out. Fortune showed her where to climb up on the roof to join him. Together they sat quietly eating their breakfast and drinking their morning brew.

"Thanks, Tish." It was quiet up there, no wind and no activity, except for the volunteer fire-brigade busy cleaning up the part of the hotel that survived the fire. "I just love the desert in the morning. Just look at how everything is so calm, so soft, the light doesn't cut things up so harshly, it's so gentle," Fortune said sipping his coffee and munching on his marmalade toast.

Tish was a city girl through and through. The only reason she was in Western Australia at all was to attend her best friend's wedding. The girls were still celebrating when the Pine Gap crew arrived and helped them party.

"Yeah, it is sort of pretty, I guess." Her voice wandered, "I'd rather Sydney Harbour though. Sunshine, water, boats, Manly and Bondi beaches, the RiverCat and the Sydney Ferries. Now that's something to wake up to, Gary."

They sat quietly watching the sunrise for a while. Tish was still trying to get used to the dramatic changes in the world, in her life. Sometimes a joke made things better.

"Gary, do you like coffee? They say that you've not had enough coffee until you can thread a sewing machine needle while it's running. That's how I've been living my life, on the edge, running from one adventure to the next. Look at me now, sitting quietly watching the sunrise. How did I ever let things get so crazy?" she said softly, her mind still trying to accommodate what she wanted with what she needed. "I love city life but the hardship and the friends I've met these past weeks have changed something inside me."

"Ah, you city girls," the quiet Delta replied. "I came from the big city, Chicago. I couldn't get out fast enough. Give me the wide open spaces any day to the cramped houses, the noise and smell of the city." He sighed and picked up his binoculars again, sweeping the countryside for 360 degrees. "I know it's been tough travelling through the desert but at least we can see the enemy miles away before they can get to us. When I was fighting in the jungle... sorry, I shouldn't talk of war, we've been through enough... even I've had enough of it."

Tish put her hand on his leg. It wasn't sexual or even intimate but it was comforting to feel the touch of a woman in times when you've lost friends.

"I'm sorry about your friend. Burger was our saviour back in Geraldton and again in Shark Bay when the terrorists were shooting at us. He had a funny laugh didn't he," she smiled and then stopped, she began to cry softly. Tish pushed her face into Fortune's shoulder and clung tightly to him. "I just have to get this out, Gary, I'm sorry.

Each death makes me feel so alone. I have to get this blasted sadness out of my system before it destroys me."

Corporal Gary Fortune put his arm around the young woman's shoulder and drew her into his broad chest. He held her tight, tighter than he expected.

The tough Delta, the best of the best, felt tears of his own forming in the corner's of his eyes – but Delta's don't put those he is responsible for at risk. He deliberately disengaged his feelings and switched his mind-set back to the task at hand – and continued to watch the desert approaches.

"Right, everyone, time to move. We've got a long drive ahead of us." Obi-Wan turned to Joey. "Joey, if you don't mind guiding us to that farm-house you mentioned, we'd be grateful."

Earlier, at Obi-Wan's request, Joey had agreed to take them to visit that friend of his, Bluey. Bluey was a city-bred prepper, a survivalist who lived alone on his property in the desert. His home was one of the mines he'd dug prospecting for gold. It turned out to be so pleasantly cool down there that he decided to live in it.

The 'gold' that Obi-Wan was interested in was his radio system which was apparently state of the art. Joey said that Bluey was a whizz-kid, he'd worked for military intelligence until a few years ago. He'd had a 'bit of a breakdown' and was medically retired. He and Joey would sometimes listen in on the astronaut's conversations from the space station; to Pine Gap; even to some of the military operations in Afghanistan and Iraq.

"We're sorry we burnt down your hotel, Maisie; and we're sorry that the terrorists will probably come out here to check out why their patrol won't answer their calls; but if everyone pulls together and fights together, you should survive." They all shook hands and wished each other well.

"Good luck, and thanks for your hospitality. I hope one day to find out that you've survived this damned apocalypse and are living Part Two, Walt."

They hit the road and drove as hard and as fast as the dirt road allowed them. The convoy focused on putting as much road between them and the terrorists who would certainly return in force once they found out what had happened at Meekatharra.

It was some hours later that they saw the turn-off to Bluey's. An innocuous dirt track that looked like it rarely, if ever, bore the weight of a car.

"I'd better go first," said Joey, leaning through Obi-Wan's open window. "Bluey has some strange ways and his paranoia sometimes gets the better of his common sense. If you guys wait at the next gate I'll let you know when it's safe to come in." They drove for another hour before arriving at a cattle grid and gate. There was no fence, just the grid and two posts that precariously held a closed metal gate.

"Why don't we just drive around the stupid gate?" asked Tish perplexed as she watched Joey carefully open the gate, drive through, then close it behind him.

Joey heard her and yelled through his open window. "It's got a mechanism thingy that tells Bluey when someone's visiting. Besides, it's good manners, that's all. No-one would dream of driving around a gate in outback Australia anyway. We're all bloody nutters aren't we?" He laughed as he drove off leaving the three vehicles parked in line waiting for the signal to pass through the gate.

Obi-Wan stood on the roof of his vehicle and swept the area with his binoculars. He followed Joey's dust as he approached what looked very much like a miners camp. There were mountains of dirt piled into mullock heaps. Surrounding the mullock heaps was a series of poles wired together. There were dozens of solar panels, satellite dishes and a shed that was probably where he had his radio. Besides that the place was barren and empty of life.

Chapter 9 – Goldmine Bluey

"Hey'dy, hi'dy!" shouted the small, muscled man who ushered them into his empty shed. He looked like a dwarf from JRR Tolkien's 'Lord Of the Rings'.

"Welcome to my portal." The dwarf chuckled to himself. His beard was long and straggly, it was a mixture of colours ranging from black to grey to red and even some blond streaked through it. "You'll have to be careful, these steps are steep and if you fall you'll take everyone down with you." Again he chuckled as though he expected to see just that, a tumble of bodies bouncing their way into his subterranean home.

"Hi, Bluey," said Skip as he stepped forward offering his hand. But the man blanched awkwardly, pulling his whole body backwards as though Skip's hand was a white-hot cattle brand.

"It's OK, mate, I won't touch you. I just wanted to say thanks for inviting us into your home and out of the heat."

Bluey's eyes opened wide in pleasure. Skip realised that this was the complete opposite of what the little man expected.

"You know what?" he asked of Skip, who was the last to head down the stairs into the well-lit cave below. "I was going to blow you all up when I saw you stop at the highway. I've got sensors and imaging systems everywhere, you'd never escape me if you came to kill me, you know." He smiled again. "I saw the news on the internet, the terrorists have taken out the whole world. You could have been terrorists in disguise coming to take me out. It was lucky that Joey sent me a message first."

"We're the good guys, Bluey. We're here to ask for your help, we're not interested in getting killed," stated Skip clearly, and somewhat firmly. Skip had worked the old man out quickly, he wanted to make it clear to Bluey that he wasn't going to let the old man play mind games with him.

"It's lucky I called before we left," offered Joey as he called the two to join everyone, "otherwise Bluey would have blown you all up for sure. He's a proper mad bastard," he said. Joey tried to force a laugh but Skip could tell that he meant every word.

"Bluey, is there anything you need from us? Just ask and we'll help out if it's in our power. I hope Joey explained to you that we're here because we need your help." Skip's eyes focused on Bluey's to make sure the old fellow knew what he was getting at - the subtext was clear, 'we won't hurt you, you won't hurt us, we're not a threat'.

Skip's brother had a mental illness and there were times when he'd had to talk him down from harming himself, or someone else. He recognised that same crazed stare in Bluey's eyes.

"Ah, OK, yeah, we're all good aren't we?" He turned to Joey for confirmation, Joey nodded. "OK, well come on into my lounge, it's a bit mixed up because I don't usually get many visitors." He showed the visitors around his underground home. It had rooms the size of cathedrals and some so small that it appeared Bluey had forgotten what he was doing half-way through cutting them out of the ground.

There was a flurry of black fur as a cat leapt from one of Bluey's seats and introduced herself to the guests. She immediately began rubbing her cheeks on Danielle's legs.

"Hey, a pussycat!" called a delighted Emily bending down and putting out her hand to the cat. As soon as the black ball of fur saw Emily she raced across and smooched all over her.

"What's your cat's name?" called Emily, smiling with delight, she loved cats.

Bluey was watching, mesmerised, it was as though he'd never seen anyone pet a cat before.

"She's called 'Piggy'. Do you like cats?" asked Bluey, truly bewildered by the girls' attention, as one after the other, they crouched on the floor to stroke little 'Piggy'. Even Hooky joined the group fussing over the black cat.

"Yes, I love cats," announced Emily trying to lift the tiny cat. It was built much the same as Emily, petite and compact.

"Better watch she doesn't claw you, she hates to be picked up." Indeed it was true. The black cat wriggled and squirmed out of Emily's hands to immediately return to the crowd to be petted again.

"What's happened to her tail, it looks like she doesn't have one?" called Danielle stoking the purring, prancing, and tailless cat.

Bluey chuckled, he had been waiting for someone to mention his cat's absence of a tail.

"Piggy's a Manx, they don't have tails. See how her back legs are longer than her front ones? She looks like she's always walking downhill. That's why she's called 'Piggy', because her tail is so tiny, like a little piggy's." He chuckled delightedly when he heard the girls 'ooh' and 'ahh' at his answer.

When their interest finally ebbed the group looked around at their host's stunning underground home.

"Hey, Bluey, how do you get fresh air so you don't suffocate?" asked Tish, an architect in her past life.

"Simple, warm air rises and cool air falls. I installed piping and solar-driven fans through all the rooms when I decided to live here. There are pipes going up through the roof, other pipes draw air back down through the soil to cool it. I simply apply Newtons' Laws of Thermodynamics." The old man pointed out his pipes and the rooms they led to. Bluey was overjoyed at the attention from everyone. He was obviously proud of the work he'd done on his home beneath the desert.

"We've brought some food for you too, Bluey," said Skip lifting a large bag of dried kangaroo jerky from Fortune's backpack. He handed it to Bluey. "We added some chilli to give it some taste, I hope you don't mind some hot spices."

The old man's eyes lit up a second time, he couldn't remember the last time a stranger did a kind turn for him - and he loved chilli. "Thank you, thank you, wow, that's nice of you people. Here, let me make some tea for you. I've not got much in the way of food for visitors, I never get visitors except Joey here, and sometimes his wife, Gina."

"Bluey?" called Tish, "What do you feed Piggy?"

"Whatever she wants," smiled Bluey as he bustled around his kitchen. The questions came thick and fast. He was in 'survivalist' heaven as he answered every question put to him about himself and his cat's survival in the middle of the Australian desert.

Eventually everyone found a comfortable position to sit in the sparsely furnished lounge, most sat on the hessian-bag covered dirt floor. Bluey's home was enormous, having been excavated to find the odd nugget of gold.

Soldier of Fortune had put Kerrie's arm in a sling to support it. Danielle helped her friend sit on the floor while she sought a cold drink for her. Fortune noticed that his patient's temperature was up and she was looking pale. It was unexpected because she had recovered so well up until now.

Obi-Wan was restless, he wanted to get down to business as soon as possible. While Murphy, Emily, Tish and Julie helped Joey make tea and prepared their refreshments, Obi-Wan went to sit with Skip and Bluey. They spoke quietly, well away from everyone else.

"Yeah, I know you blokes want help to contact your base, Joey told me. But it's off limits. I can't help you." He accepted a plate of sandwiches that Gina and Maisie made for them before they'd left Meekatharra.

Obi-Wan and Skip looked at each other then back at Bluey. Obi-Wan pushed forward, "I can see you've got quite a set-up from the dishes outside. It looks like you can contact the satellites from here." He noticed Bluey's eyes light up at the special ops' observation. "We're not asking you to breach your security or divulge any secrets, we just want to get home, back to Pine Gap. We've lost our Black Hawk and we've lost our Taipan. We can't contact anyone because the Pine Gap communications are compromised and we've been kicked from the network. Bluey, we need your help."

The small man turned his face sideways as he listened, his mouth chomping vigorously as though he'd not eaten in years. His head nodded up and down as he listened and his eyes turned up, down, then back up again. Finally the small man stared at the radio at the other end of the room.

"I guess you fellas can keep a secret?" he asked, his face a mixture of fear, dread and excitement.

" 'Secrecy' is our middle name, Bluey. We're both Ultra-secret, special ops and we're also the top crypto-analysts at Pine Gap. We just don't have the equipment to do a damn thing to help ourselves right now. We hoped you could help us."

Obi-Wan waited patiently, sipping his black tea and grimacing, *'how the hell do these Aussies drink this stuff, it's like burnt water',* he thought. He swilled the tea around in his mouth looking for a place to spit it - there wasn't any.

"Well, if you promise not to tell your Commander Cullen, I guess I can show you a few things. Besides, QE3 thinks highly of you guys so maybe I can trust you." He didn't wait for a response but got up and motioned for the two to follow. A few of their team noticed but didn't interfere.

"This is my baby. I've sourced the best quality hardware and created my own software. No one will ever crack my code. I'm completely immune to being tracked, cracked or broken." He tittered into his open hand. Both Skip and Obi-Wan smiled at each other, it was easy to like this wizened little man.

Just then Piggy jumped onto Bluey's computer desk.

"Hey! Piggy! Get down, now!" he said sternly as he tried to gently shove the little cat across to a space on his desk. "How many times have I told you not to jump on my computer?" But the little black cat immediately walked straight back across his keyboard to be petted and rubbed.

"Darn it, I said move you pesky darn bundle of fur and nuisance," he said repeating his act to move the cat aside without upsetting it. He clearly loved his Piggy. Once more the cat stepped back to his computer and walked across his keyboard. That did it, Bluey exploded.

"Damn it, Pigg'n! I'm gonna throw you outside and you can find you're own bloody home to live in!" Bluey tried to pick his cat up but he too failed. She skilfully squirmed and leapt from his arms onto the floor. Piggy raced back to the group of admiring girls, who, just as quickly, began petting and entertaining her.

Bluey sat for a moment as though he'd lost track of what he was doing. He then recovered and went back to where he was before the cat-attack.

"Darn cat," he muttered under his breath. "What would you like to know first? I've been listening to the goings-on in Geraldton, I listened to their communications when you lot escaped. I've been monitoring Perth, Sydney, Melbourne, the space stations and even overseas. I even know all about you two blokes." He winked at them. "I've had a hell of a time keeping up with all that's going on. Europe's down and out, America is down and out, parts of China, Asia and India have gone up in smoke. Those diseases the Revelationists released have killed billions, get that, 'billions' of people. We're lucky to be here in Australia, no one cares about us. But we're our own worst enemy, our own people have turned against us and now we're killing each other." His voice petered off into silence at the end of the sentence.

He started up again, like a motor that's been throttled back on a curve only to be revved back up to speed on the straight. "The Revelationists have everyone frightened. Everyone that's alive that is. The poisoned water hit every major city real bad. But look, you're here, and I'm here, so it can't be that bad can it?"

By now Skip was getting a bit tired. "Bluey, can you tell us what happened to the helicopters? We saw Wagontrain, our Taipan, hit and go down. We know that's lost. We saw Maverick, our Black Hawk, shoot off into the heavens and that's the last we've seen of it. We've not been able to contact them and we don't even know if they were shot down or what." Skip stopped as he watched Bluey carefully move his mouth close to Obi-Wan's ear.

"They got away," he said so softly that Obi-Wan could barely hear him.

Obi-Wan turned to Skip with a wide smile, "The Black Hawk got away!" but Bluey hadn't finished speaking. He spoke into Obi-Wan's ear once more.

"But they did get hit, and they didn't make it back to Pine Gap. They're out there now, patching up their helicopter so they can fly it home." Bluey sat back and resumed eating his sandwiches, a cheeky smile played across his weathered face.

"Skip, Bluey said that they're down somewhere. They got hit, they're still repairing the chopper," relayed Obi-Wan.

Skip now leaned across to speak softly in Bluey's ear. "Bluey, mate, I've got ears too you know. You can talk to me as well, I won't eat you."

Bluey immediately laughed out-loud spraying bits of his sandwich over the floor. "Ha, ha! I got you did I? I was waiting for you to break! Got you!" He jumped up and ran a few paces then came back and sat down.

"I know where they are too." He stopped moving and waited for a response.

"Where?" Obi-Wan instinctively responded. "Where are they, Bluey? They're our friends, if they're close we can help them."

Speaking loud enough for just the two to hear, Bluey said, "Oh, you'll never get to them from here, they're miles away up north. They're up near the RAAF Base at Learmonth, Exmouth way. They had engine trouble and decided to head to the base but came down before they could get to it. It was a stupid idea anyway, there's nothing at Learmonth, it's dead."

"Damn, they're in the opposite direction to Pine Gap. What's their situation now, Bluey? When will they be ready to head back to Pine Gap?" asked Skip, excited to know their friends were still alive.

"I can ask them if you want?" offered Bluey as he finished his sandwich and started on another.

"WHAT?" both special ops said in unison.

Bluey looked perplexed, " 'What' nothing. I can call them up now if you want me too, you can talk to them yourselves."

"Bullshit!" exploded Skip, his face wreathed in smiles.

In response Bluey lifted the microphone, flicked a few switches and said, "Maverick, this is Goldmine, come in."

After a few seconds there came a response. "Goldmine, you're early, what's up? Over." The special ops recognised the voice of Captain 'Curly' Moe.

"I have some friends of yours here with me, do you want to talk to them, over." Bluey turned and smiled at his new-found friends, he was enjoying this beyond his wildest expectations.

"Goldmine, this is Maverick Actual, your time is not for another hour, what news do you have, over." This was Major Samuels, there was some interest behind his usual professional demeanour.

"Hey, that's Major Samuels!" cried Obi-Wan unable to contain his enthusiasm. "Here, let me talk to him!" He reached for the mic but Bluey pulled it out of his reach.

"Wait your turn, Mr Skywalker, we have to catch up on our gossip before we can let you talk," ordered Bluey. "Maverick, I've got Obi-Wan Skywalker, and his side-kick, Skip Chewbacca here with me. Do you wish to talk to them? Over." There were excited yells in the background as Samuels called to his crew to come over and listen.

"Hey, thanks, Goldmine, you'd better put Obi-Wan through. We're in a hell of a pickle right now and in need of his assistance, over." Bluey smiled broadly and handed the mic to Obi-Wan.

The two visitors noticed that when Bluey spoke on the radio he became a different person. He spoke like a professional, as though he had done this before.

"Maverick, this is Obi-Wan, glad to hear you're all alive and kicking. What's your situation, over." It was back to business.

"Obi, glad to hear from you. We're sorry that we had to bolt like that, we took hits over your position. We saw Wagontrain go down, damn shame. How are you lot doing? Over."

"We're down to ten of our group. It's been hell but we're still in the fight, over."

"Sorry to hear that, Obi-Wan. We're near Learmonth RAAF Base. We need parts but can't organise transport, there's no one around that can help us. We need very specific parts and Bluey has generously built the replacement parts for us. That wizard has everything, in fact,

I think he could build a Black Hawk by himself. Is there any way you can get them to us? We can then get the bird into the air and back to base as soon as we put them in, over."

Obi-Wan looked at Bluey's bright face, Bluey nodded excitedly and said, "Yep, I've got their parts. If you can get them there your bird can fly."

"Maverick, that's affirmative, over."

"Bluey has the details of our position. If you send a vehicle with the parts we'll fly the boys home, over."

"Consider it done, out." Obi-Wan handed the mic back to Bluey who confirmed the news and closed down.

"See, I told you I knew a few things," said Bluey with a wink. He stood and placed a large map on the desk in front of them. He pointed out exactly where the helicopter came down and the best route to get there. Obi-Wan accepted the map and started writing and drawing all over it to catch every word of advice from the dwarf-like, electronics wizard beside him.

"Bluey, you're a champion, would you like to come with us to Pine Gap, or maybe visit the Maverick?" asked Obi-Wan.

Bluey's mood changed immediately. His face closed and his eyes darted about. "No! I'm not going back there, never, you're not going to force me are you?" He looked like a lost little boy for a split second.

Skip quickly took over. "Hey, Bluey, you can come with us but only if you want to go. We're not forcing you to do anything." He waited for a few seconds then said, "So I guess that means you don't want to go?"

"Go? No, I'm staying here. I think you'd all better leave now. The gear you need is upstairs, Joey can show you. Take the maps, I've got spares, I can print more if I want." Bluey stared at them, then spoke venomously, "I wish I'd never met you." He stood and withdrew into one of the rooms pulling a blanket down to cover the entrance.

Bluey was going to tell his new friends about the virus-like Trojan that he'd released to control the military satellites. He was also going to tell them that he also knew things they were desperate to find out, secrets. But now he wouldn't tell them a damn thing, they didn't deserve to know - they could all go to hell.

Bluey clicked his fingers. Piggy immediately looked up from her ring of admirers. She then artfully leapt over several pairs of legs and arms to join her master in his den.

Joey saw his friend storm into his bedroom and knew what that meant. He stood up and called to the group, "I'm sorry folks, Bluey's unwell, we'd better be leaving now." The team members turned to look at Obi-Wan and Skip. They saw them confirm Joey's words so they began packing up.

As they walked up the stairs, Joey called out, "Bluey, we're leaving now, I'll give Obi-Wan the gear. They said you can keep the food. I'll talk to you on the radio soon. See ya, mate!" he yelled, then followed the last police officer, Danielle, up the stairs into the hot, fresh air of the Little Sandy Desert.

The group held a quick meeting outside the shed. It was just on dusk and the heat in the air was less intense. Obi-Wan addressed the questioning faces around him.

"Good news, I've just spoken to Maverick, they're all fine but the chopper needs parts. This," he held up the bag containing the components Bluey had prepared for them, "needs to go to Learmonth, or near abouts. I want one vehicle to head back to the coast and deliver it. You'll then fly back to Pine Gap with the Black Hawk."

"I'll go," said Murphy before anyone else could open their mouths. Immediately his SEAL friend, Pipeline, put his hand up as well. The two girls, Emily and Tish quickly followed.

"I'll go too if they'll have me. I want to stay with my friends," said Julie quickly, not even turning to look at Skip. Skip remained silent, gently nodding to himself. *'Of course Julie would want to be with her friends,'* he said to himself, *'so stop being a silly bastard feeling sorry for yourself'.*

Obi-Wan looked at the group and nodded. "OK, let's prepare to move out. Murphy and Pipeline, you'd better have a look at this map of Bluey's." They examined the map while Obi-Wan explained Bluey's suggestions for the best route to take through the desert.

While the girls helped Julie carry her scant kit and pack it into Murphy's vehicle the two SEALS discussed their return journey to Meekatharra with Joey. It seemed that Joey knew quite a lot about the arid desert regions of Western Australia and suggested he escort them, at least back to Meekatharra. They would then plan their second leg to help repair the helicopter.

"Staff Sergeant," called Pipeline. "I'd like to help Joey and his townsfolk prepare for a terrorist assault before we head off to Learmonth. We'll just be a single day then we'll be off to visit Maverick. It's the least we can do for all they've done for us."

Obi-Wan rubbed at the itchy growth of his blond beard. "All right, Pipeline, do that, but your first priority is the Black Hawk. Nothing comes between that bag of equipment and Maverick."

The two SEALs extended their hands to Obi-Wan, Fortune then to Skip. Immediately the others lined up to hug and shake hands with the crew before they set off on their mission.

Julie squeezed Skip's hand. "I'm sorry but I have to go home. I've got someone there I need to sort things out with. You know, unfinished business." They embraced a little longer than two friends normally would. They had supported each other through hell and back and Skip had actually started to fall in love with the tall lawyer.

"Good luck, Julie, I'll miss you. I hope things go well for you." He turned so she wouldn't see the grief he felt plastered all over his face.

"Boss," said Pipeline in his deep voice, "we'll deliver that bag to Maverick, don't sweat on it."

The two groups were soon back on the road, dust billowed behind them as they headed in opposite directions. One to Pine Gap the other back to the hell they'd just escaped.

Chapter 10 – Return to Meekatharra

Petty Officer Third Class Peter 'Pipeline' Liner, sat in the back and napped, while his US Navy SEAL buddy, Petty Officer Second Class Matt Murphy, drove. Emily sat beside him in the passenger's seat trying to stay awake.

Joey shared the driving with Tish and Julie. It made sense and it also made room for everyone to get some sleep. They drove as fast as conditions allowed. There were times Joey would slow down to a crawl to avoid particular areas where the kangaroos gathered on the side of the road. Hitting a full-grown kangaroo can do serious damage to the kangaroo, the vehicle, and to those inside.

After two hours driving in the dark Joey pulled to the side of the road, Murphy pulled in beside him, they both got out.

The stars above shone like sparkling fairy lights at Christmas. Together, with just a sliver of moon, every detail on the side of the road was clearly visible. It was one of those spectacular nights that must have inspired the ancient aboriginal desert dwellers, sitting around their camp-fires, to create their myths of the dream-time.

"What's up, buddy?" asked Murphy, completely oblivious to the beauty above him. He stretched his hands upwards, then to the sides, his back crunched loudly in the still night air of the desert.

"Murphy, I've got to rest, I'm starting to hallucinate. I'm done. The girls have had it too. I think we need to rest before we fall asleep at the wheel or hit a 'roo. We'll still get home in time for breakfast at my mum's place," replied Joey. His yawning almost put Murphy to sleep. Illuminated by the starlight his wiry frame made him look like an elf from a fantasy movie.

Murphy, mindful that they were all exhausted not having slept for two days, agreed.

"Yeah, that's sweet. Take us off the road and we'll sleep until 5 am. How's that?" he asked.

"That, my friend, is a cracking idea," said Joey, his eyes felt like they had sand in them. He was sure that for the past hour he'd stayed on the road by sheer instinct alone.

They pulled into Maisie's house not long after dawn. Walt was in the kitchen cooking eggs and bacon, he looked up as the group came in through the front door.

"Back so soon? How'd it go fellas? How'd Bluey cope with the visit? He's not had that many people drop on his doorstep ever. I bet he was feeling a bit paranoid," said the old man flipping eggs and bacon onto slabs of thick, buttered toast, "and that cat of his, Piggy, I bet she won everyone's hearts."

Joey called for Gina to get another dozen eggs from the pantry, "and grab some more bacon, will ya?"

Emily grabbed a pair of tongs and began helping Walt while Julie and Tish toasted and buttered the bread.

Joey sat wearily at the kitchen table. "Bluey managed OK, Walt. Obi-Wan and Skip did well to keep him relaxed right to the end. He lost it when they asked him to come with us, but he'll get over it. I'll jump on the radio after breakfast and check up on him." Joey leaned over the plate handed to him, wearily poured on a liberal amount of tomato sauce and started eating, the conversation forgotten.

Over breakfast Murphy explained their return, minus certain details. He then asked Walt about the townsfolk and their readiness for a possible assault by the terrorists.

"We had a meeting last night while you blokes were gone. There were about four hundred in the hall and they were mighty pissed off at Obi-Wan for burning down our hotel I can tell you." He laughed remembering the night. "We've got some of the home-brewers working overtime to make up for the loss."

"Walt, any news on what the terrorists are doing?" asked Emily.

"We don't know, if anyone does it's Bluey. He's been monitoring the radio non-stop. Didn't he say anything yesterday while you were there?" Walt looked at his step-son and waited for him to finish his mouthful of egg and bacon.

"Nah, you know what he's like," mumbled Joey, "he wasn't all that comfortable once their business was finished, he closed up and locked himself in his bedroom."

Pipeline asked, "Did anyone at the meeting come up with a plan for your defenses? And have you and the boys collected the spare ammunition and weapons in the terrorist's vehicles?" He looked at Walt expectantly.

"Yeah, we did, we've got our own rifles too." The old man sipped at his hot tea and smiled. "If the terrorists show up we've got a few good ex-army and shooters, you know, dingo and kangaroo shooters. The rest of us can fire off the half-dozen automatics they left behind. The fire only burnt part of the hotel anyway, we managed to scrounge enough ammunition for a fight or two."

"What I mean, Walt," said Pipeline softly, "is that Murphy and I will spend today with you and help you set up a defensive perimeter.

We've got another job to do which means we can't stay any longer, I'm sorry about that. Do you think you could organise some of your people to come around with me and Murphy? We'll walk through what we think would make good defensive positions and possible strategies. I'm afraid we might have terrorists dropping in here by nightfall."

"By tonight? Huh, yeah, we can do it." He gulped the last of his tea and stood up. "You lot stay here and finish your breakfast, I'll do the rounds with Maisie. We'll be back in a half hour with the Meekatharra Volunteer Army." He chuckled loudly, grabbed Maisie by the arm, together they marched out of the front door.

By late afternoon the two SEALs were satisfied that the Meekatharra residents had developed a plan of what to expect and what to do. The volunteers had already started preparations and had set up a veritable labyrinth made of derelict cars on the roads leading into the town. There were outposts complete with CB radio's in their sniper positions covering every possible entrance. They had plastic explosives buried in the road where the terrorists would have to stop at the barricades. If anyone made it into the township there were vicious booby-traps and set points for defense that the civilian soldiers could retreat to and fire from.

"It's not the easiest place to defend but what you guys have done is good, damn good," admitted Pipeline to Joey and Walt, his two off-siders.

Gina had been out looking for the boys and when she saw them she called out.

"What's she so excited about?" asked Murphy.

"I bet Gina's got news from Bluey. Come on, we'd better find out."
They ran down the slight incline of the hill that overlooked the mines
and the township itself.

Gina was panting, trying to catch her breath in the afternoon heat.

"I just spoke to Bluey… he said the terrorists… are on their way…
they said they would be here… by dusk…" She stopped talking to
breathe deeply and get more air into her lungs.

"Darn, they didn't waste any time did they. Did Bluey say how many
terrorists?" asked Pipeline, now in action mode.

"He said a 'squad', I think that means a car-load?"

"Hmm, they lose a half platoon and they only send a squad to
investigate? Maybe they've got other things on their minds, or they
think that maybe their friend's radio has broken… what else did Bluey
say?" asked Murphy.

Gina was now a lot calmer, her breathing and nerves settled. "Bluey
said they don't know about the fight, they just think that it's a broken
radio, like you said they would."

Pipeline and Murphy moved away from the three and talked softly.
They came back to their friends.

"Sorry folks, we've got orders to move out as soon as your defenses
are complete and that means we'll be leaving before the enemy
arrive." Murphy and Pipeline said that they were confident in their
friends ability to hold off the Revelationists. "OK, we'd better start
packing."

While the men were out preparing their defenses the girls had been
busy with Maisie and Gina preparing meals and organising how to

manage any of their townsfolk who may be wounded in the coming fight. Tish and Julie enjoyed the easy manner of the townsfolk. By the end of the day, the two girls had decided that they would stay at Meekatharra and not repeat the horrendous drive across the desert to rescue the helicopter crew.

"That's a good idea," said Emily. The three were busy cutting sandwiches and wrapping them for the fighting men. She looked carefully at Murphy then back at her girlfriends, "but I'm going to stay with Murphy, we've got something going, I think."

"Go girl, you're always the one to get the handsome boys," said Julie. "I wish we'd never had this stupid damn apocalypse in the first place. I was happy where I was. Perth, men, career, money, travel… you name it I had it. Now look at us, stuck in the desert miles from nowhere."

"At least we've got nice companions, look how lovely these people have been to us. Can you imagine another week driving in that bloody car over the stinking desert? No shower, hardly any water to drink let alone wash in, and my hair… yuk!" Tish didn't need to say anymore. The girls giggled and swapped stories of how bad it was crossing the desert from Shark Bay to Meekatharra.

"If it wasn't for the odd farmhouse and dams we'd have sprouted mushrooms down there," said Julie. Maisie had just walked in and snorted with laughter.

"So you girls are going to stay here or are you going off with the soldier boys?" she eventually asked as she studied each in turn. She knew what they were thinking and quietly agreed that another crossing like that was something no city-girl would want to repeat in a hurry.

"Tish and I are staying. We don't want to go back to the desert when we can stay here, in this lovely town with you lovely people. If you'll have us, that is?" Julie looked at the tough country-woman with the bright, red apron and blue-rinsed hair.

"So you're staying? Goodness, my dear girls, the men here will certainly enjoy having fresh blood to prey on." Maisie smiled broadly. She liked these city girls, they pitched in and didn't shirk the dirty jobs either. "You can stay with Walt and me, we've got a spare room and double bunks that the grandkids used to sleep in. I'm sure Walt would enjoy the company of a couple of pretty young girls too."

"I hope one day we can get back to our homes. We've got family and Julie and I have boyfriends. No doubt they're all worried about what's happened to us," said Tish.

"We don't even know if they're alive, Tish. If these Revelationists did what we heard they did with the poisoned water; then the executions like they did at Geraldton; Perth and Sydney could be ghost towns for all we know," added Julie, chewing her lip worried about her future.

"So what's their ETA now?" asked Pipeline, his mind was in so many places that he had to fight to bring it back into focus.

Walt replied calmly, knowing the huge black man in front of him was doing his best. "Bluey said they've had a break and will now be arriving around 1 am, so after midnight."

"I'm pretty certain that you won't be needing us. It's going to be your war, Walt. As you know, Murphy and I have that top priority mission to get to and we can't let anything get in the way of that."

"Hey, big fella," said Denny, one of a small group of ex-military gathered around the giant SEAL. The defenders included a mix of miners, prospectors and farmers from the Meekatharra district. "Don't worry about us, we know how to kill, just ask Bob here. We've both done two tours of Vietnam, 1970-72. We know how to fight, mate. You've done enough, thanks for your help, but your friends need you now."

"We've got the approaches mined all we need do is blast the bastards when they pull up at the road-block. From what Joey said they don't know what's happened to their friends. For all they know the radio fell over and doesn't work anymore," said Bob standing beside Denny. They looked to be in their late sixties or early seventies, it was hard to tell with their faces weathered to an almost leather texture by the harsh Australian sun. They were dressed in khaki shirts and trousers, and, like everyone else, they wore wide-brimmed felt hats. Each of the small group held a rifle, some were ex-World War Two, Lee-Enfield .303's, others had expensive hunting rifles of various makes and designs.

Pipeline looked at the stalwart group and nodded, he could see they were staunch and would give whoever turned up a proper reception. Perhaps as good as he and his SEAL Team Six, back in the states, would have given them.

"Thanks, fella's, I'm real glad to have met you." They all shook hands warmly. "I hope one day to come back and spend some more time to enjoy your hospitality. Maybe the hotel will be renovated by then and I can get a decent cold beer." They all smiled and nodded in agreement, already a work crew was repairing the bar and cleaning up the undamaged lounge.

Pipeline called for Murphy to join him. They walked back to their dual cab four-wheel drive together.

"Hey, Pipeline, someone's inside our vehicle!" said Murphy suddenly. He pulled his pistol from its holster at his hip.

"Hey, you, inside that vehicle! Come out or I'll shoot you!" he yelled. By now Pipeline had converged to the other side and had his pistol held at the ready.

Just then a balding head appeared above the dashboard. "What? Oh, hi guys! I'm nearly finished, just give me a minute." Joey's head disappeared again from sight. It was clear that he was oblivious to the SEAL's drawn pistols.

Pipeline looked at Murphy and grinned, they both holstered their weapons and peered inside. There they saw Joey just finishing up with his radio renovations.

"There, it's done!" said Joey putting his screw-driver into his toolkit and exiting the cabin. "Now you can talk to Bluey, myself and the Black Hawk. It's a little contraption Bluey gave me. Just screw it into the CB radio and it connects you to the satellite right above us. It's a bloody beauty. And what's more," added Joey with a big grin. "It's all coded by Bluey so no one knows you're on the network, you're invisible."

"Wow, how do we work it?" asked Murphy peering in to look. "Hey, there's nothing different, didn't you put something inside?"

"Yep, it's screwed right at the back of the radio," said an excited Joey. "Just click to the alternative channel that comes up when you switch it on then you're live on the network."

"Did Obi-Wan get one? Is he on the network too?" asked Pipeline. "I don't remember you screwing anything into his radio before we left."

"Bluey didn't give me one for him," said Joey. "This is one I've had sitting in my shed waiting for a good home. Bluey would be really pissed if I'd given it to just anyone. It's top secret and Bluey would kill me and I mean that literally if I'd given it to Obi-Wan without his permission. You're just lucky, he suggested I put this one in for you, otherwise, I'd have to let you guys drive off without it."

"Thanks, Joey, this is going to make a heap of difference." Pipeline flicked the switch on the CB and found the alternative channel that appeared where none had been before. "Can I test it out?" he asked, his grin was almost wider than his face.

"Sure, call signs are 'Maverick' as you know, 'Goldmine' for Bluey and 'Tonto' for me." Joey blushed when he gave his call sign. His call sign, 'Tonto', was the name of the Lone Ranger's sidekick. "Go on, call Maverick now. No one can hear you except those on the network. Bluey, Maverick and me are the main ones. There are a few others but they won't talk to you until they've been given the clear by Bluey, personally," said Joey, delighted to be able to contribute to the rescue of the Black Hawk.

"Maverick this is Pipeline, Obi-Wan's rescue team, do you copy?" There was no reply, nothing. Pipeline and Murphy looked at each other, then at Joey, who continued to smile. He reached across and took the mic from the big man's giant hand.

"Maverick, this is Tonto, we have a new member of our family, Pipeline, do you copy?" he said brightly.

There came a crackle of static then a voice came through, loud and clear, "We copy you Tonto, so this is our rescue team, Pipeline? Over?"

"Roger that Maverick. I'll pass you over to Pipeline, over." He handed the mic back to Pipeline.

"Pipeline, I wasn't sure if that was you, we don't get many visitors on this channel. What's your situation, over."

"Maverick, we're heading off at sunset with one vehicle and three crew, one is a civilian. We will no doubt need a week or maybe more to get to you. Bluey has supplied us with maps and plotted fuel and water depots at friendly farmhouses on the way, over."

"Roger that, we'll stay in touch and provide whatever information we can. We're looking forward to seeing you…" there was a pause then Major Sam Samuels came on the air. "Petty Officer, you do have those parts Bluey prepared for us? Over"

"Roger that, Major, we've got it and we'll deliver it whole, over."

"Copy that, OK, have a safe trip, talk to you at sunrise tomorrow, out."

The goodbyes and tears were genuine, not just from Emily's two girlfriends but from the rest of the townsfolk who had warmed to the two hard-working SEALs. Their vehicle was packed to the brim with fuel and supplies as they waved goodbye knowing that soon enough the townsfolk may soon be in a fight for their lives. If all went well they would talk to Bluey and Joey in the morning.

The sun had already set when they hit the dirt track leading into the arid deserts of Western Australia on their Black Hawk rescue mission.

Chapter 11 – Obi-Wan's War

Ranger Staff Sergeant Ben 'Obi-Wan' Kennedy had other things on his mind that sunset as Murphy and his team drove off into the desert. He had a very sick Senior Constable Kerrie Black on his hands and nothing to stop the spreading infection she now suffered as a result of her wounds.

According to his map there was a farm, a 'property' or 'station' as they called it in the Australian outback, not too far away. They were traversing a region where there were occasional cattle stations and mining villages, often surrounding a cluster of open mines and deep pits. Obi-Wan's map showed some stations that might still be occupied.

"Damn it," Obi-Wan hit the steering wheel with the palms of his hands causing the car to vibrate. "We've come too far now to lose anyone." He turned to Kerrie, she was hunched over in the back seat, shivering, wrapped in a blanket despite the heat.

"Obi, she's got twenty-four, maybe forty-eight hours if we're lucky. I suggest we drop anchor at this farmhouse… here." He pointed to a dot on the map that suggested a largish cattle station. "If they have any antibiotics she might pull through, but as it is… she's not in a good way." Fortune didn't need to spell it out any more than that.

"Yep, that's what I was planning to do. There's another property a couple of hundred kilometres farther east. Damn it, I hate to see anyone on my team suffering like that. Her arm's twice the size it should be, it must be hell for her." He folded up the map and rested his head on the steering wheel.

"Right, we'll sleep for a few hours. Hooky?" Obi-Wan leaned out of his car window and called the WA Tactical Response Group police officer over. The ex-SAS's arm rested in a dirty sling. "Hooky, we're going to have one of your Aussie 'kips', I'm so damn tired. We have to grab some sleep. It's been hell driving this past few days with barely a break. Wake us in four hours."

Hooky nodded and settled the fold-up chair beside the two vehicles so he could watch the road some distance away. He leaned his Heckler and Koch G36 against the side of his chair and relaxed, planning to walk around regularly to stay awake.

That evening the two vehicles approached what appeared to be a small village. There were sheds, houses, pens for cattle and an enormous warehouse. What struck them as odd was the number of cars, mostly four-wheel drives and a dozen or so trucks. Although it was approaching midnight the warehouse was lit and there appeared to be movement inside.

Before they proceeded they sat together and discussed their options.

"It could be a standard cattle station, everything appears pretty much right for it. Maybe everyone for miles has joined together to form a community, you know, strength in numbers, 'let's stick together' sort of thing," suggested a very tired Danielle.

Skip said it might be a drug laboratory. "There are too many vehicles here. That warehouse can't be lit up like that at this time of night for any other reason than the manufacture of drugs or growing marijuana."

They continued discussing options when they heard Kerrie groan.

"Damn it, I need to know if these people will help us or hinder us. Danielle, Skip, and you, Hooky, position yourself to provide covering fire if we get fired upon. If one of us is caught or hit then withdraw and regroup," said Obi-Wan. He and Soldier of Fortune were armed with their AK47 assault rifles, pistols and prepared for just about anything. Everyone was nervous. That many cars meant a lot of people - and a lot of people meant complications.

"OK, Fortune, let's go." The two set out in stealth-mode to investigate.

They approached some of the vehicles first and checked them over, they saw nothing suspicious. Next they crept to the first building which looked like an office or administration building. The door creaked softly when they opened it. Fortune covered the entrance while Obi-Wan searched inside. Again they found nothing of interest except a chair with straps on it. Obi-Wan thought it would make a good chair for interrogation - or torture.

"The warehouse," Obi-Wan whispered. They stealthily passed through a half-dozen parked cars then crossed a cleared area to get to the enormous shed.

'*Listen*,' indicated Fortune, he pointed to his ear and then the shed wall. They could hear noises, human noises. They crept slowly to a window and looked in.

The warehouse was large enough to hold a dozen massive harvesters, some of which were parked outside. But the inside of the warehouse held nothing of the sort. Inside they saw fifty or more people. Most were sleeping on the floor, these appeared to be prisoners. Three guards chatted over a game of cards while another twenty or so slept in bunks lined up against the wall. Behind them was an enormous laboratory and warehouse, clearly set up for drug manufacturing, and glasshouses for growing marijuana.

Obi-Wan pulled Fortune back to a space between the vehicles so they could plan what to do without being heard.

"There was something wrong here after all. Prisoners, men, women and children, I wonder who they are and who those armed men are. They aren't wearing uniforms like we've seen with the Revelationists, they've all had some form of identifying clothing. These are dressed like bogans - T-shirts, thongs, jeans... more like a drug gang, an organised drug manufacturing and distribution business..." Obi-Wan's voice tapered off.

As they watched, a group of armed men entered the building, so the two special ops returned to see what was developing.

There appeared to be a power struggle happening. One man was seated playing cards. He was tall with long, dark hair that fell straight down his back, he had the body of a dancer or a boxer. The other was short, ruddy and powerfully muscled. They appeared to both be in their thirties. The shorter man stood over the seated, taller man.

The smaller man moved to push the seated one, there was a rush of guards, weapons were drawn and a stand-off ensued.

"Hey, Obi, we might be lucky and they'll end up killing each other." Fortune had one hand on the wall to steady himself and the other flicked the safety off his weapon.

The tall man now stood up, the smaller immediately got into his face and they began screaming at each other. Obi-Wan and Fortune could hear it now, the argument certainly was about who ran the 'village' and who owned the drugs and the prisoners. The smaller man finally left with his gang and things seemed to settle down. The tall man then walked over to what appeared to be a CCTV monitor, probably making sure the smaller man wasn't up to something.

"OK, so we now know it's a drug lab. These people, the prisoners, could be locals forced to work here or they could be from a tourist bus or something like that. But they're right in the middle of the desert, it doesn't make sense," whispered Fortune.

"They could be a biker gang. It looks like their leader, that tall fellow, is their warlord. The other fellow might have been his second in command before the apocalypse." Obi-Wan stopped for a moment. "OK, we'll head back to the vehicles and get out of here. I doubt these folk will be interested in helping us. We'd just end up sleeping on the floor with those prisoners. These people are edgy, anything could set them off. We've got to find a friendly cattle station or a mine site where we can get some treatment for Kerrie. This one's not worth tackling, we're compromised enough as it is."

Obi-Wan stayed back to cover the retreating Fortune, when he was satisfied his buddy was safe he started to move.

"Don't try anything stupid, mate. Drop your weapon and stand up - slowly," came a voice from behind him. It wasn't just the one person behind him, he could hear perhaps a half dozen mumbling voices.

Obi-Wan slowly placed his weapon on the ground then put his hands in the air.

"Good, now where's your buddy we saw on our monitor? There were two of you, weren't there, where did he go?" asked the voice. It contained a gentle menace, yet it was also friendly. Obi-Wan was unconsciously alerted to the resonance of kindness and charisma in that voice. It came from the tall, muscled male they had just seen arguing in the warehouse.

There was something tapping Obi-Wan inside his head - something he had witnessed in his years with intelligence, a particular personality characteristic he was trained to notice. Then it came together - he was in the presence of a psychopath.

'Great, I get caught by a psychopath and his henchmen,' he thought to himself. *'So this is the warlord and I guess that he's looking to build his business into an empire. That's what psychopath warlords do.'*

"Mate, you've just joined my army, whether you like it or not." The man laughed and the others around him joined in. Obi-Wan wasn't laughing, he was waiting for the psychopath's games to start.

"Luke, go out and get the bastard that got away. See where their car's parked too and if there's anyone else." He stared at Obi-Wan noting his casual clothing and military webbing. He also noted the AK47 rifle. "Toby, you'd better go with Luke."

Turning back to Obi-Wan the tall man spoke. "So, you're WAPOL? Tactical perhaps? You look the police type but something doesn't look right with this picture." He spun and with a round-house kick to the chest he knocked Obi-Wan to the ground.

Obi-Wan was winded and in considerable pain. *'Damn, I bet I've now got some cracked ribs'*, he thought as he struggled to breathe through the stabbing pain. He slowly curled into a ball trying to get his breath back.

"Like my kung fu?" laughed the tall leader and once more his men joined in.

Just then there came the sounds of gunshots and the sound of cars revving then racing through the gears as they sped off.

"Well, well, the big fella here brought some friends. That's not one friend driving away, that's two." He stopped his friendly banter and viciously kicked Obi-Wan in the stomach. "Who the hell are you? The world's finished, you idiot, there are no more police, get it!" He bent down and screamed in Obi's face. "It's ended! Everything has ended!" He stopped when Luke and Toby returned, panting.

"Khan, there was more than one, sir, there were two cars. They drove off as soon as they saw me. Sorry, sir, I couldn't stop them." He stammered a little then cowed when Khan suddenly swung his fist at him. Luke automatically swayed his head back a fraction causing Khan's fist to miss its mark.

"Prick! Move closer and don't sway back this time. And get your hands down away from your face!" Khan screamed. He held the luckless teenager by the throat with one hand and punched him in the face with the other. The teenager's nose broke, the sound was clearly audible to the group. Luke's eyes rolled upwards and he collapsed.

"Toby, get here," Khan ordered. The group went quiet, some snickered which made their leader even more animated.

Khan smiled as he teased his next victim. "Come on, Toby, come closer, you didn't do anything wrong. I like you, you're one of my favourites." Khan reached out his hand and pulled Toby into an embrace. He put his mouth in the boy's hair and spoke, looking at the group surrounding the two.

"Luke got his punishment because he was a loser. You're not a loser, you had no choice but to follow behind Luke, you didn't fail me. THAT PIECE OF SHIT ON THE GROUND DID!" he screamed and kicked the prostrate Luke.

Toby wasn't sure what to expect. Sometimes Khan was generous and kind while at other times he was cruel and vicious.

Khan now took Toby by the hand and put the boy's arm around his own shoulder. "There, we're friends, that wasn't too hard now was it. I told you I'm not angry at you." He kissed Toby on the top of the head. "You know what happens to those who disappoint me. Just don't disappoint me, simple isn't it?" He let Toby's hand go. The shaken young man eased himself to the back of the group.

"Come on, get this pig inside, we'll ask him a few questions." He thumbed towards Obi-Wan on the ground and two of his men picked the big Ranger up and helped him walk into the warehouse with the rest of the men.

It was just starting to lighten in the eastern sky when Obi-Wan woke and looked around. He was seated in a chair facing the civilians. Most were awake and talking softly, some remained asleep. He tried to work out where he was and what was happening. When he moved he felt his broken ribs, they reminded him of the night before.

'Genghis Khan, that's right.' He stopped thinking and let his mind probe his body for injuries. He found some, ribs, back, neck, face and stomach, but both arms and legs were functional. *'I've got a lot of bruising, some cracked or broken ribs by the feel of it, and my back and stomach muscles are killing me. I'll be fine if I can just stand up and move.'* But he was tied tightly to his chair.

It wasn't until midday that Khan came to visit his new prisoner. Obi watched as the people in the warehouse were organised into work parties, none fought back or argued. A few punches or the jab of a rifle butt in the ribs or face soon settled any possible dissent. Where they went Obi didn't know. He counted over fifty individuals with weapons, it confirmed his earlier suspicions.

"So, you're awake I see. I think it's time we talked." Khan pointed to two of his guards who untied Obi-Wan. They half carried half dragged the injured Ranger out of the warehouse and into the administration building. He was thrown into the interrogation chair he'd seen the night before.

"We'll start civil-like. What's your name?" Khan fingered a long, sword-like machete as his two henchmen stood lazily nearby enjoying the show.

"Ben Kennedy," Obi-Wan replied.

"What organisation do you belong to? And it better not be that piece of shit Spiro's who's trying to take over my empire. If I find out you're one of his, Ben, then I'll be using this machete on you." Obi-Wan noticed that it had a two-foot blade and the handle was about half that, it looked very much like a martial arts weapon.

"I don't belong to any force, or to your… whoever it is you're talking about, and I'm not police."

Khan settled a little. "Ah, so you do belong to a force of some kind then, but not the police, I like this game." Khan laughed. "I've got more questions for you. What force do you belong to if it isn't the police?"

"I'm military, as you already know."

"Yes, everything about you smells of army. I was army once, Corporal Khan, supplies, Q-stores and all that. I made my fortune selling weapons and materials to the biker gangs, terrorists, anyone who had the money. I then bought myself a property and an army of my own. I manufacture drugs, I have a harem of gorgeous women on tap… the army was good to me, eh?" He paused, wanting to go on but his curiosity got the better of him.

"OK, so what rank are you? Officer, NCO? What regiment? You're not Aussie either, so what the hell is a yank doing out here in the middle of the Australian desert?" He kicked Obi-Wan in the shin, it hurt. Pain flared behind Obi-Wan's eyes and he breathed deeply to quieten it down.

"Ahhhh," he sighed slowly releasing his breath as he calmed his mind. "I'm American, yes, on leave to visit friends in Perth. We got caught up in the apocalypse and escaped into the desert. We saw your light was on and investigated. We'd almost run out of fuel and water, we needed a place to rest up." Obi-Wan stopped, he was used to this game, he'd played it himself.

"Right, good, now I can see why you're here. OK, but who was that other bloke with you, the one who ran off. And who else was in the cars?" asked the Khan, his eyes began to roll upwards as he tried to control himself and remain focused. "And that assault rifle... what... what..." Obi realised that the warlord was entering a substance-induced high so decided to take the conversation to its obvious conclusion.

"That was my friend, Gary, he was the fellow I was visiting. He and our girlfriends obviously didn't want to hang around when they saw Luke and Toby running at them. I guess they're half-way to Adelaide by now, the bastards."

Khan rubbed his face then picked vigorously at a lump on his lip, splitting it open. Next, he scratched at his scalp and armpits. Obi-Wan watched patiently knowing the warlord would wind down soon enough then the fun would start all over again.

It was warm inside, he wondered if the air-conditioning system was working properly. When Obi-Wan glanced up he saw the air-conditioning system was fitted to the walls but there was no sound or air flow. *'Good, let's hope he overheats and makes a mistake'*, he thought.

It was about now that Obi-Wan started a special form of breathing, packing energy into the muscles and tissues surrounding his broken ribs. He knew Khan would soon want to fight him so he needed to pack energy into his wounds as quickly as possible.

"So your friend is military too, eh?" asked Khan, his mind and voice came back for a moment - then he grew broody and quiet. Obi-Wan braced for another kick.

"No, he's an accountant, a dumb-arse who plays paintball and Counter-Strike, he thinks he's a hero. I guess he's much like me, a wannabe."

One of the men looked up at Obi-Wan's comment. "Khan, he's built like a brick shit-house, he's like a weight lifter or something. Watch out, he's dangerous."

Khan looked at his guard and blinked rapidly. He stood up and leaned over the man. "Did I ask you a question? Did I say you could speak?" He put his face into that of his henchman and pushed him in the chest. "Who the hell asked you for advice anyway?" Khan wanted to hit the man but instead he yelled in his face, "Do you think I'm a dumb shit like you? Eh?"

The man came back quickly trying to ease the situation and prevent it from escalating. No doubt he'd done this before.

"Sorry Khan, my mistake. I was out of line. I should have known there was a plan behind your questions, sorry," the younger man pleaded.

Khan breathed deeply, blasting the breath from his mouth several times. To Obi-Wan, it looked like he was reaching his high. *'He's probably on methamphetamine, ice,'* he thought.

"I… I…" Khan was now drifting into another dimension, his face appeared to close off from the world and he started to smile, he found a chair and sat down. "I don't remember where I was at. Chucko, what was I saying?"

Chucko, the man closest to Obi-Wan, answered. "You were asking this dick here questions about his friends who drove off."

"Yeah, now I remember… sorry, mate, what's your name again?" Khan once again exuded charm, he sounded friendly.

"Ben Kennedy," Obi-Wan replied politely.

"So… Ben, you're army and you're here on holidays." He now pulled out a plastic bag containing a white crystal then poured some onto the glass top of the admin table. He chopped it into a fine powder snorting two thin lines.

"Yeah, now I remember… wow, I feel good. I could kill someone right now!" Khan was storming back up into another high. He swung his fists like a boxer giving an opponent an uppercut followed by a six-punch combination. He then stepped forward and kicked the air to the side of Obi-Wan followed by a series of martial arts moves.

Obi-Wan watched, noting the tall man's style. He also noted that Khan favoured his left leg, he might be carrying an injury. He also noted that Khan's style wasn't karate but a mainland Chinese kung fu style.

'Damn, what is that style, I know it…' Obi-Wan said to himself, his mind raced through a series of files he held of the many fighting styles he'd studied as a teenager and then as part of his special ops training. *'Yes, got it, Tiger style. He's obviously done…'* he thought for a moment, *'four or five years training. He might be a competent opponent one on one.'*

"Hey, not bad, eh!" Khan put his face in Obi-Wan's and laughed. "What did you think of that kung fu, eh?"

'Nice work, Obi-Wan, we've done it, he's now yours.' Staff Sergeant Ben Kennedy smiled to himself.

"Not bad, Tiger style is it? It looks like you're pretty good too. My preferred style is Bagua with a smattering of Praying Mantis." Obi-Wan now looked Khan directly in the eyes. "I think I could teach you a thing or two about kung fu, Khan." He goaded his enemy deliberately, certain that Khan would accept his challenge.

There is a traditional insult, or challenge, among martial artists and that's to offer to 'show' or 'teach' your opponent how much better your style is compared to theirs. There has always been fierce rivalry, particularly among the older, more traditional styles, for prestige as the superior martial art. Obi-Wan saw that Khan's style kept strictly to traditional forms - Khan must have been trained by a traditional custodian of the Tiger style. Tiger style is an ancient kung fu style rarely taught to non-Chinese. Whoever taught Khan did it well and didn't seem to have held back enforcing a perfect execution for each move.

"You seem to know a bit about kung fu, Ben. Perhaps I can teach you a few tricks myself." Khan glanced at his two companions now lounging in their chairs only a few metres away. They were armed with Steyr automatic rifles, Australian army issue. These were no doubt some of the weapons Khan traded while working in the military Q-Stores. The two men laughed, they knew what was next and they anticipated some entertaining violence.

"I was taught by an old Chinese kung fu master, he worked as a chef in Sydney. He was a tough old man, very strict, very traditional. His family lived in China and he needed money to bring them over here. His granddaughter had cancer and he was desperate. I traded him lessons for money, a lot of money I might add." Khan was artful in both his manner and in how well he spun the machete in his hand.

"Did you like that?" Khan asked and did it again, following up with a pattern involving a series of slashes, stabs and leaps as though fighting an invisible adversary.

Obi-Wan noted his form and style, 'now that's more a northern Shaolin kung fu than the southern style', he considered and let his brain unconsciously develop counters to the moves he'd just seen.

"How about I teach you a few tricks, Ben, what do you say? Want to go a few rounds with me?" Khan again flicked his machete into a series of patterns with yells, leaps and thrusts. It was impressive and his two henchmen smiled, they looked forward to the entertainment.

"Sure, I'd like that, Khan. I've not faced a Tiger style for some time, this should be interesting," replied Obi-Wan. No one noticed his breathing had begun to change again. He could tell that Khan knew the patterns of his style but not the energy breathing that goes with it. It appeared that his teacher deliberately failed to teach his student how to breathe, deep into his dan tien, that vital space between the navel and the spine, the martial artist's source of power.

Obi-Wan wanted to keep Khan off balance while he prepared himself for the fight. "So, that piece of shit, Spiro, he's good at martial arts too? Is he good at Tiger style like you?" It got a reaction but not quite the one he was after.

"That piece of shit Spiro, is a wanker. His only weapon is a gun. He worked with me, helped me collect weapons and sell them on the black market. But his greed is bigger than his balls, he'll never challenge me to a fight, he's more likely to shoot me in the back. I've got him covered though, don't you worry about that," replied Khan confidently.

While Khan was busy talking Obi-Wan continued to breathe slowly and deeply forcing his energy deeper into and around his cracked ribs. Slowly he built a web within the fascia surrounding his rib cage, an armour that would hold his ribs in place for the vital few minutes he needed to kill his opponents. It would also serve to protect his ribs in the event of a kick or punch. He knew well enough that he could only hold the power in his fascia for a limited time. It needed to be long enough to take down all three enemy in the room.

By the time Khan ordered Chucko to untie him Obi-Wan had centered his energy in his dan tien, armoured his ribs, and was on a mild high himself. He felt the energy 'high' that only elite martial artists enjoy.

Chucko pulled Obi-Wan upwards and sliced the rope binding his legs then stood to do the same with his prisoner's hands. The second his hands were free Obi-Wan flicked his fingers into the man's eye bursting his left eyeball. As Chucko dropped screaming to the floor Obi-Wan snatched his guard's knife and thew it into the throat of the second henchman. It happened so fast the man had yet to raise his rifle from his side.

"Now we're even, Khan, one-on-one, mano-a-mano," said the injured but resolute Ranger.

Khan hadn't quite registered that he was alone. It hit him when he saw Obi-Wan stand before him, smiling, in his Bagua kung fu stance.

"Hey, dick-head, let's pretend I'm Spiro and you're my bitch!" taunted Obi-Wan.

"Fuck you!" Khan was in shock at the speed of his enemy's assault. Instead of flying into a rage, as Obi-Wan had hoped, Khan settled quickly. "Don't you worry about Spiro, I've got him under my thumb - he's my bitch, just like you're my bitch." He smiled, a disarming smile as though the two were drinking together at a bar and about to play pool.

"I did notice you used the Bagua Monkey Flick on Chucko. Nice, you popped that eyeball real good!" He laughed out loud then turned to yell at the man clutching at his eye and screaming on the floor. "For fuck-sake! Chucko, shut up or I'll give you something to cry about!"

Khan then turned to focus on his opponent, he flicked his machete into a forward fighting position.

"Come on, yank, show me your style," he said. His voice was soft, empty of emotion, he had now become pure, cold evil. Torturing Obi-Wan was for pleasure but killing him was just business.

Obi-Wan felt, for just a moment, that the energy surrounding his ribs was waning after he had expended most of it in the Monkey Flick and knife throw. In the space of a heartbeat he pumped several short energy breaths bringing his 'armour' back to full strength. He knew that he had about ten seconds to end the fight before the pain overwhelmed him. Against a trained opponent that would mean death.

"You're just a jerk-off wannabe, Khan. Your stance is weak, your patterns sloppy, you're a loser. No wonder Spiro thinks he's a better man to lead this little empire than you." Obi-Wan taunted one more time, his next move had to be the decisive one.

Khan did exactly as Obi-Wan wanted this time. "You arse-licking yank. I'll show you who's worthy to lead." He slashed his machete in anger at Obi-Wan's face, then twisted to send a flying kick at his opponent's ribs - Obi-Wan noted that Khan balanced his kick on his weaker leg.

It was the opportunity Obi-Wan was waiting for. He easily swung his head backwards avoiding the machete, his feet slid across the floor into position ready for Khan's follow-through. As the kick came in Obi-Wan timed his own kick to send Khan's leg flying towards the ceiling. Khan's groin and torso were left exposed and vulnerable for that split second.

This was the opportunity Obi-Wan needed, but that split second was too short. The energy armour surrounding his ribs simply couldn't withstand the demand for his ownfollow-through.

The Ranger had the opportunity for a Baboon Snatch to Khan's hanging arm, or an Eagle Claw Grip to his exposed groin, but he simply couldn't do it, it was too late, the moment had passed. He was losing power fast and the pain was breaking through. A dribble of sweat ran down his cheek and onto the floor.

Obi-Wan unconsciously closed his mind and went on autopilot. His body immediately positioned itself for a Praying Mantis jab into Khan's exposed stomach. His right fist sank deeply into his opponent's midriff. Khan's core-muscle training had been severely neglected and the fist sunk nice and deep. Next, Obi-Wan twisted his wrist causing Khan's muscles to contract around it. This had the secondary effect of fracturing his stomach and bowel muscle tone causing Khan to automatically open his bowels. As Obi-Wan twisted he let out a loud grunt, the pain from his cracked ribs had broken through - he was at breaking point.

To complete the combination he slammed his elbow into Khan's rib cage causing his taller opponent to lean forward. All Obi-Wan needed to do next was flick the knuckle of his index finger into Khan's temple.

Khan collapsed to his knees on the floor, a stream of faeces dribbled out from the bottom of his trousers. Obi-Wan also collapsed, the pain from his cracked ribs had broken through. At that moment he was completely powerless to protect himself. If Khan stood now he could easily kill the brave Ranger and the fight would be over.

With enormous effort Obi-Wan stood, breathing deeply he shut out his pain and snatched up the dropped machete. Just as Khan began to rise Obi-Wan brought the blade down, it cleanly sliced Khan's head off.

"Fuck you," he grunted, surprising himself. Obi-Wan never swore, but this was an exception he decided.

Chucko was still on the ground groaning, holding his hand over his burst eyeball. He had remained completely oblivious to the fight and its violent outcome. Obi-Wan had just enough strength to finish off Chucko, using Khan's sword-like machete.

Reaching for the Steyr lying on the table he picked it up, slowly rummaged through both henchmen's pockets for ammunition. He now had six magazines of thirty rounds each. He stepped over to the man with the knife in his throat and pulled it free. It was a thin-bladed stabbing knife, well balanced too, so he decided to keep it. He held onto the machete, it had a good feel to it as well.

'I'll keep this too, it might come in handy one day,' he thought to himself.

The pain in his body was almost unbearable so he sat down. After a minute of slow, deep breathing he felt a little better. Obi-Wan knew that it wouldn't be long before one of the gang members came snooping, then he might be in a bit of trouble.

The smell of Khan's spilled faeces filled the room but Obi-Wan just smiled. That was the most skilled execution of the Praying Mantis move he had ever performed.

Chapter 12 – Skip the Skipper

Skip saw Fortune running towards the vehicles and he knew something was wrong. Then he saw flashlights and several men running. As they had agreed earlier, if the mission was compromised get the hell out. He gunned the engine of the four-wheel drive and yelled at Fortune to jump in.

Danielle knew what to do. With the mission going pear-shaped they were to pull out, at speed. Although it went against every cell in her body she knew there was no other option. The two vehicles pulled away as instructed leaving Obi-Wan in the hands of the enemy.

No-one bothered to follow so after a few kilometres Skip pulled off the dirt road and drove into the desert some distance. Danielle followed. The red-haired SAS corporal swore to himself as he walked to the back of the vehicle and started kicking in the overly-bright tail and brake lights. Skip was grief-stricken, distraught and furious.

"Damn things, I should have thought of this before. Damn! Damn!" He then went to the headlights and did the same, venting his frustration, grief and anger out on the vehicle's lighting.

"Skip, I've got the road covered. When you're ready go and rescue Obi-Wan," offered Hooky, trying to ease Skip's loss, giving him a direction to express his painfully raw emotions. He'd seen it before when he was in action with the SAS. When a mate was killed or wounded people react in disturbing ways. In this case a redirect was the best thing to do right now. Hooky knew that Skip was a professional and once he had somewhere to direct his frustrations he would slip back into his usual controlled, professional mode. Expending his frustrations Skip soon rallied back to his usual practical self just as Hooky expected.

There was a simple rule among the special ops: get the civilians and wounded to safety, then come back and attempt a rescue - then send the bastards to hell.

Skip called everyone together. "Fortune and I are going back in. Danielle, you will drop us off and come back here. You and Hooky wait and provide back-up if they come chasing after us. We might not be back until tomorrow night." He pulled out his flashlight and checked his weapons. "I'm sorry we have to leave you both behind with a sick officer. Kerrie will either tough it out or she will die. I like her, we all do, she's brave and she's been a good friend to all of us. All I can suggest, Danielle, is that if you want you can head east and find the next property, drop her off and come back. That's about the best we can do for her right now."

Danielle thought for a moment then said, "I think we should all see this rescue to completion first - we stick together, Kerrie knows the score."

Skip was anxious to get to the farm and rescue his friend. Constable Danielle nodded and started the vehicle as Fortune and Skip entered. They only had a few kilometres to drive before they would exit the vehicle and make their way to the farm and surrounding buildings on foot.

It was just on dawn when Skip and Fortune found a good position to observe the activity on the prison farm. There were work groups heading into various sheds and some were being driven off into the desert scrub towards unknown destinations. It seemed like the usual workday on a cattle property in the outback.

"Where the hell have they put Obi-Wan?" asked Skip, musing out loud as he peered through his binoculars. "There doesn't seem to be much excitement... they have armed guards out too."

"They have a bunch of prisoners in that warehouse and they're using them as slaves," offered Soldier of Fortune. He had gone silent since the escape as his soldier's mind kicked in. The Delta specialist wanted revenge, on his terms.

The two special ops wanted to put themselves inside the farming complex before the light improved, but there was too much activity and movement. They agreed that they would make better progress around noon, the hottest time of day, when there would be fewer observers. As heat and fatigue from being in the sun would soon strip them of energy they decided to lay back in their shallow ditch in the grassy paddock and sleep. They took turns to keep watch.

It was midday and Fortune was on watch. He lay with his binoculars in his hands observing the movement of prisoners and guards at the farm. He saw movement and shifted focus. Sure enough it was a bound Obi-Wan being dragged across the dirt and into the administration building they had both examined the night before. It was right up against the barbed-wire fence and the closest building to the two watchers.

Fortune dug his foot into Skip's side, "Skip, we've got activity."

"Huh? What?" came Skip's sleepy answer.

"They've taken Obi-Wan into the admin building right against the fence. It's the one closest to us. Just three enemy and no one else in sight." Fortune handed the binoculars to Skip as he crawled beside him.

"Yep, I've got them, they're inside. I can't see much more than shapes. I guess we should make our way over and introduce ourselves," replied Skip with a smile, now fully awake and keen to go to the next level.

They waited to see if there was going to be any more activity but it seemed to be the only action on the farm. There was no one else to be seen, there hadn't been any movement for the past hour.

"OK, let's do it, I'll go point." Skip eased his body into the long, dry grass in the paddock and began the painful crawl to the barbed-wire fence where the building was situated.

In the arid regions of Australia the ground was usually covered in tough bushes, many of which were covered with spines that stick into the palms and backs of hands, fingers and sensitive faces. There were also countless thorns, some with spines an inch long.

The two armed men carefully but painfully made their way to the fence under the hot sun. They were grateful when they made it to the shade of the building against the fence. They silently cut the wire and leaned against the building. It provided just enough shade to protect their roasted bodies. There they paused to drink from their water bottles.

"OK, time for a sneak-peek," said Skip rising slowly to the level of the windows. He checked each window until he found one that would provide enough vision while also remaining unobserved from those inside. Just as he raised himself to look he heard a commotion from inside the building, it sounded like someone dropping to the floor.

Skip looked into the building just in time to see Obi-Wan slice through Chuko's neck. In stunned silence he watched the henchman's head fall to the floor.

"Fortune! Get up here and have a look. Obi-Wan's settled things for us." Together the two peered into the building. All was safe to enter so Corporal Gary Fortune placed his hands together and lifted Skip high enough to push the window fully open and climb in.

"Hey bro, I see you've sorted things out for us," Skip said brightly.

Skip quickly placed himself into a defensive position while Fortune wrapped a bandage around their friend's chest. They all drank more water and munched on a snack of slightly stale cheese and beetroot sandwiches, left-overs from their stay at Meekatharra.

Soldier of Fortune spoke to Skip as soon as his mouth was empty. "We're pretty much compromised. We may want revenge but Obi-Wan's going to be useless in a fire-fight."

The Ranger had nothing left, his face was pale, his breathing laboured and he could barely raise his head. They'd given him food and water which helped but he'd used up every ounce of reserves in the fight.

"Skip, Fortune's right," Obi-Wan grunted, he struggled to even speak. "Let's just get home, to Pine Gap."

He gasped as he stood, then wavered, Skip leapt up to hold him upright. "One more thing, Skip, there's another psycho here. He's the second in command, Spiro, short guy. I haven't seen him since yesterday though." Obi-Wan closed his eyes and breathed in slowly, settled then continued. "There's about fifty, maybe more armed men here. Fortune… you'd best set up some sort of incendiary in the vehicles… but watch it, they've got security cameras." He had to stop, he was about to cough and that would hurt, he was in enough pain as it was.

Skip was thinking. "Fortune, what if you sort out our escape vehicle first, then light-up the one next to it. Then get yourself to the back of this building. I'll take Obi-Wan there. That's where you can pick us up. As we head out I'll open fire on the parked cars, hopefully, some will dribble enough fuel to catch fire. Not a great plan but it should work to distract them."

"Yeah, we can do this. Pity we don't have any explosives." Fortune quickly looked around the large room and noticed a pile of plastic sheeting. "Incendiary, plastic, perfect. OK, give me two minutes and I'll meet you out the back near their driveway."

It still wasn't that easy. It was lunch time but there was now some activity - a group of men led by Spiro, were walking towards the warehouse a hundred metres away.

The open ground directly in front of the building held a half dozen vehicles. Fortune was certain the keys would still be in the ignition in at least one of them.

He was right, the first vehicle he came to, a comfortable Honda SUV, had its keys in the ignition. When he turned the key it showed a full tank of fuel. Fortune left the motor running while he packed plastic beneath three of the vehicles beside it, setting each alight as he did. Knowing that he was probably on their security Closed Circuit TV, he hoped that no-one bothered to watch their monitors. It was lunch-time and they would most probably be eating.

Gary Fortune slowly drove to the back of the administrative building and opened the side door. There was still activity around the warehouse but now some of Spiro's men started to walk towards the administrative building. It looked like they expected to see Khan.

Instead they saw smoke, flames and someone stealing Khan's favourite SUV.

There came a crack as a rifle was fired, then another crack. Fortune heard raised voices and then a burst of automatic fire smacked into the side of the Honda. The Delta corporal didn't wait any longer, he leaned out of the window to fire on the three cars he'd already lit up. The bullets ripped into the fuel tanks of the first two and the cars burst into flame.

"Get the hell in!" he yelled, pulling in closer to the rear of the building where Skip and Obi-Wan waited. More bullets hit the SUV and he could see six or seven armed men running towards them. Some of them stopped to aim and fire. Another group veered off to move the remaining vehicles away so that they wouldn't be caught in the flames.

Skip helped his friend into the back seat, he chattered calmly, as though they were on a Sunday picnic.

"Come on, mate, get yer arse inside, away from those nasty bullets. Don't worry, I've got you covered, Obi," Skip said cheerily.

Obi-Wan had just settled into the back seat when he heard a sharp cry from beside him. Skip slowly bent and collapsed into his best friend's lap.

"We're in, let's go!" cried Obi-Wan as he awkwardly grabbed at Skip's shirt to pull him fully into the SUV. The pain was too much, it flared and he collapsed. Obi-Wan closed his eyes for a few seconds then, leaning over his friend he pulled the door closed. Fortune spun the steering wheel and he raced along the winding driveway towards the main road. Their enemy had yet to do more than fire at their disappearing SUV. Some of them stopped firing to climb into two of their remaining vehicles.

"What's happening? Are you both all right?" asked Fortune pushing the accelerator to the floor, it spun the SUV's wheels leaving a cloud of dust. They were out of the compound but they were sure to have a convoy of angry gang members racing after them.

Fortune looked into his rear-vision mirror and sure enough there were now two vehicles racing to overtake them.

"We've got bandits on our tail," called Fortune as he spun onto the dirt road heading towards their support only a few kilometres away. He expected to hear the sounds of firing but there was silence from the back seat.

"What's your status, Skip?" The silence continued, it worried him. "Skip? Obi-Wan, what's your status back there? Is Skip OK?"

Obi-Wan's voice was empty. "Skip's dead, Gary. He's gone."

In a daze the tough, unforgiving Ranger staff sergeant, took up his newly acquired Steyr and began firing through the rear window. He had the back seat to lean against but every bump sent flames of pain shooting through his rib cage. Obi-Wan re-engaged his energy breathing to stop himself from blacking out. Deliberately clearing his mind he dropped his grief into a deep pit which allowed him to continue firing throughout the chase. But it didn't bring his friend back to life.

Hooky knew they were in trouble the moment he saw the enormous dust cloud approaching on the dirt road. He yelled to Danielle to arm up and prepare for a firefight as he steadied his good arm to hold the

Heckler and Koch G36 resting it carefully on the roof of their four-wheel drive.

"Are we going to stay or should we join Obi-Wan and drive off with them?" called Danielle who was readying her automatic copying Hooky.

"Damned if I know what Obi's got planned. Our orders were to wait and provide cover, so we wait… and provide cover." He let out a light chuckle when he realised how silly that sounded.

Danielle was still recovering from Burger's death and tried to keep her mind from wandering back to that special place she had found with him. It didn't work, in some ways, she wished she were dead too. She had caught herself fantasising about what it would be like to die. The dusky-skinned police constable forced herself to stop thinking about it as Fortune sped past them pursued by a loaded utility and a four-wheel drive. The two defenders opened fire but their target drove by so fast that they weren't sure if they'd hit anything.

"Bloody hell!" exclaimed Hooky emptying his magazine into the last vehicle, "did we even hit anything?" Their vehicle was camouflaged with bushes pulled up from the surrounding area fifty metres from the road. At that distance and the speed of the enemy's vehicles it was possible they'd missed with every bullet.

But sure enough, as they watched, the front vehicle careered off the dirt road and flipped over. It spun spectacularly into the air, bodies were flung out of the ute tray and doors into the desert scrub. The other vehicle slowed and stopped, they drove back to check on their mates.

"Hooky! Hooky!" called Danielle loudly, "they'll see us, let's get moving, come on!" She grabbed his good shoulder and spun him around to look at her, "are you all right?"

Hooky nodded to clear his head. "Yeah, I'm fine. Come on, let's get moving," he sighed, his shoulder injury was hurting like hell now.

Danielle automatically jumped into the driver's seat. As he got in beside her Hooky looked in to see how Kerrie was doing, he noticed she was awake.

"Hey, Kerrie, how are you feeling? We're going to get some action and you'll be bumped around." Hooky reached down and touched her face, it was hot and fevered. "Hold tight, darling." Kerrie smiled then screwed up her face in pain as the vehicle took off at speed over bushes and sand dunes away from the road.

"Hooky, I don't think they're going to follow. Can you get back there and try to help Kerrie, please. This trip is going to be pretty damn tough for her," suggested Danielle.

Fortune slowed when he saw that the race was over. A deep sense of grief hit him in the chest now that the adrenaline of the chase was over. He watched in his mirror as Obi-Wan settled into the seat and nursed Skip's head in his lap.

The quiet, tough Delta, took control of the situation, he knew that he now needed to give his buddy time.

"Obi, I'll get us to that farmhouse we discussed, we've got a few hours. Take it easy, grab some sleep, I've got this." Obi-Wan nodded but said nothing.

"I saw Danielle and Hooky, they're heading out too. We'll either meet them at the farm or at Pine Gap." There wasn't much else to say so he stopped talking. He switched on the CB and set it to 'roam' listening to the chatter of the enemy at the drug lord's warehouse.

The news was that they'd found the bodies of Khan and his two henchmen. Their new leader, Spiro, immediately took control. Elements of the previous faction weren't too happy, they were now in the process of fighting for dominance. Over the course of the next hour Fortune listened to their arguing and eventually the compromised negotiations as the two groups sought to take control. When the signal faded it appeared that Spiro had positioned himself to take leadership of the gang. Clearly they weren't interested in their escaped prisoner, or the lost vehicles, it was all about gaining control of their drug empire.

When Fortune looked in on his buddy he saw that he was asleep, his head resting on Skip's chest.

The two vehicles met at the farmhouse they had decided upon the day before. It was abandoned, empty of food and anything that might have helped Kerrie. It was too late for her anyway. The four survivors were exhausted but they wanted to keep a vigil by her side as the brave policewoman drifted into a coma.

As they sat at the kitchen table Danielle made them all something to eat and drink. She kept busy as she struggled to manage her own grief.

Fortune and Danielle explored the house and out-sheds in the darkness looking for fuel. Everything had been taken so they drained the fuel from the farm equipment. There were tractors and a half dozen caterpillars and other heavy farm vehicles, one truck held eighty gallons of diesel. They had enough to fill their jerry-cans and vehicles to capacity. They were now good to go once they had grabbed some sleep.

"Guys, I'll stand watch for the rest of tonight. I've got all of tomorrow to sleep. Go on, I'll be fine," ordered Hooky. He was tired but couldn't sleep anyway. He had a problem and this was a good time to wrestle with it. Outside in the mild evening air was too good an opportunity to pass up.

It was doubtful there would be unwanted visitors. From the CB chatter they'd heard it sounded like the gangs were still busy negotiating. It sounded like they were quite happy to leave their escapees in peace.

Hooky's problem was that he liked Danielle, had for years. His other problem was that when he was single she had someone. Their timing was terrible. Being a year younger than Danielle meant that age shouldn't be a problem. But after silently courting her for the past few years he didn't know how to cross that line and ask her to go out with him. There were times he even doubted she knew he existed. Feeling like a school kid he decided that he should just ask, no harm in that, he thought.

It was just on sunrise when Fortune went outside to dig the double grave. Danielle brought out a blanket from the farmhouse and lay it over their friend's bodies. They each said a few words but it couldn't express their sadness or how they felt about these past weeks of fighting and running.

Danielle looked at her friends standing beside her, their heads bowed, she saw that they had all lost something precious. Obi-Wan was lifeless, he'd lost a mate, sure, but so had they all. Skip was different, he'd brought a vitality to their group that few people had the ability to do. His charm and charisma made the day to day challenges bearable. The red-headed soldier always had a nice thing to say and never a nasty word escaped from between his lips. It was hard for any of the group to speak, the emptiness of loss just enveloped them like a choking cloud.

Danielle had always thought fondly of her friend, Kerrie. They had trained together as new police recruits and would sometimes meet for lunch right up until Kerrie was invited to join the anti-terrorist team, the Tactical Response Group. It was Kerrie's dream to be part of the action, to be the best - with the best. She remembered how proud Kerrie felt that day when she was called up to start her anti-terrorist training. It all seemed so long ago now, so pointless.

As she watched Fortune cover their friend's bodies she had plenty of time to think about her own situation. It gave her time to put her own journey of recovery into perspective. She understood that grief was a process, it went around and around until it gained enough momentum to reach the velocity it needed to escape its destructive orbit.

Over the past twenty-four hours driving across the desert towards Pine Gap, Danielle faced her demons of lost loves and the many betrayals. She was old enough to be married with kids yet each time someone looked like they were the 'one and only' something unexpected happened. It was time she took control of herself, and looking at the drawn, exhausted men around her, she decided to make a suggestion to bring them back to their task at hand.

The dusky beauty stepped in front of the three men. "I don't give a shit if you don't like it but I'm going to suggest some changes to our patrol. We need to get to Pine Gap and not by dragging our sorry arses like we are now."

Hooky looked at her. Slowly, a smile crept onto his suntanned, lean face, he slowly nodded his agreement. Danielle noticed, she appreciated his acknowledgement. It showed that he believed in her, that she was now part of this group of elite professionals. She smiled and nodded back.

Danielle then looked at Obi-Wan and Fortune, she addressed the senior members of their group. "I think it best if Hooky travels with Fortune and Staff Sergeant Kennedy, maybe you might want to travel with me for a change."

Obi-Wan nodded, he'd barely slept all night, wrestling with his grief and the pain of his cracked ribs. "Yeah, I'm fine with that. A change of scenery will do us good, besides, you're better looking than Gary."

"Yeah, that's a go. I'll help Obi shift his gear over," was all Corporal Gary Fortune could say. He was emotionally flat and drained. He and Skip had enjoyed playing games on their cerebrally-gifted mate, Obi-Wan. They often swapped stories of how they always lost to him. Now Fortune wasn't quite sure how he would relate to his Ranger friend, or anyone for that matter.

As he carried Obi-Wan's gear from his vehicle Fortune realised that Danielle's plan was simple but good, they needed to change something, and with change came opportunity.

"Danielle," he called from his vehicle, "I'll lead."

Chapter 13 – Escape from Danger

It was false dawn when Murphy pulled up under the sparse branches of a lonely tree in the arid landscape of Western Australia. It had been a rough night with dry creek beds and large ditches carved by the monsoonal rains and floods. The two SEALs had decided to knock off for a few hours and get some sleep.

Emily was thrilled to be part of this rescue adventure and took it upon herself to mother the two handsome men. The boys said it wasn't an 'adventure' as such, rather it was just a job.

"Who in their right mind wants to drive for days on end, smelling like a pig, a sore butt from sitting in you're own sweat all that time, eating dried food, no decent coffee, no soft bed and these blasted pesky flies everywhere?" said Pipeline. Emily loved how his deep voice and accent always made her stop and listen, it simply fascinated the petite girl from Perth.

"Well, Pipeline. I've got some eggs cooking, tea brewing and there's toast waiting. Maisie gave me enough marmalade jam... no, you guys call it 'jelly' or something strange like that don't you? Well I've got enough marmalade jelly and that Aussie favourite, vegemite, to feed an army." She smiled, none of the Americans that she knew could stomach the taste of vegemite. "And I sure get it about the flies. Holy cow, no wonder the Dutch sailors had no interest in settling here back in the 17th century."

"I've given up pushing them away. If they crawl into my mouth I just eat them," said Murphy, yawning. The flies were only now waking up with the coming sunrise and as he lay back in his camp chair he pulled his cloth cap down to cover his face and was soon fast asleep.

"Isn't it time to check in with Maverick and Bluey?" asked Emily. "I wonder how the townspeople got along last night with the terrorists."

"Yeah, you're right. You dish out that food and I'll get onto the team." Pipeline was tired too, fatigue seemed to be a given since the apocalypse.

"Maverick, this is Pipeline, do you copy?"

There was some static then a clear voice came on the air, "Pipeline, Maverick here, what's your situation? Over."

"Good morning, Major. We're about eighty k's out of Meekatharra. We've had a lot of creek crossings and soft sand to contend with, it's slow going. We've followed some of the tracks, but this cross-country driving is hell, over"

"Just do what you can, buddy. What's your status regarding fuel and personnel?"

"There's Murph, myself and Emily, civilian. We left two female civilians at Meekatharra. Fuel is holding up. We've got a stop-over coming up in a day or two, Bluey organised it for us before we left. He's contacted the family there so they're expecting us. Over."

"We're doing OK here, we'll need some more water soon though. The puddle we're using is shrinking fast in this heat. I've yet to contact Tonto about their contact with the terrorists last night, do you have any news? Over."

"I'm about to do that, sir. If you stay connected we can have a conference call... Tonto? Do you copy?" Pipeline was hoping to hear the news from Meekatharra but Joey was either busy, knocked out, running, or maybe he was still asleep.

"Pipeline, Maverick, this is Goldmine, Tonto is busy. We spoke late last night, the terrorists are exterminated - like the stinking vermin they are. The fella's at Meekatharra have been celebrating. Over,' came Bluey's distinct voice.

"Goldmine, this is Maverick, that's good news indeed. Any news on numbers and casualties? Over"

"Yes, good news indeed, Maverick. One terrorist vehicle, five occupants killed, no survivors. No casualties our end either. Our Meekatharra miners and bushwhackers know how to fight. Over."

"Thanks, Goldmine, this is Pipeline. Is there any other news? Anything from Obi-Wan? Over."

"Radio chatter suggests a contact with the biker gang out Warburton way. It seems like they had some fun, your friends left behind some casualties and upset the leadership there. Obi-Wan and crew seem to be fine, over."

"Copy that, OK, we'll catch you all this afternoon at dusk, Maverick, out."

"Goldmine, this is Pipeline, what can you tell us about Obi-Wan's contact? Did anyone get hurt? Over." Pipeline's face creased in worry. Emily stood at the door and listened.

"Pipeline, all I know is what I just told you. They had a contact and got away. It sounds like they shot the place up a fair bit because there was a lot of arguing going on and the gang leadership has changed hands. But other than that I know nothing, over," replied Bluey.

A moment later they could hear the crash of something falling over in Bluey's cave.

"Bloody cat!" they heard the sounds of Bluey trying to straighten whatever it was Piggy had knocked over.

"Thanks, Goldmine, I'll catch you this evening. Good luck with your Piggy. Pipeline, out." Pipeline kept the radio on to scan the frequency channels and accepted a plate of food from Emily.

"So they've had a fight but got away, and from what Bluey says they must have taken out the gang leader," offered Emily who had moved her camp chair next to the vehicle and began eating her own meal.

"Yup, sounds like Obi-Wan must have run into some bad people and decided they needed a new leader. I hope they got away OK though." The enormous SEAL finished his meal then cleaned up the remaining food left in the pan. "Emily, my darling girl, you don't mind cooking a meal for Murphy when he wakes, do you? I'm sorry but I seem to have… eaten everything." His broad smile made it easy for Emily.

"Sure, I'm going to have a sleep now too. Leave everything by the fireplace, I'll clean up later." She opened the car door and climbed into the back seat, she was asleep in moments.

Their stop-over was at a cattle station in the middle of the Western Australian desert. They arrived before dawn after a heavy night battling the boggy sand, dry sandy creek beds and just impossible country covered with scrub. There were very few tracks heading the way they wanted to go so part of their trip was bush-bashing.

"Murphy, I think we'll sleep where we are, no use waking the poor folks up this early," said Pipeline pulling over at the gate and switching the vehicle engine off. "You guys get some sleep, I'll reconnoitre and come back."

The homestead was a kilometre from where Pipeline had stopped the vehicle. He checked the ground for tracks to make sure there had been no unexpected visitors.

The giant SEAL walked slowly along the dusty drive with his AK47 over his shoulder. The sunrise was still a half hour away so he relaxed and enjoyed the predawn stillness, it was pleasantly cool. To make things better there were no flies.

He looked up at the night sky to see an enormous expanse of light from the stars above. The Milky Way hung low over the horizon while to the east there now appeared the rosy streaks of dawn. He stopped and checked the homestead very aware that if he went much closer the dogs that every farmer has would start barking and wake their hosts. The SEAL didn't want to start their visit on the wrong foot.

Pipeline was feeling lonely, watching Murphy and Emily courting reminded him of his other life in the US and his wife. He never chased the girls and he didn't flirt, he always played a straight game. He thought of how many times he could have bedded the most gorgeous girls on the planet. He was tall, had a body-builder frame, and with his ebony skin and ready smile, he was always being asked out. He had charm, personality and turned girls and many men's heads. But his eye's were only for his wife back in the US.

As he walked slowly back to the vehicle he remembered how he chased Janice, the girl he liked in high school. She vowed she would never go out with him, "*Not even when hell freezes over, Peter Liner, not even then would I go out with you,*" she'd say. He chuckled, she said it like a mantra. He persevered through high school and college until finally, on the day before he was to leave for military training, she said 'yes'.

The high school and college football hero, the best running back in the game, finally took the quiet, library-girl Janice, to the movies and then dinner. He had her home by 10 o'clock, like he'd promised her father. There, on the doorstep, they kissed.

"Janice, will you wait for me? I've waited eight long years for tonight's kiss and I'm not going to wait that long for what comes next." He looked into her eyes, "so it looks like I'm going to have to marry you."

Janice simply smiled back. "No you won't Peter Liner, I'm going to university and you're going to court me properly. Now that I know you're a gentleman I expect you to continue to behave like one." He chuckled to himself again, remembering. To Janice, everything was always '*proper*'.

That was twelve years ago and they'd not spoken a single bad word to each other. The two shared a love he didn't understand but there was no way on earth that he wanted anyone else. Not even now, knowing that he might never make it back home. He put the thought of his loss away but it often crept out when he was feeling low.

'Maybe Commander Cullen has a submarine up her sleeve, then we can all go home,' he mused.

Behind him, the low clouds began to glow red and pink, ahead of him the stars slowly faded. By the time he had their breakfast fire started and the billy of water boiling for their morning cuppa the dawn had broken and the sun was shining. And, of course, with the sun came those pesky bush flies.

At full sunrise he called for his team to wake up and grab some food and a cup of hot tea, they'd run out of coffee. Sometimes even a cup of boring tea was good enough to start the day, he thought.

"Come on you two, get yourselves untangled and ready to go door-knocking," he called to the lovers through the open window.

"Hi, Pipeline, what's it like, the house and stuff?" asked Emily rubbing the sleep from her eyes. She turned and held Murphy's hand as she stepped out of the vehicle. He then put his arm around her shoulder. It was so natural that Emily felt instinctively safe with him.

"All looks normal. I'll call up Bluey in a minute. I decided to give you a break, Emily. I made breakfast for us all. Try some of my grub." He saw the look on her face. "It won't kill you. It's just eggs, kangaroo jerky and cornflakes – protein and carbs."

Murphy shrugged when Emily looked sideways at him, "Don't worry Emily, we've lived on Peter's cooking for years, no-one's died yet."

"If they did they haven't complained, eh," she added.

Within a half-hour Pipeline had confirmed all was ready for their visit to the homestead. It was now a case of driving through the gates and introducing themselves.

Once through the front paddock gate the three were met by a pair of cattle dogs. They raced up to the visitors barking, they then stopped to sniff their visitor's hands curiously. It was a stand-off until Pipeline bent down to pet them. He threw a stick for the dogs to chase, they played chase all the way to the front door.

The homestead door was opened by an apprehensive, weather-beaten man in his late fifties. His similarly weather-beaten wife joined him at the door.

"You must be those soldiers Bluey called up about?" asked the man. He seemed awkward, cautious and a little afraid of the giant Pipeline standing over him.

Pipeline put his hand out and introduced himself. "I'm Pipeline, this is Murphy and this little girl is Emily. Thank you so much for inviting us to visit."

The woman looked at the three of them. A simple up-and-down inspection told her that they needed a bath, a decent feed and a few days rest.

"Come on in, you look like you could do with a few luxuries. We ain't got much but you're welcome to what we have. Bluey said you've been fightin' them bad church people we've heard about. He said they've stopped all TV and radio and have been killing people. Is it really that bad?" she asked.

Emily took control when she saw that the two Americans struggled to understand the woman's country accent.

"Hi, I'm Emily. We sure could use a bath, even a dam or well will do us. We've still a long way to go and some food and a wash would be more than welcome." As the three were invited inside, Emily continued, "and yes, those terrorists are bad, Mrs…?"

"Oh, I'm so sorry, how rude. I'm Becky and that's Adam. He's not good with people, you have to tell him what to do otherwise he'll just go off and do nothing. Since there's no more radio signal he's got nothing to do with his spare time, poor beggar." Emily smiled, she liked the woman already. "Come on inside, it's going to be another hot one."

The homestead, apart from the radio, was stuck in the 18th century. They had their bath in a big metal tub - they had to change the water several times. The water was pumped by hand from a well outside the house. The stove was a wooden fireplace which heated the water for their bath also heated the house when things got cold in winter.

Emily was pleased to note the house was clean, even the animal skins and hemp sacks covering the dirt floor were spotless.

Emily spent the day helping Becky around the house. Pipeline and Murphy helped Adam fix the roof, they also did some fencing in one of the paddocks where the farmer kept cattle and some goats. They had several horses that Adam used to get around the enormous property - not having to worry about fuel made a difference.

"Adam, do you have any diesel? We need to top up our fuel tanks and jerry-cans, if you have any to spare," explained Murphy, pushing one of the dogs off his foot.

"Sure do." Adam took them to his storeroom. He explained that he'd spent months digging a deep pit until it was large enough for a cellar. He covered it with iron sheeting and then a layer of earth for insulation. "It's nice and cool down here. You boys come on down and take a look."

He turned towards the homestead to see if his wife was watching then cupped his hand around his mouth and whispered, "I've got a few bottles of home-brewed beer you might like to wash that desert sand down with." It was the first time they'd seen him smile, they now had a new friend.

"My father home-brews, I've helped him heaps of times," said Pipeline as they walked down the stairs into a tidy earthen cellar. "He sometimes distils his own whiskey too." He saw Adam's eyes light up.

"Hey, you don't say, he makes his own whiskey, eh?" Adam was all ears now as he took down two dusty bottles of beer. There were several glasses on a dust-covered bench, he cleaned them with a rag from his pocket.

"There you go youngn's," he said as he poured, "some lovely ale to celebrate your visit."

They sat on wooden boxes containing home-salted meat and chatted while they finished a half dozen bottles.

"That's damn good, Adam. What do you reckon, Pipeline? Is it as good as your old man's?" asked Murphy pouring the remaining drops from the bottle into his glass.

"Yessiree, that's mighty fine beer, Adam. My old man would be proud to say he brewed this." Adam scrutinised Pipeline's face to make sure he wasn't pulling his leg. The lonely farmer smiled, satisfied the boys were giving his beer their honest appraisal.

"Here, take some beer with you, you'll need it on your trip." Adam handed the boys a half dozen bottles which they gladly accepted when they saw he had a whole wall of beer.

"Thanks, Adam, that's right good of you," said Murphy, "but we'd better get that fuel for our vehicle sorted out."

"I'd forgotten about that. Come over here fella's, help me roll this 44-gallon drum up the ramp and we'll fill 'er up, eh." He smiled again and proudly showed the two SEALS his one-man winch and ramp setup.

While the boys were bonding over their beers, Becky and Emily were bonding over a huge pile of bread dough. Becky had decided the three visitors needed some bread to take with them on their trip. If they made the dough this afternoon it would have all night to prove and be ready to bake in the morning. Emily and Becky worked solidly as they mixed and then kneaded the dough until it was silky smooth.

All through the process they chatted about everything from terrorists, to desert herbs, to cooking in the bush and eventually to relationships. It was then Emily realised that Becky had been hedging towards this topic all day.

"You seem to get along well with that nice soldier, Murphy. I think he likes you." It was both question and statement.

"I do, he's gentle and strong, but he's also fragile. Did you know that we haven't had sex yet?" Emily flushed bright red, she really didn't expect to say something as intimate as that, especially not to a stranger. She began to giggle, the next thing she knew Becky started giggling too. The two couldn't stop and had to sit down before they fell over.

"I'm so sorry, Becky," Emily said between outbreaks of the giggles, "but it just came out."

"Don't worry darling, Adam and I didn't have sex straight away either. He was too scared that I'd laugh at him. These days I have to send him outside for a few beers before he gets the courage to come to bed with me." They burst out laughing, the two kept breaking out into the giggles as they covered the enormous pile of dough sitting inside an old, enamel bowl the size of a baby's bathtub.

"We'll let this sourdough rise overnight and it should be ready to bake in the morning." Becky touched Emily on the arm affectionately, "you know, I've not had so many laughs as I've had with you. I'm going to miss you when you leave." Instead of giggles, her face softened. "And don't worry about your boyfriend, it's going to be all right, I just know it. My mother had the sight and I've got it too. Relax, he wants you but he's been hurt - so have you, I can see it. But love heals and the love I see in you and Murphy... it's a healing love."

Becky called the boys inside for the evening meal and a bath. For the boys, it had been a busy day - working, drinking and preparing their vehicle for the second leg of their trip.

"Do you boys really have to go so soon? I mean, I could do with a bit more help with the cellar," said Adam, he struggled to keep his eyes open. They'd had a second visit to the cellar after they filled and serviced their vehicle and were all feeling quite merry.

Murphy decided he should answer, besides, he was the senior SEAL so it was his decision.

"Adam, we've got to get to our rendezvous, but we'll rest-up tonight and get away before lunch. I think we can put in some hours driving through this never-ending desert before it gets dark. What does everyone say?"

"Yeah, I'll second that. I'm bushed, my heads like cotton wool from all that driving. A good night's sleep and a relaxed morning will make all the difference," added Pipeline. They looked at Emily.

"Me too, I love it here, Becky's a beaut cook. I think that's the second best decision you've ever made, Murph." Emily smiled at her lover. He reddened hoping their hosts wouldn't understand what they were talking about. "Besides, Becky said she'll show me how to bake bread, bush-style. I can't leave without a few loaves to take with us."

"Wonderful," smiled Becky, clapping her hands, "and we can play a few games of cards tonight, five-handed Five-Hundred, it's my favourite. Then we can have a sing-along - I've got that old pianola in the corner. It hasn't heard a tune for the past twenty years but I think I can still play her." She was so excited the three would never think of disappointing her.

That night they played cards and sang along with a very out-of-tune pianola. They eventually gave up trying to tune it so the boys sang some of their navy songs. The two farm-folk were beyond happy. Adam was allowed to bring several bottles of beer into the house and even Becky shared a drink with them. At midnight Emily had to call it quits on the evening's entertainment.

By candle-light they enjoyed another bath in the 'sleep-out', a large semi-attached stockmen's dormitory beside the homestead. It held six rooms with bunks that had no doubt been built some hundred or more years ago. For Emily it was just right, the sheets were clean and the beds soft and that's just what she needed.

Emily felt safe, and recalling Becky's words she decided to chance fate again as she snuggled up to Murphy. Neither knew what the future would hold and both could feel the ghosts of failed relationships hanging over them.

"Murph, where are we heading with this?" asked Emily softly. She placed her lips on his neck and kissed him, slowly. Murphy groaned, he didn't want to answer but then she stopped and waited.

"Em," he said, looking at her in the dim starlight slanting through the open window. "I really don't know. The world is no longer the same one we were in a month ago. We've left behind something broken and this is our opportunity to fix it. But that means us, the first generation of survivors need to sacrifice parts of ourselves to achieve that." His reply came softly as he weighed each sentence carefully. He now lay back with his arm around Emily's shoulders.

There wasn't a lot of room in the single, wire-framed bed, but Emily was small enough to squeeze right on the very edge without falling off. By curling into Murphy's arm and lying partly on his chest she was connected to him, heart-beat to heart-beat.

After several failed relationships, betrayal, loneliness and finally pushing everyone away so she wouldn't be hurt again, Emily knew that she desperately wanted this man. Not just sexually she wanted to be with him forever. That simple realisation confused and frightened her. They had been so close to losing their lives and could still lose each other through the hardships they were yet to face, she reminded herself.

"Em, what are you thinking? You're too quiet, you're never quiet and now you're scaring me," whispered Murphy, pulling her on top of him hugging her to his broad chest.

Emily lay there enjoying his manliness, his scent of sweat and beer. She breathed it in, deeply, to savour the moment before she had to answer.

"I'm worried that we won't survive this. We've got everything against us, terrorists, deserts, starvation, thirst, getting lost. I don't know, it's just that so much can go wrong and I'm afraid that if I love you anymore I might lose you." She stopped not wanting to spoil this special moment by crying.

"Well, if it's going to be like that, then, I'm going to be brave and say it - I love you." Murphy lifted his face to kiss through her salty tears.

Rolling onto his side Murphy propped himself on his elbow to look at her. He could see the stars through the open window. The light they cast made her look as though she was covered in sparkles - all over her tear-streaked face.

"Emily, you've shown me what a special woman you are. And I've fallen so damn hard in love with you. You're kind and you're gentle, you don't make a scene and you don't make demands, ever. You know what, I think you and I might have a chance. Even if all hell breaks loose and we have to run away to live in a cave together."

Emily laughed lightly. "Murph, I've run away from life too many times. I don't know if I can trust myself to love again, but I love you so much it hurts." She buried her face in his shoulder.

It seemed as though they made love all night. Each time they woke the stars were still shining outside their window signalling that there was still time for more lovemaking.

Just as the sun was rising they were woken by Pipeline's singing and the dogs barking the chorus.

"Now that's clever, he's teaching the dogs to sing Motown," said Murphy loud enough for Pipeline to hear.

"If I didn't know better I'd say that you two spent the night singing another kind of music," Pipeline called out in reply. This was followed by peals of laughter as he opened the door on his way to splash some water on his face and freshen up. "Come on you pair of lovers, the sun's up and there's work to do, and not that sort of work either."

They spoke to Maverick and Bluey before breakfast. Once the dawn checks were done Adam took the boys for a drive in his old World War 2 jeep. They came across a mob of Red Kangaroos resting in the shade under some low bushes. Adam pointed them out for the two American's to see. Before the kangaroos could move the three men had shot one each. It only took a short time to skin and prepare the animals. Adam kept some meat for himself and he helped the boys salt and pack the rest for their trip - the dogs had a feast.

"Yer gonna have to cook some of that over the next day or two," he advised. "Keep the rest salted for a few more days in that tub of salty brine then string 'em up and let them dry out. You'll have enough food for a few more weeks if you do that."

When they returned Becky and Emily proudly showed them the loaves of bread they'd baked. Becky had been up before dawn getting the fire prepared to make sure the oven was 'just right' for baking later that morning.

It was hard to say goodbye, for all of them. The outback farmers belonged to Bluey's network so they could keep in touch. Pipeline said he would check in with them when he could.

The dual-cab four-wheel drive set out after lunch loaded with bread, meat and food enough to feed an army.

Chapter 14 – West Lyons River

Petty Officer Second Class Murphy and his team were within shouting distance of their destination. It had taken them nearly two weeks of bush-bashing but it seemed like a single day to Emily. The time Murphy and she had together was way too short.

Some days were spent locating suitable water sources and digging down into the sand to access the cool, refreshing water. When they came across emus or kangaroos it was an opportunity to refill their larders. They salted the meat so that they would have meat supplies for the now starving aircrew.

Towards the end of their journey the reports from Major Samuels grew more disconcerting. The helicopter crew had run out of food and were almost out of water. Once the shallow pools of algae-covered water dried up they began to suffer the terrible symptoms of thirst. On Murphy's suggestion the aircrew found a soak. It was a damp, wet area in the dry creek bed. They dug into the moist sand and collected a cup of clean water every half hour. It simply wasn't enough to keep four men alive in the sapping heat of the Pilbara.

To make matters worse Major Samuels was vegetarian. Once his vegetarian meal rations were gone he had to square-up and eat the meat dishes that were still available. It didn't make him sick but it did go against his morals. He was fortunate that his crew, normally rowdy and chummy about things like this, never said a word. They were afraid that if they did then Sam would stop eating and die of starvation. They had crewed together for some years and knew just how stubborn and proud their aircraft commander was.

The SEALs kept up the pace to get to the crew as fast as possible but their limitations were almost overwhelming. Sand, lots of sand; rough patches of saltbush and spinifex that cut the tyres to shreds; countless punctures and now they were running low on the patches Adam had provided. They were frequently forced to make long detours around insurmountable barriers which slowed their progress. Some days they followed vehicle tracks but there was always the concern the terrorists would be on the lookout. At the forefront of their mind was getting Bluey's parts to the helicopter.

The boys knew that the terrorists were primarily city-centred but the Revelationists wanted to expand into every corner of the west Australian coast. Every township, holiday park and tourist destination were being trawled for survivors. At the time of the apocalypse Western Australia was a haven for tourists and the terrorists executed every one they found.

Bluey relayed the horror stories he had heard on the CB network from tourists set up with their own CB radio. He advised them of what they could do but, because the terrorists monitored the network he had to be careful what he said. So did the 'grey nomads' trying to create their own sanctuary.

Emily was a city girl, she loved the city life of Perth, her hometown. In fact she loved any city where she could get a latte and croissant for breakfast. But somehow the desert was special, more so than the city, especially at dawn and dusk - at these times magic happened. She loved dawn, the magic of the world awakening to a flush of reds and pinks, building to a heat that bakes everything. At dusk the sky pulled its star-lit bed-covers up to rest and recover from the heat of the day.

The nights weren't too cold but it was enough for the two lovers to snuggle up in each other's arms; enough to enjoy the feel of their naked bodies against each other. They made love as often as they could but once dawn came they stepped back to becoming part of the team.

Pipeline didn't seem bothered, as long as she and Murphy shared the load he was as bright and chirpy as ever. In fact Emily noticed that he smiled a lot more, he even hinted at how happy he was for his friend, Murphy. On one occasion he even remarked that he'd only ever known one Murphy: the miserable, unhappy bastard who should have divorced his wife before they had kids. Emily was sad about the children but silently pleased he had been so miserable and that made her feel guilty – but only a little.

The desert honeymoon ended when they saw Lance's smoke signal. Murphy carefully navigated through deeply cut gorges and around dry water-holes to finally arrive at their destination to deliver the helicopter parts as promised.

As Emily exited the vehicle cabin she could see four skinny, filthy, flight crewmen. As she got closer she could smell them too. It made her think that perhaps she didn't smell all that good either.

"Good afternoon, gentlemen and lady. It is a pleasure and a relief to see you," called Major Samuels from beneath the canvas where the crew were resting.

The tall, thin man stood up and slowly, painfully, ambled across to the parked dual-cab. He gently extended his hand to the three arrivals.

Murphy glanced at Pipeline and saw the same look of concern on his buddy's face. The aircrew looked emaciated and the major was barely able to walk.

"Good afternoon, Major Samuels. It looks like you haven't had it all that easy either. And here we were thinking that all you fly-boys lived like princesses drinking straight bourbon, eating lobster and caviar and sleeping on goose-down mattresses." Pipeline's eyes took in the empty water bottles and unkempt state of the crew.

"Sir, we've brought a heap of edibles and water for you and your crew." Murphy leaned into the rear of the cab and lifted out a jerry-can half filled with water. Pipeline held a bag of kangaroo and emu meat which they'd shot and salted only a few days earlier.

"We're sorry we don't have any vegetables for you, sir, but we're sure you'll enjoy this," said Murphy as he handed out the strips of jerky to Samuels and his crew.

Emily and the two SEALs carried the rest of the supplies across to the crew's makeshift shade and began filling the crew's mugs left lying on the camp-table. The crew were thirsty and ravenous and showed it.

"Slowly guys, you'll make yourselves sick if you drink and eat too much on an empty stomach," offered Emily. "If you eat too fast you'll get diarrhoea. Now that would be a darn waste of good food."

BB asked, "Where'd you get all this water and meat from? Our puddles dried out a week ago and we haven't seen a kangaroo or emu since the day we landed here."

Murphy sat down after filling the billy with water and placing it on the fire.

"We've done what our friend Adam said we should do in the desert. To find water he said we should look for the edge of a big sand dune and dig down. Or beside a big rock, or better still find a rock-ledge in a dry creek bed and dig. Even though the creeks are dry there are still places you can get water," he said.

"We were lucky, BB, we've got a shovel. Adam gave us a heap of survival tips and gear and that bag of tyre patches was a life saver. We've managed to find food and water all the way here. The meat was easier to find than water. We went hunting around dawn, sometimes we'd see kangaroos and emus while we drove. But it wasn't very often." Pipeline was eating some of the jerky too, though he didn't seem to be enjoying it as much as the helicopter crew. "We've been eating this jerky for two weeks and I can tell you, I'm sick of it. I just want a nice beef burger with ketchup and mustard, now that's what we should have brought you."

As the sun set, they gathered around the camp-fire and the two groups shared stories of their adventures. The aircrew shared how they had caught a snake but were too afraid to eat it in case it poisoned them. That caused a few laughs. Then they told of how Major Samuels, a vegetarian, was forced to eat the remaining meat rations once his own vegetable meals ran out.

Only BB could get away joking about vegetarians in ear-shot of Major Samuels. "Hey guys, when I took my vegetarian girlfriend on our first date, I gave her a bunch of flowers. She said, 'Oh, that's so nice of you.' I told her, 'Well, I didn't know what you vegetarians ate.' "

Pipeline, who was sometimes known for his tactfulness, saw Samuels' face redden. He quickly jumped in to support the vegetarian chopper commander. "As they say boys, if slaughterhouses had glass walls everyone would be vegetarian."

Samuels wasn't impressed about being the brunt of his crew's jokes. "Boys, you think it's funny, but I have a responsibility to you, my commander and to humanity to stay alive. If it means I compromise my morals and eating habits, that's what I'll do," he said stiffly.

BB had laid his bag of electrical components beneath the helicopter. He planned to start the repairs the following morning. But by the next day the aircrew had exactly what Emily warned them about - gastric diarrhoea.

Despite her warnings the crew ate, on and off, all evening. She tried to tell them to slow down each time they reached for another piece of jerky. As each strip of kangaroo or emu jerky was only the size of a pencil it didn't seem like they were eating very much. Even Samuels ate until he couldn't eat anymore.

"We should have listened to you, Emily," groaned Lance, "this is so embarrassing. Can you promise to turn your eyes somewhere else when we have to go poop in the bushes?" Lance's hands fell to hold his trousers as he ran off into the bushes for the third time that morning.

"That reminds me of the South Park episode where everyone ate green apples," laughed Pipeline, "but we can't call it the 'green-apple squirts', can we, it just doesn't sound right."

Emily called out, "What about 'explosive diarrhoea'?"

"Or 'speed poopin'?" Pipeline added.

"Well, there's always 'extreme pooping' or making 'butt-butter'," offered Murphy.

Not to be outdone Pipeline continued, "maybe they're having an 'assquake'?"

"They say that love is the best feeling ever. But I think finding a toilet when you've got diarrhoea is better," called Lance, who once again grabbed at his trousers as he ran off into the bushes.

Captain 'Curly' Moe was recovering from a busy night trotting back and forth to dump a load. He wasn't in a mood for jokes.

"Pipeline, put a sock in it. Just wait until you get a dose of bum-gravy and see how you like it." He tentatively sat by the fire to drink some of his fresh herbal tea.

BB was nowhere to be seen and at first Murphy and Pipeline worried that he might have gone off into the bushes in the middle of the night and got himself lost. They found him asleep under the helicopter frame among his tools.

"Hey, buddy, BB, wake up," called Murphy at the request of the major. "Did you start work down here and fall asleep or something?"

Crew Chief 'BB' Bingley, explained that he'd fallen over coming back from the bushes during the night. There was a blanket beneath the aircraft where he had already made some repairs, he was so exhausted that he decided to just crawl in and sleep there.

"I was too tired to get into my bed, this was closer."

By now Emily had a large metal pot on the fireplace and soon had the dried meat simmering in water. Feeling sorry for the crew she'd also gone out into the bush, away from their toilet, and collected some bush herbs that Becky had shown her. She hoped that adding them to the stew might help sooth the crew's tender stomachs.

"I'm cooking up some stew, it might help settle your bowels. It shouldn't cause more diarrhoea either, you can drink it like soup." She was initially a little shy of the aircrew but their discomfort and Pipeline's morning banter made her relax around them.

"Hey, Major, have you had any news from outside yet? How are things going in Perth?" she asked. Even though Pipeline and Murphy spoke to Joey and Bluey every day she rarely heard the news of her home city.

"Well, I did ask Bluey a few questions about other contacts but he won't tell me a damn thing. I guess he doesn't want us to know, why I can't fathom. He's a funny old coot that one," replied the major.

Pipeline said that Bluey was as 'silly as a cut snake', and proceeded to tell the crew what happened when they visited him in his cave home and how he ordered them to leave.

"I didn't know that. I guess since Bluey runs the whole communications system no one would be brave enough to mention it over the air." Curly chuckled softly, worried if he got up to a full belly laugh he'd be in serious trouble again.

"Major? Pipeline and I are going to head out and find some water for you, what we have won't last another day. We'll be back for lunch. Emily? Did you want to come with us?" called Murphy pulling gear out of the dual cab to lighten its load. They knew that once the helicopter was repaired the vehicle would be left behind.

"Nah, I'm going to stay and rest up. I'll play nurse to these boys here. Have fun." She waved to them as they headed off to search the dry creek bed looking for a suitable place to dig for water.

By evening the water bottles were full, the helicopter parts installed and the stew was tasty. They all had a quieter night and planned to run checks on the morrow and fly out the day after. Major Samuels decided that a few days recovery was needed just in case they had another electrical failure and ended up in the desert again. He spoke to Bluey at dusk, the crew gathered to listen.

"Goldmine, this is Maverick, do you copy?"

"Maverick, I copy. So what's the news with those repairs?"

"We're running our checks tomorrow and will most probably head out in two days - we've been unwell and need some time to recover. What news do you have for us, and... is there anything from QE3?"

"Nothing new, just make sure you keep me connected so I can run my own checks on your software and hardware. Those components I gave you can be fine-tuned from my end..."

Samuels broke in, "Goldmine, I'm not comfortable with you doing that. These machines are already fine-tuned masterpieces, any tinkering should only be done by the experts who made them."

Bluey went quiet, everyone waited for him to explode. "Samuels, you are such an arse! Who the hell do you think helped test and write the code for these bloody systems?" There was silence again, they could hear Bluey breathing, waiting for Samuels' reply.

"Yeah, I guess I can trust you then..."

Again there came Bluey's explosive interruption. "I assembled the damn parts so don't you think I know what the hell I'm doing?" There came another short pause as they heard noises in the background which sounded like the little genius knocked a chair over, probably as he stood up to rant some more. "You damn yanks think you bloody know everything! Us Aussies invented the rotary motor, the Hills Hoist clothes-line and the Victa lawn mower, we even had corrugated iron before you lot did! I write code, I read code, I dream code and I hallucinate code! If there's anyone on this damned planet that can get your system running better than it ever has before, it's ME!"

Amid the quiet chuckles of his audience, Samuels spoke calmly. "OK, Bluey, settle down, I said it's fine. I'll keep our system on for you to check and run your tests." There continued the sound of muttering and expletives but Bluey eventually settled.

"Maverick," said Bluey calmly, professionally. "I do have a message from QE3. She said to drop the SEAL boys just outside Darwin. There are a few people she wants to get in touch with. I've got a few data files I'll send you… now…" there was the sound of a mouse clicking in the background, "there, done. She wants you to read it and digest it. QE3 wants Murphy to send a reply and any questions to me and I'll forward it on to her."

"Got it Goldmine, we'll reply as soon as Murphy has had a chance to go through it. What's the score on having a chat with QE3 now?" Samuels knew he had no chance of talking to Sue-Ellen but he never missed an opportunity to ask.

There came a muffled expletive from Bluey, it sounded like he was off-stage, busy moving something. "Damn it cat!" they heard the little man trying to be angry. Piggy was in strife again. "Get off me bloody keyboard. How am I supposed to look after these bloody soldiers with you walking all over me bloody computer and knocking bloody things over all the time?" It sounded as though it hadn't registered to Bluey that he was live on-air.

"I'm… I'm sorry about that fella's. Little Miss Piggy here wanted to have a chat with you as well. Major, about that QE3 communique… you've got none and Buckley's. I'm not letting you anywhere near Pine Gap - it's verboten. Each satellite is coded differently and if you get in there you'll announce to every bastard terrorist that we have control. The current situation is that the terrorists think my Trojan is either a virus or it's a systems error, they're trying to correct it. Idiots… I'll catch you soon, out."

Samuels studied the data files then called Murphy in. Commander Sue-Ellen Cullen, head of the Pine Gap Intelligence Facility, wanted Murphy and Pipeline to meet up with her spy in Darwin - it was her son, Tanner. Hopefully, it would be a simple drop-in, shake hands, smile, then get the hell out.

That night the aircrew's digestive and eliminative systems had settled and they had the best sleep they'd had in a week. The following day BB ran his tests and communicated with Bluey on several matters. They brought the motors up to speed and did a test run in the afternoon. When they were back on the ground they received another data package from QE3. Sue-Ellen had answered Murphy's questions.

The crew, sufficiently recovered from their gastric diarrhoea, were now ready for lift-off.

Chapter 15 – Sue-Ellen's Secret

The following morning the exhausted mix of police and special operatives had barely gone twenty kilometres when they came across a lone figure walking along the dusty, dry track towards Pine Gap. The man turned when he heard the vehicle approaching then sat down to wait for them.

"Who are you?" the man asked, his eyes were wide and his face tense. Danielle could see that he was clearly afraid.

"We're police, who are you?" Danielle replied.

"I'm Jake," he jerked his thumb in the direction Danielle had just come from. "I escaped the prison farm back that way. I'm trying to get to a township and tell the police. I was the tour bus driver when the apocalypse hit. Those bikers captured everyone they could find: old people on their grey-nomad adventures; people on outback tours like those nice people on my bus. They even went and collected any locals they could find."

The man had a bag beside him, he put his hand inside and pulled out an empty water bottle. "Do you think you could give me some water before you leave?"

Gary Fortune had already exited his vehicle and now held his own water bottle out to the man. "Here, drink this. Grab your gear and jump in with us, it's not safe to be walking in this heat."

When the small group arrived at Pine Gap, Commander Sue-Ellen Cullen immediately called for Obi-Wan to discuss security. There was a lot to talk about.

The attractive, middle-aged blond, interviewed all four survivors on their arrival. They had been out in a world that no-one else in the secret facility had experienced. The news they carried was vital for Sue-Ellen to take in and process. Importantly, and noticed by Obi-Wan and Fortune, she didn't include her second in command, Major Will Binks.

The news of Skip and Burger's deaths upset her, she had a special fondness for her specialists. She knew that their occupation made life tenuous at the best of times but when they didn't return from an operation she grieved.

She assigned Danielle to security and complimented her on her performance. Corporal Gary Fortune was given leave - but it was to covertly keep on eye on certain individuals.

Jake was invited to help in the kitchen until someone found a driving job for him. Hooky was interested in joining Danielle in base security but his injury required treatment before Sue-Ellen decided what to do with him.

The evening following their return Sue-Ellen sat with Obi-Wan over dinner.

They had finished eating when Obi-Wan asked for a 'cup of tea'. He explained that having nothing else to drink he had grown used to its horrible taste, he now preferred tea to his usual black coffee.

"Obi," said Sue-Ellen, "I know who the spy is. I know what to do with him too. There may be sleepers but at this moment I'm satisfied I've got the snake by the neck." She watched her friend curiously.

The Ranger staff sergeant's eyes opened wide as he listened to his commander's disclosure, but he didn't say anything. He hadn't been very communicative since Skip was killed, he was still coming to terms with his loss. It seemed to open a hole that he had tried to keep a lid on since the apocalypse. But now the lid was off and the demons crept out when he least expected it.

"You don't need to say anything I'll just walk you through it, OK?" Sue-Ellen saw that her old friend was struggling. He had a wife and children in the states and there was little chance of him ever seeing them again. She also knew that he had held his best friend in his arms as he died. She knew he was struggling but she also believed that he would come back, stronger than before. If there was one thing she knew about this man it was his resilience and his personal code of ethics to be the best.

Obi-Wan listened and nodded when he could bring himself back to the moment and hear her words. But for most of the time his mind was elsewhere, sitting in the back seat of the vehicle nursing Skip; at home with his wife and kids; memories of his courting days before he was married to the most beautiful woman in the world; all the opportunities he had to tell her he loved her but didn't… the memories and thoughts floated around inside his head and he couldn't stop them.

"Obi? Ben, are you still with me?" he heard his commander softly ask.

Staff Sergeant Ben Kennedy, 'Obi-Wan' even to his commander, looked up and saw the worry and what he recognised as fear in Sue-Ellen's eyes, he looked back at the floor.

"I'm here now, but I've been to hell and back," he paused and looked again at her. It was late evening and his cup of tea was cold. "How long have I been sitting here?" he asked.

Sue-Ellen put her hand on his. "Ben, you've been sitting like that for three hours. I think you'd better sleep in here with me tonight. I'll get the girls to make up a bed for you on the floor." She was about to get up and call her secretary when Ben put his hand on her arm.

"Sue-Ellen, you don't need to do that. In that place I just went, I remembered something that has always been very important to me: *'Rangers Lead The Way'*."

Sue-Ellen baulked and sat back down.

"I'm a Ranger, I earned the right to call myself a Ranger. I lead by example, I give more than a hundred percent, surrender is not a word in my language. I volunteered as a Ranger, fully knowing the hazards of my profession." Obi-Wan picked up his cold cup of tea and finished it. He then stood at attention in front of his commanding officer.

"Commander Cullen, Staff Sergeant Ben Kennedy, ready for duty." He smiled, his first for a very long time, then he relaxed his stance and said, "I've been gone for a while but now I'm back. I'll see you at 0600, I believe you and I have work to do." Without another word he turned and exited the office.

Sue-Ellen sat quietly for a few moments then smiled to herself. *'That's why I like the guy, he's the best of the best and probably the only person on this planet I trust more than my son, Tanner.'* Stretching her legs she finished her martini, sorted out her papers for tomorrow's meeting, then crawled into the blankets that lay like a pile of rags on the couch behind her desk. *'Now that Obi-Wan's back it looks like I'll finally put that scum-bag spy where he belongs.'*

"It's in there, Obi, it's in the background check they did when he was after ultra-security clearance." Sue-Ellen held a cigarette to her lips and drew smoke deeply into her lungs. "Pretty good, huh?" She smiled at her chief crypto-analyst, someone who could put Sherlock Holmes to shame.

"Yeah, now I can see it,"beeprep", how simple, the Boy Scouts motto, 'Be Prepared'. I was never a scout, never had time for playing games either. So he was an Eagle Scout too, did you discover this yourself? You're a clever young lady, I might find a suitable job for you if you keep this up." Once again Obi-Wan smiled, but then it was back to business. "Right, so what have you been doing with him since you discovered this?"

"Guess, smart-ass," she said, her face animated and lively, she hadn't had fun like this for so long she couldn't remember. Sue-Ellen took another drag on her cigarette then stubbed it out in her ash-tray. "Slowpoke, he's mine now. I'm going to feed him and keep him closer to me than anyone else on the base."

Although Obi-Wan was never going to be his old self again he did see the joy in his commander's, no, his friend's face, and he liked it.

"Sue-Ellen, if Reece were here today he'd jump for joy and we'd all drink to it, maybe even get a little drunk." Obi-Wan smiled a second time that day. "But there's just you and me and we can cook this grub like a frog in warm water." Obi-Wan put his head down again.

When she saw him do that Sue-Ellen felt fear, the fear that she was alone, fighting the world to right the insurmountable wrongs all by herself. It was a loneliness she had fought since Reece was killed doing what he loved, flying Navy planes.

Obi-Wan looked up and saw, and he knew, he'd seen it many times, those moments when Sue-Ellen let her guard down. He well knew her vulnerabilities, knew of her undying love for her husband. He and her son Tanner were the only ones who were allowed, privileged, to see beneath her veil of self-control.

"Hey, I'm sorry Sue-Ellen, I'm back. I won't scare you like that again, I promise. I was just thinking, that's all," he assured her. Sue-Ellen flashed a smile and waited. "That Major Daniels in Adelaide, he's on your payroll too, does he know that you know?"

"Daniels, that predatory sleaze-bag? No way, he has no idea we're on to his spy here. Ony Bluey, you and I know. I need to feed Daniels and Will the same news, and that means you and I will be spending time together monitoring their communications, developing strategies to manage them both," she replied firmly.

"Copy that, Commander," Obi-Wan said absently. Already his mind was racing through possibilities. "And Bluey, what else did he have to say? I've seen his set up in the middle of the desert. He lives under the ground, it's like a bunker. So he's running the entire military satellite system by himself is he? He's has his hand in so many pockets I just wonder what else he's up to."

"Bluey worked with Reece many years ago, Obi, he was a whizz kid way back then. Reece found out about him and invited him to work with us. He came to us via Australian Security Intelligence Organisation and the Australian Signals Directorate, he was then co-opted to work with our Navy intelligence. Reece was basically Bluey's keeper for a while. Bluey and I did a lot of work together too. I gave him jobs and he completed them. He was, and looks like he still is, the most competent communications whizz on the planet. He's forwarded Dr Tantoni information on how to take command of the supply carrier so the astronauts can return safely to earth. Apparently they've had a supply ship docked there since the apocalypse. The

Russians sent it up and when the apocalypse hit Dr Tantoni and the crew refused to release it. No one complained because the Russian base was knocked out by terrorists only a few days later."

"He wants to bring the astronauts down to earth? In a supply ship? They're unmanned, they're not designed to carry people." Obi-Wan looked at Sue-Ellen waiting for a reply.

"Bluey and Dr Tantoni said they can do it. So I guess they can. The other option is that they stay up there and die of starvation and radiation sickness. It's not very safe up there you know."

"Yeah, they really have no choice, do they... Bluey's also got control of the military satellites? And that means the laser? Does Will know about the laser too?"

"Major Binks knows everything about the satellites, his problem is that he can no longer contact nor control them. He can't even track them. Bluey has locked him out with his own code which, according to Bluey, is unbreakable. Did you... want to have a crack at it?" Sue-Ellen teased her friend.

The two had worked together in intelligence for many years. Both of Obi-Wan's Pine Gap deployments were under Sue-Ellen's command. During his first deployment he worked closely with her husband, Reece, as well. The two men got along like a bush-fire. They shared a passion for Star Wars and Star Trek. Sue-Ellen was pleased to see her husband opening up to someone. Reece was a solitary man until the chief crypto-analyst, Staff Sergeant Ben Kennedy, came along.

"I think I'll trust Bluey on this one, he can keep his code. Is there any other news? What about Meekatharra and the SEALs, how are they all going?"

"The two SEALs and one of the girls have headed off to deliver the computer parts to the Four Musketeers. It seems the SEALs are doing well, some difficulties with the terrain, flat tyres and the usual hardships of driving in the desert, but they'll get there. As for the aircrew they're slowly running out of food and water. Major Samuels sent two of his crew to look for water and anyone who might help them. Even though they've done their survivalist training it's a desert out there and they're not bushmen. If Murphy and Pipeline don't get to them within the week we might have lost our one and only Stealth Black Hawk and it's crew," replied Sue-Ellen. She took another cigarette from the packet on her desk and lit it. She noticed that her hands were shaking slightly, *'damn, this stress must be getting to me,'* she thought.

"We should plan what to do with your boys when you all get back together. I've lost half of my special operatives and the ones I have left I want to keep. How is Gary Fortune? He's gone quiet, but then again he doesn't talk much, not like Skip."

At the mention of their friend the room went cold. Sue-Ellen realised she didn't want to go there, Skip was her friend too. She knew she needed to be strong for Obi-Wan but sometimes she failed to be strong for herself.

"Yeah, Gary feels responsible for Skip's death. If anyone's responsible it's me. I got banged up and had to be helped out - that put Skip in the line of fire. But Fortune was close to Skip too. They did a lot of training together, gym and boxing, that sort of thing. When Murphy and Pipeline get back that will help Gary I think." Obi-Wan stopped, he'd said enough and didn't want to go back to the place in his mind that he'd finally managed to close off.

"What about your ribs? What did the doc say?" Sue-Ellen changed the subject, it was too soon and too raw. They'd get around to opening up about it, but not now. She held her cigarette in one hand while she lifted her mug of coffee to her lips with the other. "They seem to have improved a lot."

"Doc said they're not broken, they're cracked, which is just as bad, pain-wise. I have to take it steady. He said that I can do a lot of walking but little else." Obi-Wan went across to Sue-Ellen's kitchenette and poured himself another cup of tea. It was time to get back to work.

Senior Constable Paul 'Hooky' Pan, of the Tactical Response Group, recovered well. By the time they'd made it to Pine Gap he had a plan. He'd known Constable Danielle Ahmet for over three years, they did some of their training together. Since he was posted to the Geraldton area he spent almost as much time with the WAPOL as he did with his own team.

But his big problem was confidence. He was always the gawky guy at school, the one with the big, boofy head and gangly legs. He was just one of those kids who had to grow into his body, and he did, but it took him nearly twenty years. He worked hard at maintaining his buff abs and broad shoulders but his legs stayed skinny. At six foot 2 inches, his mother always said that his skinny calves could be forgiven.

Hooky was a soccer player, a handy forward who scored as many goals off his own foot as he did setting up his team mates with accurate crosses. Soccer was his passion, as it would be, given that his mother and father came from Glasgow, Scotland. His father was a professional soccer player back in the seventies. His mother said that she never saw him during the soccer season because his father was training and playing matches all over the United Kingdom. But as a born and bred Perth boy Hooky enjoyed surfing as much as he did his soccer.

Danielle, on the other hand, came from refugee parents. Originally from Afghanistan her parents fled to Pakistan to try to escape the Taliban's persecution of her people, the Shia Hazara's. Her family were from warrior and merchant stock. They could sell ice to an Eskimo then turn and fight a battle high up in the Hindu Kush mountains. Both herself and her brother were born in a refugee camp waiting to be resettled in Australia.

While her brother entered the army and became an armoured cavalry sergeant, Danielle entered the police force. Their parents had witnessed the atrocities of religious terrorism first hand in both Afghanistan and Pakistan. They felt honour-bound to instil in their children a love for law, order and tolerance.

Sadly, both her parents suffered post-traumatic stress. They were tortured at the hands of the Lashkar-e-Jhangvi, religious terrorists, and sometimes the tension at home was unbearable. The sooner the siblings entered the forces the better she thought.

When Danielle arrived at Pine Gap she was interviewed so many times she lost count. The first and the final interviews were with Commander Cullen. Danielle was impressed by the woman and swore to be as much like her as possible. She was invited to be part of the security team at the Pine Gap base and jumped at the chance.

Her friend Hooky was also invited to join their growing security force. She was delighted when she heard the news, the two now had plenty of opportunity to meet and talk. But once again Hooky's old problem struck him down. Every time he wanted to sit next to Danielle he became tongue-tied and stupid, so he gave up. That created its own problem. A woman as attractive as Danielle is never without courtiers and soon a swarm of potential suitors began to chase after her. Hooky was back to feeling like the great loser he was back in high school.

One lunch-time, as Hooky tried to walk past her to get to an empty table, Danielle grabbed his arm.

"Hey, Hooky, why aren't you talking to me? I have a feeling you're trying to avoid me." Danielle wasn't smiling, in fact, thought Hooky, she looked forlorn. That stopped him in his tracks, *'what would a beautiful young woman with every drone male in the facility clamouring for her attention want with me?'* he thought.

In a facility with a dominance of males between twenty and forty years there weren't enough eligible females to go around. Those women who made it to Pine Gap were usually career girls who easily dominated their targeted man - powerful females abounded. Danielle wasn't like that, she was a pushover and simply couldn't cope with the unwanted attention.

Hooky just stood there, holding his tray of food in his hand while he struggled to think of something to say, fearful he would just say something stupid.

"Ah, I'm sorry, Danielle, I just thought…" it was happening again, he just couldn't say a damn thing. Those gorgeous, big brown eyes mesmerised him.

"Well, you could sit with me for lunch once in a while?" Danielle felt hurt that her friend Hooky, of all people, would abandon her to all these strange, hungry men.

It was the forlorn attempt at a smile that made Hooky pull out a chair and sit. Over the course of the hour he began to relax and they chatted like old times - like they did on their trip from Meekatharra; like they did listening to the ocean waves by the campfire at Shark Bay. By the end of their lunch break Hooky felt he had a chance. Danielle felt safer knowing her friend was just shy and feeling a little lost.

"Hooky, let's meet up again tonight at dinner. We'll go outside and talk like we did in the desert. What do you think about that?" she asked. His eyes, bright with anticipation, reflected an urgency to say 'yes' despite his many insecurities.

'Yeah, yeah, sure, if you think that's a good idea. I'd like that." They both stood and just stared at each other. Their eyes locked as something magical passed between them, something they both felt - it felt nice. The moment was broken by a call from their team leader, lunch was over.

"See you then." Then Hooky was gone, a slight smile on his face and a pain in his chest that felt strangely pleasant.

Chapter 16 – In Darwin's Shadows

The stealth Black Hawk dropped Pipeline and Murphy at an out-of-the-way football field in Darwin. Tanner was waiting for them and ushered them into his SUV.

"Hi guys, I'm Tanner, your guide for this evening." He was tall, had his mother's charm and blond hair and his father's boyish good looks.

"You sure have your mother's sense of humour," said Pipeline as he pushed Murphy away to sit in the front seat. Murphy chuckled, it was like they were on holiday. It was hot, steamy and it was 3 am in the morning.

"My turn in the front on the way home!" said Murphy, automatically putting his rifle within reach as he pulled his Glock 18 and chambered a round. "Where are we going, Tanner?"

"I've got two operatives I want you to meet. They've got material for Pine Gap. We've lost all contact for some reason. I need Commander Cullen to hear their information," he replied. "Oh yeah, before I forget, leave your weapons in the car, the guards will definitely search you when we get to our rendezvous."

Tanner took them to a hotel known as 'Shags'. It was once a lively, pleasant place, but since the apocalypse, it was a place known to provide for everything a terrorist's black heart desired: sex, drugs and power games. Tanner led them to the guarded entrance where they were searched before permitted entry. He ushered them through a throng of uniformed, drunk Revelationists. Murphy and Pipeline noted that there were three different uniforms present and that they were generally segregated by armed security guards.

"What's with the security?" asked Pipeline as they sat on a bench looking out onto a brightly lit courtyard filled with drunken revellers.

Tanner looked around and explained the situation in the Northern Territory city of Darwin.

"We've got three Reverends here, each has his own battalion, and their own ambitions to rule them all. Whoever wins Darwin rules the north and access to Asia. There's a lot of wealth, trade and power out there to the north and Darwin is the gateway." Tanner laughed, it was light and soft, like his mother's. "We're waiting for my team, Barry and Laddie, we manage the three reverends. I want you to listen to what they have to say. No notes, nothing in writing or recorded, just listen. We've got maybe a half hour so keep the questions till they finish their reports. I want Commander Cullen to hear it directly from your own observations."

As they waited Pipeline watched the assembled patrons milling around the bar. Some were dancing, some drinking and some asleep in their chairs or on the floor. It looked like a normal Friday night crowd in a bar anywhere in the world.

"What's the security here like, Tanner?" he asked.

Tanner looked around. "Nothing for us to worry about. The security guards are there to stop the three battalions killing each other. They leave their weapons at the door. Security is run by the Priests. Anyone who crosses the Priests is dealt with. No one returns from a visit with the Revelationist Priests."

Murphy turned to look at Pipeline then at Tanner. "Hell, that's one way to control them, can't say I'm upset by it."

They watched as a group of men and women, all uniformed, enter one of the private entertainment rooms. When the door opened they could hear loud music and what sounded like some heavy partying.

"What's in there?" asked Pipeline, though he might have guessed.

"That? Oh, just one of those private parties, you know, sex, alcohol, drugs. They get high and have fun. We use it all the time as a reward for the guys and gals we use in our games. All three battalions use drugs and sex as a reward."

"They're noisy," said Murphy as the sound levels rose with the arrival of the newcomers.

"That's nothing, just wait another hour or so when the drugs kick in," replied Tanner. "I prefer to sit next to these rooms, it's a good way to disguise our little meetings. Besides, some of the battalion staff we use know me. They like me to see them enjoying their rewards."

As they were talking two well dressed middle-aged men pulled up chairs and sat at their table. They put their beers down and introduced themselves. Tanner introduced the SEALs, then got straight down to business.

"I told our friends here we have a half hour, but we're running a little late. So I think we'd better cut that down to ten minutes. I've got to get back to Reverend Albert for another meeting. OK, let's get started, you first, Barry." Over the next ten minutes the three secret servicemen told their story of how the three battalions were at each other's throats - even before the apocalypse.

The men were frightened for their own safety though. They wanted the SEALs to ask Commander Cullen for a new communication channel. The satellites were out and they had no way to contact Pine Gap. They didn't know of Bluey but they did know someone was making it hard for them to communicate via the satellites.

The spies were afraid that their current status would be compromised if they tried to change their usual practice of passing on information. A courier would be suitable but that required helicopters or desert travel and they were certain neither method would be approved. They needed another means to maintain communications with their base.

It was now time for Tanner to get his visitors back to the helicopter but as he went to leave a drunk tripped and fell on the table spilling drinks and knocking the table over. The two SEALs immediately went on alert, several of the security staff turned to look at the disturbance. When they saw the SEALs they knew something was going down in 'Shags'.

"Hey! You lot, stay where you are," called one of the guards, a squat, beefy man who looked like he was poured into his uniform then the legs and arms trimmed off. Three more security staff walked over, their night-sticks out and pistols at their hips.

Tanner took one look and realised that if he didn't step in the SEALs would go into action. He really didn't need his cover blown. Even if they managed to escape his role as 'eyes-on' in Darwin would be over.

"Piss off! You're spoiling my party," cried Tanner at the drunk on the floor. He kicked him savagely in the ribs then turned to the guard. "Dale, get this dumb shit to the Priests, he's trying to compromise my commission."

Dale, the squat, gnome-like guard, stopped and looked at Tanner and his companions. "What's happening here, Tanner? Who are those military types you're with?" He looked at the two other men, quickly recognising them as part of Tanner's group. "Sorry guys, I see you're at a meeting. I was just checking, that's all. I'll get someone to throw this bum out."

"Come on guys, we have to get out of here, quick." Turning to Dale he said, "Thanks, Dale, can you escort us to my car? I need to get them to a meeting with Reverend Albert and we're already late. I don't want to upset him with the news that Shags security held me up. You know how pissed he gets."

As they walked down the corridor to exit onto the car-park the three other security guards joined them. Tanner nodded for Barry and Laddie to melt off into the darkness. The gas lanterns at the entrance to the hotel barely shed enough light for him to see his SUV. The sound of the security staff crunching their boots on the gravel was magnified in the fading light.

Tanner stopped when the group got to his car, he turned and looked to see the guards only a few metres away, walking with a purpose towards his two SEAL friends. Dale, the squat gnome-like security staffer, was yet to realise he had more security at his back.

"There you go, Tanner, make sure you put in a good word to the Reverend for us, thanks, mate." As he turned he stopped, saw his three security staff friends only a metre or two from the SUV and realised that there was going to be some action. Dale pulled his night-stick in anticipation and spun to face the two SEALs.

"You pack of stupid pricks," stormed Tanner. "I just told Dale here that this is my commission and I don't want to have to explain to the Reverend Albert, or the Priests, that you bastards have interrupted their plans. So why don't you lot go back upstairs and look after the hotel."

"Sorry, Tanner, we have orders just like you do," answered one of the security. He had tattoos on his forearms and one of his front teeth was missing. "These two friends of yours are strangers. I think the Priest's might want to have a word with them before your Albert does. Only yesterday Priest Ambella told us to investigate any newcomers, especially those we consider military. These two certainly meet that description."

The two lean, mean SEALs took one glance at each other then at Tanner and moved - fast.

Even with their night-sticks out and the cover-flaps off their pistols the four security guards were no match for the two SEALs. Tanner froze as he watched the action, fascinated at how smoothly the SEALs disabled the four security guards. He fantasised that, given the chance, he could have done just as well as Murphy and Pipeline.

"Tanner, do you have any flexi-cuffs or rope in your SUV?" asked Murphy, his breathing was heavy and fast. Two of the enemy would need cuffing the other two were dead.

"I've got nothing, use their belts and shirts. I'll help get these two into the back then I'll cover the fight marks on the ground. We've got to get the hell out of here," he replied as he opened the trunk for the dead bodies.

They dropped the bodies into the bushes on their drive back to their rendezvous with the helicopter. There was no traffic and where they were headed, to the long-abandoned footy-field, it was unlikely anyone would discover the bodies.

"What do we do with these two?" asked Tanner, though he was quite aware what one of the options was.

Pipeline looked at him. "Tanner, leave them with us. You'd better get back to your meeting with your reverend. Good luck, we'll pass what we've seen and heard to Commander Cullen, we'll send her your love." He didn't smile, no-one felt all that happy with how things had turned out.

"Good luck, fellas. I hope to see you around in better circumstances, then maybe we can finish that drink." Tanner stepped on the gas and disappeared towards Reverend Albert's seedy headquarters.

It was early summer when the Black Hawk finally arrived at Pine Gap. Immediately Major Sam Samuels attended Commander Cullen's office to debrief.

"Commander, I never give you grief over anything. I see a snake - I cut it's head off myself. I never ask someone to come and cut it off for me. You've known me for years and not once can I recall ever asking you for help with something that I could deal with myself," he began, fast and furious, his emotions aroused. Sue-Ellen smiled, she knew what was coming.

"That's correct, Major. We go back a long way, Sam, I've always admired your individualism and excellence of service," she said.

"Well, Sue-Ellen, it's that damn Bluey. He has so pissed me off over control of the communications satellites, damn it, over everything, that I am about ready to fly down to… where-ever the hell he lives… and carve him a new ass hole."

"Sam, I don't recommend that," Sue-Ellen cut-in gently. "Bluey runs the entire show at the moment. He links me up with the rest of the world and supports me against the terrorists. I've known Bluey for twenty odd years, Reece was his mentor for a lot of that time."

Samuels didn't know any of this, it was news to him. In fact, he realised, there was no way he would normally be in touch with Bluey, he was one of the intelligence spooks. Reece, Sue-Ellen, the whole intelligence community, kept their secrets to themselves and Bluey was beyond top secret. It was only the apocalypse which had brought them together now.

"I didn't know that, Sue-Ellen, sorry. So Reece knew him? Well, that explains his bad manners then doesn't it," he chuckled. It was an old joke between them.

One night Sam Samuels and his wife took Sue-Ellen and Reece out to dinner. The normally quiet and reserved Reece took offence at the conversation of the people on the table next to them. It turned into an argument and finally to blows. When they laughed about it later they would always bring up how rude it was for Reece to listen-in on someone's private conversation. From then on the story was always about how bad mannered Reece was and not about how stupid the couple at the other table were.

"Yes, Bluey certainly is rude and bad mannered, but he is crucial to us. I have a plan to regain control, but I have to do it so he thinks it's his decision. There are still a few obstacles I have to work through before I'm ready to tackle Bluey for control of the satellites."

"I'll just have to let that one fly. On the other matter, Sue-Ellen, the SEALs met with Tanner and his team. I understand that they need a private communications channel. They've lost contact and I guess Bluey might be the one to organise that link with you - is that what you're getting at?" Samuels asked, his eyebrows raised.

"I try to play my cards close to my chest but yes, Bluey's been busy setting up communications with the entire planet, he just hadn't managed to reconnect Tanner and his team as yet. That's why I needed the boys to drop in, catch up on the gossip and find out how my son and his team are doing. It seems that Tanner has things under control. Pity about the Shags incident, the loss of a few security staff might raise a few questions. But these are violent times and things do happen." Commander Sue-Ellen Cullen, head of the Pine Gap security facility, pulled a cigarette from the packet on her desk.

"Samuels, how are the crew? You had a bit of a hard time of it in Western Australia I understand. How are the boys recovering?" She lit the cigarette and blew smoke up towards the ceiling. "And are you OK? I heard you had to eat meat to survive."

Major Sam Samuels smiled, he knew what she was getting at, another old joke between them.

"Ah, yeah, I prayed to the 'Lord on High' and he said I could eat meat to stay alive. It was the damnedest thing though - we had no food for three days, a cup of water every few hours and we all hallucinated at one time or other from the heat, thirst and starvation." He stopped talking, lowered his head and he became emotional. "I saw my wife, my kids and grandkids, it cut me up, Sue-Ellen, it damn near sent me crazy. I was at our last Thanksgiving with my family, everyone was there. They each came over to me and wished me well then disappeared. Last was my wife, Janelle, remember how she used to laugh, that funny, light giggly laugh, and we'd all crack up over it? She took me in her arms and held me, she said that I would be seeing her again soon enough. She smiled, handed me a plate of lamb chops, she giggled again as she left. I can still hear that beautiful sound. I have a feeling that they were all killed on the day of the apocalypse. I miss them all so much." He put his head in his hands and quietly sighed, a deep, soulful sigh.

Sue-Ellen got up and put her hand to his face, she stroked it affectionately then went to put the coffee pot on. There was still some vacuum sealed ground coffee left on the base.

"Come on Sam, I'll make us some real coffee. I'm proud of you my dear friend. But don't think of leaving me just yet, you've still got some flying to do before you can retire your wings."

The two prisoners captured by Murphy and Pipeline were filled with a mixture of fear and arrogance, but they soon talked. Sue-Ellen listened while Obi-Wan and Fortune reported on their interrogation. It verified what Tanner had said: the three Revelationist leaders were in a tug-of-war with each other for power in the north. Neither of them knew much more, they weren't that high up the food chain to know the intimate details.

Sue-Ellen now thought of ways to, perhaps, nurture that unrest and foment some sort of rebellion or outright confrontation between the three groups. Right now was not the time but it would come.

It had been a week since the stealth Black Hawk had returned and things were starting to normalise for the special ops team. Emily found Danielle and they decided to share a room. Emily wasn't quite ready to move in with Murphy, that would come, she wanted a proper courtship first.

The special ops four invited Hooky to hang with them when he had time, but his security work meant that his hours sometimes conflicted with theirs. They all spent time in the gym when they could and he was happy to compete with them on the rifle and pistol range.

But Hooky's love interest with Danielle was still very new, he was love struck and awkward. He knew that if he joined the special ops team he'd be putting his opportunity to woo Danielle at risk, again. Now he was in conflict with himself, his duty to his friends and his new community - he needed time to sort himself out.

It was a chance lunch with Murphy, Emily, Danielle and Fortune that convinced him to join them. Danielle sat at his side and he couldn't help but want to touch her every chance he got. He noticed how Murphy and Emily got along so well and wished that he could be as relaxed about love as those two.

"Hooky, when that shoulder of yours is fully healed I want you to join us. There's only the four of us originals left and Sue-Ellen wants anyone with experience to apply. I'd say your background in the SAS and how well you performed on our way back here is experience enough. What do you reckon?" asked Fortune, now returning to his old self.

"Now that Skip is no longer with us we need an Aussie on our team to balance it. You know, one Aussie is equal to four yanks." He grinned, then his face lit up in a smile, it was an old joke of Skip's.

Hooky looked at Danielle, she nodded her assent. "OK, I'd like that." The boys were back in town!

Over the next few weeks Hooky trained with his US mates. He still had to get back into condition after his injury though. His shoulder was problematic, it didn't seem to want to heal properly.

Over the following weeks he spent more time with Danielle, in fact, Danielle insisted he spend time with her. In some ways he was in heaven with Danielle, but it was still hell with his shoulder.

Chapter 17 – Prisoner Rescue

Commander Sue-Ellen Cullen decided that her special operatives should set up a training program for their new recruits. She now had twelve servicemen she considered suitable to go on hit-and-run patrols by four-wheel drive, dirt bike or dropped in by helicopter.

Staff Sergeant Ben 'Obi-Wan' Kennedy and Corporal Gary 'Soldier of Fortune' Fortune, ran the program. She relied on the two of them to collect data, develop plans and tactics, run the training scenarios and to then carry them out. Logistics she left with Danielle and Obi-Wan.

They continued to run with the data Bluey collected from the satellites he controlled. At this stage Sue-Ellen didn't contest Bluey's dominion over the communications satellites, to do so would put her plans for Major Will Binks in jeopardy.

Bluey was well aware of the enormous power he wielded by having sole control of the satellites and therefore control of the flow of information. Sue-Ellen had to trust him. Fortunately she'd known him for many years and although he was temperamental, some would say 'crazy', he was fundamentally a trustworthy and honourable man. His occasional episode of moodiness was expected and Sue-Ellen managed him through each one - as much as he allowed her.

Obi-Wan's first operation was the prisoner rescue at the prison farm where Skip was killed. It wasn't just revenge it was also a matter of humanity.

Sue-Ellen and Major Binks acknowledged that the rescue would be a good training operation for their new special ops team. He didn't know it but every message Binks now sent was funnelled by Bluey through Sue-Ellen and Obi-Wan's desk. Together they 'managed' his communications with Major Daniels of the Revelationist Church, Alpha army, in Adelaide.

The rescue plan was for the stealth Black Hawk to drop the teams off at midnight. They would walk in hitting the warehouse and farm dormitories right on dawn. Fortune would lead a team to reconnoitre earlier and guide the rest into their positions.

Bluey provided extensive data, photographs and video footage of the farm and the warlord's movements. Commander Cullen made sure that only the team leaders knew of the satellite data. Major Binks, the Revelationist spy in their midst, was kept completely out of the loop. As much as she wanted Sue-Ellen wasn't quite ready to move in on him just yet.

Bluey was keen to use the ultra-secret space laser. It required six satellites to synchronise, building enough power to create and fire an extremely high-intensity laser beam with a destructive radius of ten metres. A circle of intense heat that would turn a house into an inferno; incinerate a squad of terrorists and anything else it touched. Sue-Ellen ruled it out. Using the laser would signal to the terrorists that she had control of the satellites. People talk, even the special ops might let something this spectacular slip. It was certainl that any survivors would talk. It wasn't worth the risk.

Jake, the prison-farm escapee, spent time briefing the teams on enemy personnel, their habits, where they slept and the guard rosters. He readily agreed to be their guide and was given a run through in basic training, but he wasn't much for warfare. Instead he agreed to carry a handgun and would assist in identifying prisoners and in recognising the scum who kept them there.

"I want revenge. They killed the folk I was responsible for. I saw them kill all the old people - those who couldn't work, they're cruel, evil," he told Fortune when he was interviewed for the role. "They've been selling their drugs and weapons to the biker gangs and church members for years. It was apparently a big business. They intend to continue supplying the church and gangs with drugs. Khan once said that they plan to relocate to the capital cities over the next twelve months."

Danielle was kept busy organising the team's weapons, ammunition, webbing and a variety of equpiment needed for an operation of this nature. Her skill was communications and managing people. It was her ability to smooth and calm the waters when members were confused, angry or upset. She made it easier for Obi-Wan to get on with it - especially as his own moods swung according to how much pain his cracked ribs caused him.

Over the next few weeks Sue-Ellen and Obi-Wan set about managing Major Will Binks. In short, they slowly strangled him with an overwhelming workload.

"I just can't get on top of this, Sue-Ellen," he complained to his commander at one of their evening debriefs over drinks in her office. "I've got over a thousand security clearance files to examine and you want a report on each one? I've got staff who can do that."

"Will, I know, but I don't trust anyone but you these days. I'm terrified of giving this information to the wrong person. Just imagine handing these files to the spy? That information would give them the leverage to manipulate and blackmail everyone on this base. No, I need your eyes on it, and only your eyes." Where once she thought Will was a friend she could trust Sue-Ellen now felt nothing but loathing.

Every time Will sat at his computer Obi-Wan, Bluey and Sue-Ellen knew about it. They also redirected, rewrote and manipulated every piece of data he sent. It was Bluey who discovered his call sign 'beeprep'. He knew it was the Boy Scout motto but he wanted Sue-Ellen to work it out for herself. It was she who found Major Binks' Boy Scout membership data in his secret personnel files.

Major Binks' contact was with Major Daniels in the Revelationist Church Alpha Army, Adelaide. His messages now centred on getting a delivery of porn from Daniels. He had little interest in anything else, although he did complain that his workload was too heavy and that he was resentful of Sue-Ellen for making him work at something a minion should be doing. He had no suspicions that he was found out.

Sue-Ellen and her team slowly choked him, focusing his energies on his greatest desire - access to a type of porn that Daniels specialised in. As the three read every communique between the two they discovered other valuable information about Daniels - and about his spy network around Australia and the outside world.

Obi-Wan was finally able to convince Bluey that they could work together. As rude and ill-mannered as Bluey was he enjoyed sharing his time with someone who really appreciated his skills. What they eventually uncovered about Major Binks was mind-blowing. What was disturbing was that he had managed to go undetected for so long. His own secret communication went through the base satellite system which he personally managed. Without their satellite connection, thanks to Bluey, they would never have caught him.

"Sue-Ellen, Bluey and I need to show you some things that we've found," said Obi-Wan as he dropped into Sue-Ellen's office one day. "Bluey has managed to download the past six months of communication between Daniels and Binks. A lot of it has disappeared with the apocalypse knocking out older computer networks but what we have is enough to hang him."

Bluey had isolated Sue-Ellen's computer from the rest of the base computers. She was able to disconnect from the base network and reconnect to Bluey's seamlessly. Even Major Binks and his team didn't notice her absences. She sat down and began to examine the material her two specialists had uncovered but she soon stopped and put her face in her hands.

"That stinking, slimy filth!" she said under her breath. "If I had known of this going on under my nose I'd have..." she stopped and looked at her friend. "Ben, this is proof that Binks and Daniels have been running a paedophile ring for years. It shows that they've had help to stay under cover: ministers of religion, and not just the Revelationist church. There's police, judges, lawyers, politicians... as well as Australian I can see American, European, Asian... this is awful."

The commander was tough, the eldest child of a mid-western farming family. When she was 14 years old her father died. She'd gone out and found a job to provide for her mother and siblings. One could never say that Sue-Ellen had it easy. She had seen some horrific things in her intelligence role but what she saw in those files would break any mother's heart.

"I'm sorry, Sue-Ellen, I had to show you the evidence. There's more, a lot more. He even has a video diary but I won't let you see that, this is enough. We've swamped Will with tasks impossible to complete, he's exhausted and feeling low and unloved. His porn hasn't made it through from Daniels since we began intercepting it. He's now making mistakes and accessing his old files, that's how Bluey could trace these. Will is desperate, he's now demanding an immediate delivery of photographs and DVDs. Daniels has promised to leave it at a drop-off point on the Northern Territory border. I say we take him there and arrest him. We don't need him anymore, we've got Daniels."

Sue-Ellen's hand was shaking as she pulled a cigarette out of its packet, she lit it and stood up.

"Ben, do it, and do it soon." She walked to the door to her office. As she let her friend out she said, "and Ben… I don't want him back, you know what I mean."

Two days later Major Binks received a message from his contact in the Adelaide Revelationist Church, a Major Daniels. Neither knew that their communication was managed by the Pine Gap commander and her chief crypto-analyst.

Major Binks hurriedly requisitioned one of the facility's off-road vehicles and drove south to the Northern Territory / South Australian border. As he retrieved his parcel from beside a large and conspicuous tree near the border sign two AFP officers rose from behind a screen of bushes. One held a shovel the other held a pistol, it was aimed at the major's chest.

The Pine Gap police officers stood quietly, like two demon sentinels waiting to assist in their victim's departure. The only words they spoke was to instruct the major to 'start digging'. The Eagle Scout sweated profusely as he dug all the while trying to convince his captors that they really didn't want to execute him. He offered them every conceivable reward his warped mind could think of but he was quite unsuccessful.

"Major, give it a rest, we have our orders and you have the evidence," said Constable Neil Conner. When he had decided the hole was deep enough Neil said, "now say your prayers."

The single shot that rang out disturbed a flock of grey and red gallahs. They were the only creatures upset by the major's departure.

One hot, mid-summer evening a stealth Black Hawk took off from Pine Gap loaded with the special operatives and their guide, Jake, the bus driver. Some, like Hooky, Obi-Wan, Murphy, Pipeline and Fortune, were looking forward to avenging the loss of their friend, Skip.

Danielle was sitting beside Sue-Ellen in the main room with the big board displaying live-streaming video and other data. They were in communication with Bluey as well as the special ops teams and the stealth helicopter crew.

This evening the two girls plus one, Emily, were keeping vigil on the release of the prisoners at the warlord's prison farm. All night authorised staff dropped in to view the action on the big board. The military satellites streamed video footage onto the enormous screen the size of a house, keeping the base up to date on the operation.

Maverick had just dropped the boys off, they were now walking into the zone ready for their assault. Craig, the big board operator, zoomed in and picked them out with his infra-red filter. Their glowing shapes made them appear ghoulish as they slowly made their way towards the farm.

Soldier of Fortune, the only Delta specialist on the base, had gone in with Murphy and Pipeline earlier to reconnoitre. They were now waiting for the teams to arrive to guide them to their positions. There was time for the girls to grab a cup of coffee before they would need to be at their desks.

With Major Binks eliminated, Bluey had begun to relinquish access of the military satellites to Sue-Ellen. He set up networks for Tanner and his team in Darwin and invited Obi-Wan to contact Joey in Meekatharra and Dr Tantoni in the International Space Station.

There were still many things that needed to be done on the space unmanned-shuttle to make it safe for human occupation before Dr Tantoni and the two other astronauts tried to return to earth. That would take months of work. Obi-Wan was now part of the team to help make that possible.

All through their long vigil the girls and the big board team chatted with Bluey who was in touch with an old friend of the CB community, Sydney Charlie. Sydney Charlie was currently hiding in a sky-scraper somewhere in Sydney's North Shore district. The Sydney Revelationists proved to be worse than any others they had heard about. These terrorists practised zero tolerance and executed all non-church members. Sydney was going through a very difficult time, a population of five million decimated by disease and murder, it was genocide at it's worst.

The city of Sydney was beginning to break into minor regions controlled by a mixture of drug warlords and Revelationist church battalions. They existed side-by-side frequently bursting into violence. Reports from around the world showed a similar pattern in most major cities.

One such outbreak of violence between factions that Sue-Ellen heard about occurred in Adelaide recently. Two Revelationist battalions had a violent confrontation at a crossroads in the city. It was a bloodbath which required the execution of the culprits to settle things between the two army battalions.

Obi-Wan and Neil formed Charlie team to take out Spiro; Murphy led Delta team to take out the main dormitory; Pipeline led Bravo team responsible for the secondary dormitory; Fortune led Alpha team, with Hooky, to take on the warehouse where the prisoners were kept.

"Shhh, it's started, team Alpha is in position at the warehouse. They've got a tough job, they're responsible for the safety of the prisoners," announced Danielle, closely monitoring the operations audio communications. Emily was with the video monitor, they were waiting for the individual helmet cam live streaming video to come up on the big board.

They heard noises and commands. It sounded eerie, the voices and noises coming through the speakers made everything about the live stream so surreal.

"Alpha in position, ten combatants inside, four are awake, playing cards... flash-bangs at the ready. Non-combatants are not in the line of fire - this is a go," came the whispered voice of Fortune.

"Bravo team in place," it was Pipeline. They could now see the images from Pipeline's helmet camera appearing on the big board. "Dormitory is full, twenty combatants asleep. We're ready."

Obi-Wan whispered, "Charlie team ready." Sue-Ellen was certain that his ribs were causing him pain. It was the tight strain in his voice that gave it away.

Murphy then announced, "Delta ready, dormitory has thirty plus combatants, asleep…" The staff in the big board room were tense, silent, no one moved or spoke.

"Teams," announced Fortune, "check your weapons, flash-bangs on three, good luck fellas." He counted them in and the big board erupted as a series of flash-bangs was followed by shouting and screams.

"Video live," announced Emily, and there it was, live video on the big board.

They witnessed Fortune's team scramble through the windows and via the rear door of the warehouse. The rapid movements of the head cams made it almost impossible to watch. The Board was split into multiple screens, each team leader had a camera strapped to their helmet: Obi-Wan; Fortune; Murphy and Pipeline. Those in the big board room now saw one video stream settle long enough to witness the shooting of the four card players. They saw Jake, but for only a second or two, run across to the prisoners yelling at them to stay down. Other images showed the remaining enemy rounded up and cuffed.

Just at that moment three of the enemy leapt at Hooky knocking him to the ground, one pulled a pistol and fired. Fortune's camera was knocked off-line leaving the scene blank except for the audio.

Pipeline's Bravo team had taken out the dormitory with zero casualties on either side. The viewers could see Pipeline's other operative, Maine, cuffing the prisoners and pushing them down onto the floor. All of a sudden four of the men broke for the door, the Pine

Gap screen showed Pipeline's automatic M4 come into view as he cut them down.

Fortune's Alpha team had lost its video feed but they still had the audio. The audience heard the sounds of people grunting, shouting - it sounded like wrestling or hand-to-hand fighting.

"Hooky! Get out of the way!" cried Fortune, the sound of his M4 firing was loud in the big room.

Then more sounds of gunfire erupted - screams and grunts as bullets found their mark.

Fortune's voice cried out, "Down! Get down on the floor! You, get down! Drop it! NOW!"

There came another eruption of gunfire and screams.

"Someone see to Hooky! Patrick! Come here!" There were unintelligible yelled orders from someone near Fortune.

"Bannerman! Hold this position, anyone who blinks, shoot to kill." It was loud enough for all in the warehouse to hear. Fortune didn't want any more unpleasantness.

"What? What did you say?" Silence. "Patrick, get Hooky outside, I'll take a look at him when we've cuffed everyone."

By now Danielle had frozen, her heart beating like the sounds of automatic fire on the big screen. Her dark skin was cold and clammy. When Emily heard Hooky's name she leapt from her chair and ran to be with her friend. No-one else in the room had moved from the moment the assault started.

Suddenly there was more gunfire and screams. Someone called loudly, "Patrick's down!" This was followed by the sounds of a rifle on full automatic, several pistol shots, then silence.

"I can't stand it!" cried Danielle. She was sobbing, almost hysterical. Sue-Ellen quickly came over to sit with her. The three girls huddled together listening to the story created by the audio feed.

"Fortune, what's happening?" It was Obi-Wan.

"All good, one man wounded, Patrick. Hooky's gone and dislocated his shoulder again," came Fortune's terse reply.

The other video displayed Obi-Wan's entry into the warlord's cottage. From Jake's description and their satellite surveillance there would be up to six male combatants plus up to four women, non-combatants, in the three bedroom cottage.

Obi-Wan was paired with Constable Neil Conner, a hard-bitten AFP constable based at Pine Gap. He was a specialist in unarmed combat, third dan in the Japanese martial art of jujitsu. Neil and Obi-Wan often worked on their martial arts forms together, he knew how good Neil was. He had also seen Neil settle a few disputes between the residents at Pine Gap and was satisfied he would be ideal as his off-sider in this operation.

Obi-Wan and Neil entered the back door together before Fortune gave the order to start the assault. The drawings Jake provided were clear in their minds-eye. They had the task of securing the cottage where Spiro, his girlfriend, and his henchmen would be.

They had already completed a circuit of the house. Satisfied, Obi-Wan entered the first bedroom while Neil covered the hallway.

Obi-Wan switched his weapon-mounted flashlight on right at the moment the flash-bangs exploded in the warehouse and dormitories. Immediately the short, barrel-chested Spiro awoke and leapt from his bed. His pistol was in his hand as he landed on his feet. Obi-Wan thought the little man did it well, then he fired and Spiro dropped to the floor. The naked girl in the bed screamed, Obi-Wan cuffed, then ignored her as he cleared the room.

Neil was similarly armed, he too wore an armour-plated vest and weapon-mounted flashlight. His silenced automatic cut into the two disorientated men who staggered into the hallway from the second bedroom. They dropped to the floor. Neil remained still as he shifted his weapon to cover the bedroom door. They could now hear voices, male and female.

Obi-Wan spoke as he tapped Neil on the shoulder. "Flash-bang the bedroom where these two came from and clear it." His breathing was heavy and Neil recognised his commander was in considerable pain.

"Sure, I've got it." Neil pulled a flash-bang from his pocket and threw it into the second bedroom. There came an eruption of light and sound. Neil ran in and cleared the room, it was empty.

"Clear! Coming out!" he yelled.

Obi-Wan could hear that the third bedroom held non-combatants as well as the males he could hear arguing. When Neil was in position he nodded to his leader - ready.

Neil threw a flash-bang into the third bedroom. There came mixed screams of men and women.

"Police! Come out with your hands up or we shall fire," Neil yelled.

Two naked women ran out into the hallway straight to the two men. They were crying and shaking, they appeared to be half asleep and struggled to even walk.

"They've been drugged," said Obi-Wan. To the girls, he asked, "Is there anyone else in that room?"

One of the girls nodded, her eyes couldn't focus so she closed them.

"There are two men, kill them," she groaned then slowly leaned against the wall, her legs were shaking. As she spoke there came the sound of gunfire from inside the room.

"Neil, another flash-bang. If they don't come out, grenade them."

Again Neil pulled a flash-bang from his pocket and threw it into the room. It exploded and the men inside continued to yell abuse and fired several times through the wall.

Neil looked at Obi-Wan who nodded. He pulled a grenade from his webbing pouch and primed it. Obi-Wan helped the two girls down the hallway to the end of the house. When they were safely gone Neil pulled the pin and threw it into the room. The yells of shock were cut off by the explosion.

Neil raced into the room and cleared it.

"Fortune, coordinate the teams," called Obi-Wan in a tight voice. "Charlie is clear, no prisoners, three noncombatant females. We're coming outside."

Murphy's Delta team had responsibility for securing the primary dormitory. It was the stockmen's quarters where the majority of the enemy were sleeping. The big board displayed his live video feed.

It was dark, at first the viewers could only hear the sounds of flash-bangs followed by screamed orders to stay still and not move. The thirty-plus enemy stirred then came the shouts and orders of their own leaders. All of a sudden the listeners heard sounds of gunfire, a mixture of AK47, Steyrs and M4 automatics.

The video steam showed gunfire flashes and people moving around the dormitory, some tried to escape out through the back door but were cut down; some tried the windows but they never made it. It was a bloodbath that only took five to ten seconds before the firing stopped leaving behind smoke and muffled groans and cries from the wounded.

They watched Murphy's video showing one of his team walk through the dormitory cuffing the survivors and checking the wounded and dead. It was gruesome and bloody but it was quick.

"Murphy, what's the status of your objective?" called Fortune.

"Delta has now cleared the primary dorm, no casualties," Murphy replied. "Twelve dead, same wounded. We are now moving prisoners out into the open."

Murphy spoke again, "Fortune, I've sent our medic, Andy, over to your position, he should be with you by now." There were sounds of muffled conversations.

Andy's voice came across clearly. "Fortune, I've had a quick look at Patrick outside, he has serious internal wounds. Blood pressure is dropping, he's not good."

"Line the prisoners up and get them outside. Anyone who moves, kill them," was Fortune's simple orders as he went to check on Patrick.

Danielle was still crying but now there were smiles. "It was his bloody shoulder again. I told him he shouldn't go," she said, laughing and crying through her tears. "I can't lose another one. That's it, he's grounded from now on."

Even Sue-Ellen smiled at that, she nodded in agreement.

There were three buses on the property, Jake commandeered one to load the surviving members of the warlord's prisoners. Obi-Wan spoke to the survivors and in conversation with Sue-Ellen they agreed that the gang members should be loaded in one of the buses and dumped somewhere - "a long way away". No one wanted to execute them, not even Jake or the survivors.

The last thing Sue-Ellen wanted was to be invaded by useless, corrupted prisoners. *'There aren't enough men to guard them and not enough food to feed them.'* Her executive decision was to leave them to the elements, an old-fashioned banishment to the wilderness.

Major Samuels and his Black Hawk raced the survivors in poor health and the two wounded back to base. Obi-Wan and the rest stayed behind to collect information on their links to the Revelationists and biker gangs.

They found an abundance of food and water so they decided to turn it into a bolt-hole, a place where anyone could escape to in times of unrest. Things were changing fast, a safe-house in the middle of the desert was as good a place as any in a time of need.

Epilogue – Sundown's Apocalypse

"Commander Cullen!" called Tammy, one of the big board operators, as her commander walked into the room for her morning debrief.

"Yes?" Sue-Ellen replied, head down as she examined the list of briefs on her work desk.

"Bluey sent us some material he found among Major Binks' files. It seems that we have neighbours, just down the road. They've caused quite a stir with the local Revelationist battalion too," said the operator staring at Sue-Ellen, trying to get a response.

"Yes, General Hughes and his toy soldiers, they keep knocking on our front door and we keep sending them away." Commander Sue-Ellen Cullen sounded bored, she didn't even bother to look up.

"This is another mob, in Marree. They knocked out the Leigh Creek battalion in the morning, then defeated the Deaths Heads in the afternoon," announced Tammy. This time she said it a little louder and with a little more animation. "We've received recorded conversations and data the battalion have been sending back to Adelaide. These locals know how to fight, Commander."

Now Sue-Ellen looked up. "What? Someone else is out there? Let me see what you've got." She briskly walked over and leafed through Tammy's material. "Well, well, well, at last someone we might be interested in sharing our load with."

Looking at the big board Sue-Ellen called across the desks to the board operator, Craig. "Hey, Craig, can you swing that satellite around and bring us in on the Marree township, South Australia?"

"Sure, we've been thinking you might be interested in having a look around Marree. Just give me a minute and I'll have it ready for you."

Craig sipped at his morning mug of coffee and munched on his breakfast of oatmeal porridge.

The base's kitchen was manned by volunteers as well as the original kitchen staff. The base kitchen catered for everyone, including the staff and their families who had been living in Alice Springs when the apocalypse hit. Sue-Ellen allowed anyone who wanted, to leave, but very few did. They all saw what was happening around the world on the big board. Sue-Ellen had kept it running twenty-four-seven through the first days of the apocalypse. Everyone on base was informed and could make their decisions based on accurate information rather than sentiment.

The kitchen was one place Craig liked to frequent. Not just because his partner, Linda, worked there, but because he loved to cook and help out. Sometimes he made special meals for Linda and himself. He could get lost in his cooking and forget the world outside. But this morning's breakfast was a snatch-and-grab because he wanted to have the big board up and ready for Sue-Ellen when she arrived.

The staff at the big board enjoyed her company. It wasn't just because she was the commander of the facility but because she showed her appreciation for a job well done. She actually took the time to understand the big board operators work and praised them when they deserved it.

Craig worked exclusively with the base communications and especially with the satellites. When he worked under Major Binks he did his job and that was it. He had his suspicions but could never find any actual evidence. Craig did speak about it to his supervisor but they both agreed they needed hard data before bothering Sue-Ellen.

Craig was once heard to say, "Binks is so crooked that if he swallowed a nail he'd shit a corkscrew."

They never found evidence but weren't surprised when they were informed that Binks was their spy. He had been passing top secret information to the church for years and he was the one who had cut satellite communications during the vital rescue at Shark Bay. It was Major Binks who was responsible for the loss of the Taipan helicopter and crew.

Sue-Ellen never kept the truth from her staff and Binks' execution was news she wanted everyone to hear. Binks was not a popular officer. His masked, sleazy nature wasn't lost on his staff. They quietly celebrated when he failed to return from his rendezvous with death.

By now Bluey was a regular with the Pine Gap communications and big board staff. Sue-Ellen and Obi-Wan made sure that he felt accepted and part of their team. He didn't want to join any organisations, he'd done his bit and it sent him crazy. But with the end of the world in full view he decided to re-enter the spook business and was even beginning to open up. It helped that, for a short time, he had the world in his hands – and he loved it.

Today was another opportunity for celebration as the room filled to capacity. The view showed the damaged, historic Marree Hotel and the bodies strewn on the ground. This was much like what the Pine Gap staff had witnessed throughout those first days of the apocalypse. Although generally unmoved by its horror, they were encouraged to know that they were not fighting the war alone.

"This is from Bluey's archives, he filmed it a while ago but only gave us access to it this morning. I think he'd forgot all about it with all the action he's had to cover. I'm sorry we have no footage of the actual fight, Commander." Craig explained as he shifted the satellite view. "The place was attacked by the Revelationist Church from Adelaide, Alpha Army's Major Lunney, Deaths Head Battalion. If you want you can listen to his running tirade against some sergeant. He blamed him for sacrificing the entire battalion. He's nuts.

"They arrived in company strength, about one hundred and fifty soldiers, and left with about fifty. We don't have accurate numbers. Lunney's superiors were right pissed-off at him for losing their first class battalion… here it is everyone." Craig zoomed in on the damaged hotel itself. "Bluey has done a great job so you can see the destruction of the building… hey, look, there are two people, armed…" he zoomed right in to the two lone figures wandering the battlefield.

Roo and Bongo were large on the screen, these were two of Sundown's Commando scouts. The walked slowly among the dead bodies examining the scene, trying to understand what had happened. Viewers saw one of them bend to pick something up from the ground then walk into the damaged hotel itself. It was just on dawn, the light was poor but the satellite image was crystal clear.

"Look, Commander, these close-ups show one is carrying a sniper rifle, that looks like an AK47… and that bloke has a Bren-gun. Blimey, that's a World War Two light machine gun. I wonder where he got that from?" Craig kept up his commentary as they all watched, mesmerised.

Commander Sue-Ellen Cullen leapt straight into action mode.

"Right everyone, listen-up. Tammy, I need information on who these people are, their strength and where they're based. They can't have stayed at Marree, the terrorists are now based there and they'll be wanting revenge." Sue-Ellen's voice was fast, vibrant and animated, it showed just how excited she was. "Craig, check out the rest of the township and surrounds, see if they've got a base nearby."

Sue-Ellen paused as she became aware of the crowded room, she suddenly realised she hadn't done her hair. '*Oh dear, I must look terrible. They'll all think I never wash,*' she thought to herself. Smoothing down her birds-nest hair she decided to just get on with it, she can wash and brighten up later – this was important.

"That place doesn't look all that habitable anyway. Craig, I want to know where those two men are based. They look like new arrivals, they're walking around like they've never seen the place before. Stay on the project and keep me updated. Tammy, I want to know everything about them and what the Adelaide Alpha army has to say about their contacts. That bastard Binks had kept all of this information from us, damn his eyes. Get onto Bluey and see what else he has on them… and see if they're part of General Hughes' army in Alice Springs."

Now that the excitement was over, Commander Sue-Ellen Cullen stood beside the two operators. "Nice detective work, Tammy. And Craig, another eye-opening display and commentary. Well done to the both of you and your staff."

Before she left the big board room Sue-Ellen called Danielle to her. She had been too busy to pass this on to her new special operations staffer, but now was a good time.

"Danielle, I've some good news for you," she said coyly, knowing this might cheer her up after listening to the horror of the prisoner rescue.

Danielle looked up from her work. "What is it, Commander?" she asked politely.

"You have a brother I believe, a sergeant in the armoured cavalry, based in Darwin?" Sue-Ellen could barely keep the smile from her face.

"Yes, Sergeant Inmar Ahmet, he's in charge of a Bushmaster, why?" Danielle had stopped breathing. She waited, hoping against all hope that her brother was still alive.

"He's doing fine and stationed at Alice Springs Command. He's been there since just after the apocalypse. He's a very popular and highly respected NCO too, I believe," continued Sue-Ellen. Danielle let out a squeal of relief that startled the staff, she then threw herself into her commander's embrace and bust into fresh tears of joy.

"I can't believe it! I've been so lucky today! Thank you, Commander, I needed a lift after all we've been through," she sobbed and laughed at the same time.

"I can't let you two meet, not just yet, but you will, in due course. There's a fair bit I need to work through before I make contact with the Alice Springs Command. But don't worry, I won't keep you separated for too long." Sue-Ellen, now straightened her shirt front and kissed her staffer on the cheek, then quickly raced back to her room for a shower.

Looking presentable and professional sometimes had to take a back seat to her staff's needs.

Obi-Wan and his team were licking their wounds after the prisoner rescue. At their debrief they decided that Hooky would act as logistics and support with Danielle - much to his delight. During the rescue he was knocked to the ground by one of the enemy and his shoulder dislocated again. Hooky wasn't happy, he'd let his team down and his shoulder was back to it's dull, numbing ache. The injury was examined by the base doctor who recommended Hooky be grounded for twelve months, allowing his shoulder to heal properly. They had a base therapist who would oversee his rehabilitation.

"We did well and Patrick's loss is something we grieve. It reminds us that every action is dangerous. Gary Fortune and I have examined the assault and we're satisfied that Patrick performed his duty honourably and professionally. The rest of his team did their utmost to prevent casualties, no one is responsible for his death, people die when there's bullets flying around." Obi-Wan paused to give everyone time to settle and process what he'd said.

"Hooky, you're now our man on the ground. We'll be passing a lot of work your way for planning and preparing future raids from here on. You and Danielle will cover our backs here at the base. Anyone who needs anything, and I mean that, anything, first see Hooky or Danielle." Obi-Wan looked across at the couple sitting among them.

He then patched through to Bluey and put the video on the large monitor for all to see. As the special ops team watched a small black cat walked stately in front of the camera.

"Bluey, we've got you and Piggy on our monitor, can you see us?" asked Obi-Wan amid the chuckles in the room. There came muttered curses as Bluey gently guided his cat across and away from his keyboard with his arm.

"I'm right now," he said in relief when Piggy decided she'd had enough of stardom. "I've got you on my screen, Star Wars man, nice work. I watched it via satellite, they don't have cable where I live." Some of the men smiled, they were getting used to Bluey by now.

"The warlord's men are out in the scrub as we speak, they've formed into three gangs and fighting over everything you left behind. I expect they'll perish before they get to civilisation. Congratulations boys, for a job well done." Those who hadn't met Bluey were impressed at how professional he sounded when he put on his communications expert hat.

"Thanks, Bluey, keep us informed if anything develops. I've got a few things to talk to you about too. I'll contact you this evening, out." Obi-Wan shut down the monitor and closed his connection.

"Some of you may have heard that we have friendly neighbours. They've shot up the Deaths Head battalion at Marree and we have news that they'd had another battle at Birdsville. Commander Cullen is investigating if they are suitable allies or just rogues. We don't know much about them as yet." Obi-Wan paused to gather his thoughts before continuing.

"General Hughes of Alice Springs Command, head of the Australian Third Army, will remain in Alice Springs. Commander Cullen and our senior staff agree that General Hughes will not play a role in our organisation, nor in any of our actions. At this time they are a rag-tag bunch, they'll need some time to settle into a fighting force that we can count on. Until then we'll keep sending their visitors away empty-handed."

Commander Cullen now stood to address her special operatives. "Thank you all for your work in rescuing the prisoners. I'm sorry we lost Patrick, he will be missed. Every loss we have is one less to protect us all. We are one big family pitted against a world gone mad." She picked at her fingernails, an old habit she had when she was nervous, she wished she could stop it.

"We have some more information from Bluey. His archives contain material on a civilian commando in Birdsville. From the reports we have coming in from Bluey, Craig and Tammy's excellent research and monitoring we now know that they have a dozen or so soldiers and a community of women and children. They're calling themselves Sundown's Commando. I like that name for some reason, sort of reflects the end of the world a bit doesn't it." She paused again to keep the excitement from overtaking her. "We'll keep an eye on them for now. We know that Alice Springs Command wants to contact them and form an alliance, but we'll just sit back and let things develop before we move." Sue-Ellen sat back down.

Corporal Gary Fortune now stood. "We still have a lot of work to do, training, recon, monitoring and we'll continue to harass and sabotage the enemy every chance we get. The rescue was just a trial against amateurs, from what we have seen and know the Revelationist terrorists are quite different. Over the coming months we'll be selecting targets to hit and each member here will be assigned a role to play in our team." Fortune looked at Obi-Wan then went on. "I'll be taking over as team leader, Obi-Wan will remain as special ops commander. Murphy and Pipeline will lead the recon and assault teams with myself. As you guys gain experience you'll be given your own responsibilities."

Obi-Wan now stood as Fortune sat down. "We all have our jobs to do. Commander Cullen and I will now leave you with Corporal Fortune, Danielle and Hooky to sort out your rosters. Well done and I'll catch you all at dinner tonight."

As Obi-Wan walked Sue-Ellen back to her office a line from an old movie, one of his favourites, entered his head.

He turned to his commander. "Sue-Ellen, do you remember that movie starring Tom Cruise, Jack Nicholson, Demi Moore and Kevin Bacon?" He paused for a moment, "it was set in South Korea and…"

He didn't get any further, she was a walking movie encyclopedia. "It's called, '*A Few Good Men*', it's from a book by Aaron Sorkin. Why?" she asked.

"I've got that line Jack Nicholson says stuck in my head… it sort of describes us both," he said.

"I know what line it is too. The one that goes, '*I have neither the time nor the inclination to explain myself to a man who rises and sleeps under the blanket of the very freedom that I provide, then questions the manner in which I provide it.*'" Sue-Ellen giggled lightly and turned to her friend.

"Well, am I right?"

"As always," he said with a wry smile.

THE END

Glossary of Australian words

Australian Light Horse – name given to the Australia cavalry in the 1st World War

AFP - Australian Federal Police

ASLAV – Australian Light Army Vehicle, armoured cavalry troop carrier with mounted 7.62 mm machine gun and 25 mm cannon.

Bearcat - Lenco Bearcat, armoured command vehicle used by police and military services

Billabong – water hole, a lagoon or small lake, often filled with water lilies, fish, crustaceans

Billy – tin to put on the fire to boil water in, for tea making and heating water

Blimey – crikey, strewth, darn, damn

Bloke – man, male, fellow or fella

Bloody – damn or darn

Lowed – confused, no idea, can also mean exhausted (out of breath)

Blow-hards – full of 'piss 'n wind', noisy complaining types

Bogans - unsophisticated, lazy-assed people

Boofhead – meat head or beef head

Brumbies – wild horses

Bull-crap – bullshit, not true

Bushmaster – six-wheeled cavalry armoured personnel carrier with 7.62 mm machine gun.

Cameleer – someone who rides and cares for camels

Comms – communications, radio operator

'Cooee'- a long-drawn aboriginal call of welcome, similar to an alpine yodel

Crikey – strewth, blimey, darn, damn

Cuffs - flexi-cuffs - nylon handcuffs used by police

Cut – a tracking term to find tracks by coming at them on an angle

Dab hands – experts, good at what they do

Dingo – Australian wild dog

Fellas – fellows, people

Flaming – bloody, damn, darn

Flexi-cuffs - nylon handcuffs used by police

Football – also used to describe soccer, Aussie Rules, rugby league and rugby union

Footy-field - where football is played

Four-wheel drive – SUV's designed for travel in the desert, all four wheels engage for better traction

Fussed – bothered, worried

Gangardi – fictitious tribal group

G'day – good day, hello

Goolies – crown jewels, what hangs between a man's legs

Hot chips – hot French-fries, potato fries

Jam - jelly - Aussies call a sweet spread on bread or toast 'jam', like apricot jam, plum jam, etc.

Kip - nap, a short sleep, a power nap

Marmalade - a jam (jelly) made from whole pieces of lemon and orange rind, it has a bitter-sweet taste

Mate – friend, buddy

Men of high degree – fully initiated aboriginal men with elevated status in their tribe – some would have nangarri, sorcerer or 'medicine men' abilities and training

Mikiri – a hole in the rocks filled with water often shaped by hand to allow entry to collect water

Mob – mobs, a lot of, usually associated with a group of people and of kangaroos

Nangarri – aboriginal medicine man or sorcerer – see also 'men of high degree'

Neddys – horse

On the back foot – uncertain

Outback – the desert country

Reefed – yanked, grabbed and pulled hard and firmly

Rollie - self-rolled cigarette from loose tobacco and rice paper

Roo - short for 'kangaroo'

Salt-pan – salt covered plain, flat as a saucepan, also called salt-flats because it's flat – the desert has many such salt covered plains

Shemagh - scarf worn by middle easterners and desert warfare soldiers to keep dust and wind out of their faces

Smoked – aboriginal method sometimes used to enter an altered state of consciousness

Soak – a shallow water hole, a spring

Spec – spot, a tiny object

Spew, spewed – vomit, vomited

Stations – property or large farm in outback Australia, some larger than Texas

Steve Waugh – famous Australian cricketer

Stockmen – cattlemen, cowboy

Stockyards – stock pen or yard where cattle, horses and other animals are collected or trained

Stosstruppen – German for 'storm trooper'

Strewth – damn, darn, crikey, blimey

Stuffed – exhausted

Swags – bed roll, blanket or sleeping bag wrapped in a waterproof canvas

Tactical Response Group - specialist Australian anti-terrorist police, like a SWAT team

Tajna Sluzba – Revelationist secret service, have a reputation as ruthless killers

Tanked – drunk, also 'half-tanked' nearly drunk

Tomato sauce – ketchup

Tyres – tires, as in car tires

Unit – apartment, small one bedroom room in a motel or hotel, also called a 'flat'

"viens et rencontrer ta mort!" - French, "come and meet your death!"

Vegemite - a bitter tasting spread for toast and bread made from yeast, popular Aussie spread

Vorschlaghammer – German for 'sledge hammer'

Walers – horses used in the 1st World War for their quiet, strong and courageous manner

Walkabout – aboriginals would 'go bush' to get back to their roots, sometimes it involved spiritual works as well as for a vacation

Wallaby – small kind of kangaroo

WAPOL - Western Australian Police

Whacked – hit, smacked

Willy-willy – dust devil, mini desert tornado, whirlwind

Worked a treat – worked well, great, terrific

Yabbies – fresh water crayfish

You've done for me – 'you've killed me' or 'you've got me'

Characters of Sundown Apocalypse 5: Special Ops

WA Tactical Response Group - Police

Senior Sergeant Wayne Dyson - ex Aussie Infantry captain

Senior Constable Kerrie Black

Constable Russell Efferent

Sergeant Guy 'Lover' Luvini

Senior Constable Nancy Haurenier - Bearcat

Constable Titch 'Twitch' Frances

Constable Lana Wosniac

Senior Constable Paul 'Hooky' Pan - ex-SAS corporal

AFP – Australian Federal Police Geraldton

Senior Sergeant Bill 'Frenchy' Wahib - ex French Foreign Legion

Sergeant Ogden 'Oddie' Danse - ex Aussie commando

Constable Ray Bidder

Senior Constable Phillip Knox

Constable Lucy Taunton

WAPOL – Western Australia Police

Senior Sergeant Brad Hopkins

Constable Chad Chopah

Senior Constable William Franklin

Constable Danielle Ahmet

Constable Cindy Briggs

Special Ops - Pine Gap staff

Ranger Staff Sergeant Ben 'Obi-Wan' Kennedy

Delta Corporal Gary 'Soldier of Fortune' Fortune

SEAL Petty Officer Second Class Matthew Murphy

SEAL Petty Officer Third Class Peter 'Pipeline' Liner

SAS Corporal Ollie 'Skip' Stone

Ranger Corporal Laurence Burger

Girls from Geraldton

Emily, Julie, Tish, Gracie

Fortune's new special ops team

Andy AFP, Patrick, Constable Neil Conner AFP, Bannerman ex-infantry, Maine

Meekatharra

Joey call sign 'Tonto', Gina, Walt, Maisie, Bob + Denny ex Vietnam veterans, Bluey call sign 'Goldmine'

International Space Station

Dr Tantoni, call-sign 'Asimov'

Desert warlords

Khan, Spiro, Chucko

Jake - escapee - bus driver

Desert Farmers - on the way to West Lyons River

Becky and Adam

Pine Gap - call sign 'Downtown'

Commander Sue-Ellen Cullen - call sign 'QE3'

Major Will Binks - ASIO - call sign 'beeprep',

Big Board - Tammy, Craig

Revelationists - WA - Perth Hades Battalion - 'Flaming Damnation' + Tartarus Battalion - "Be Damned"

General Ethan Lawson

Tartarus Battalion "Be Damned" - senior commander of the Geraldton operation, Lt. Colonel Brandon Newport

Head Priestess 'The Black Widow' - Lauren McIntosh - mother to David McIntosh AFP and Colonel Harry McIntosh

Colonel - Harry McIntosh - head military Perth Revelationist church battalions

Sergeant David McIntosh - AFP, Revelationist spy - wife Debra, daughters Nina and Gina

Captain Landan - Intelligence

Captain Lim - infantry

Lieutenants - Norton, Serri

Sergeants - Bobbi Francis

Corporals - Maitland, Zee, Mandy

Privates - Sammy, Ivan, Tiny,

Darwin

Tanner - US Navy Intelligence

Barry - Australian intelligence spy

Laddie - Australian intelligence spy

Dale - terrorist security guard

MH-X Stealth Black Hawk - call sign 'Maverick'

Major Sam Samuels - pilot

Captain 'Curly' Moe - copilot

Chief Brian 'BB' Bingley

Sergeant Lance Trudeau

90 MHR-Taipan - utility helicopter - call sign 'Wagontrain'

Lieutenant Panela

Reviews for the Sundown Apocalypse series:

"I just now finished no.5. WOW!! I wasn't really sure how I would feel looking at things from a different point. But it was entirely engrossing and I got so darn involved that I'm now exhausted from all the action. And I cried, so many good people lost to the Revelationist greed. Now see there I go. It's all fiction and I know that but the characters are so real, it's easy to sink into this world you created. I loved the story and wouldn't change it. You, sir, are a genius! I'm so glad that your books will be in libraries. I've read other books by Aussie authors but none like yours. It feels great that I can go back to them." KM

"Where do I start? This is the best Sundown Apocalypse novel by far. You have slowly brought the MAIN characters together... Mate, you have scribed a great story. To use an old Naval term, Bravo Zulu (BZ), and well done, a great story, well written." PC

"I have read all five of Leo's books, and enjoyed every one of them. If you want excitement and enjoyment, read this Author's books. I will be rereading than at a later time.!" LL

"Again as before a very good read. All of these books keep your attention and keep you wanting more. Looking forward to reading the next book in the series." BR

"This is an outstanding series... am waiting with baited breath to get all of the books. An outstanding wordsmith...each page jumps alive as you read. Keep up the great work!" GA

"Reading this series has been one of the highlights of my life. As an Aussie who has lived in the Northern Territory, I have such wonderful memories of places and people, so much like those Leo Nix has given the reader. The author has created a truly wonderful story that

encompasses all that is good, and bad, in human nature. Beginning with the Apocalypse and following groups of people who gradually come together. There is so much to experience that it's a rush to turn page after page in order to keep up. I dream of maybe a 9 book series, Mr Nix!" K